FLY CATCHER

LITTLE PEOPLE AGAINST BIG POWERS

P C CUBITT

FLY CATCHER

http://pccubitt.com

Cover Design by Jem Butcher

ISBN-13: 978-1-7398897-1-5

❀ Created with Vellum

For David

ONE
SONGOLA

The black Land Cruiser had been following them ever since they left the lorry park at Bo. It was new and highly polished with blacked-out windows but no identifiers. No government plates or private registration. No company or agency logo.

This was strange, because in Sierra Leone it wasn't customary to hide your wealth.

Songola had noticed the cruiser in the motorbike's mirror as they'd rounded a bend near Blama intersection. Miles back. It was sinister the way it hung behind, passing them several times on the stretch from Bo to Kenema, and then dropping back again. It had parked near the place where they'd stopped to pick up water and phone credit; unknown faces obscured behind the tinted glass. The motorbike would soon be turning off, heading south along the cratered track toward the plantations. What would the cruiser do then? Keep following, or stay on the highway?

The cruiser stayed on the highway.

The motorbike taxi bounced along the track, weaving through a landscape of stumpy bush dotted with banana trees, Songola seated behind the driver.

Songola was a young mother and political activist, on her

way up country to investigate a death on the plantation. The village headman had said conditions on the estate had deteriorated and that there'd been an accident involving a child, who had died. The villagers had taken photos of the boy and wanted Songola to go into the plantation with them to see conditions for herself – the dangerous working environment of the palm oil company that employed them. They believed she could help. That she could get justice for the daily abuse they suffered at the hands of the vast corporation that had stolen their land. *Arranoil.*

Songola felt the weight of their hope.

When she arrived at the village, the workers showed her photos of the boy.

The headman explained, 'This boy…maybe his age was seven years.'

'Do you know his village, or his name?' Songola asked.

'Nobody knows,' the headman replied. 'He come every day with the others…many boys…they work together. Their scars…' he drew two fingers across his forehead, '…these tribes are far, far. Maybe he come from Bomba, maybe Kambia.'

Songola feared what this might mean.

She asked, 'The child was working with many others?'

'That is so,' the headman replied. 'At first…a few. But now we have many boys working. They come from nowhere.'

The boys' tribal scars indicated they were from many different regions of the hinterland; unique patterns of scarification etched on their cheekbones or foreheads, that suggested they were not from those parts. But when the villagers questioned the boys, they were fearful, not even giving their names.

Songola examined the photos. The little boy's frame had been crushed by a falling palm fruit of immense weight and proportions. There were other injuries: spikelet perforations to his skin, and old and new lacerations to his legs and feet.

The muscles of his arms and shoulders were overly-developed for a boy of his age. The child had been worked like a man.

Songola was reminded of her own child, just six months old.

The next day, Songola travelled to the heart of the plantation. There'd been rumours about child slavery, gangs roaming the countryside buying or abducting children, selling them to companies who then forced them to work. But until then people had not wanted to talk, fearful of forces they did not understand. When the child died, the workers had brought him back to their village. They did not alert the foreman. They'd feared a cover up, that the child's body would simply disappear, and that no-one would even acknowledge his existence.

When Songola arrived at the harvesting site on the plantation, the boys were afraid to talk; shy and nervous, perhaps not understanding the Mende language of the southern people. But she cajoled one lad by offering food. He approached shyly, rubbing rough hands against grimy shorts, munching barefoot among the sharp-edged fronds that littered the plantation floor. He said he was from a remote area of the Eastern Province, close to the Liberian border in the heart of diamond country, and that he had a brother working in a different part of the plantation. Songola suspected his parents had sold the brothers to traffickers who paid a good price for healthy boys.

That night, Songola spent many hours in the hut trying to get a signal on her phone. It was hooked up and charging from a car battery provided by the old woman who owned the hut who rocked to and fro in her chair, her mismatched earrings – one gold hoop, one turquoise drop – glinting as they swayed in the lamplight. Network coverage was weak in this remote area, but Songola persevered, tapping well into the night in the glow of the screen.

At dawn the motorbike taxi arrived for the return trip to Freetown, and progress was good as they travelled northwest in the early sunshine, warming rays on their backs.

The landscape rolled by like a picture show, groves of raffia palms, dark green mango trees, banana copses among tall tussocky grasses. And the occasional thatched settlement. Everything dry at this time of year, waiting for the rains.

Songola felt the hot metal of the motorbike's engine through the rough denim of her jeans but she felt cool in the breeze, her jacket flapping open, her hands on the grip bar behind. Her driver was well-known to her and trusted, and he leant forward concentrating on the road, the muscles and sinews of his forearms tensing with the vibrations of the rutted track beneath the wheels. Before long they were back on the highway, which was starting to fill with laden trucks heading for the Liberian border.

Keeping a discreet distance, the black cruiser slipped into position behind. Songola recognised the car from before.

The sun rose higher, its rays growing stronger on her back, her head beginning to sweat under the weight of the helmet, the perspiration lubricating the cushioned interior. Instinctively she moved her hands from the rear grip, wrapping them around the driver whose body tensed, alarmed at the break in cultural norms. But he kept up their speed, clocking up the miles on the dusty highway.

Songola checked the mirror and saw that the cruiser had settled into position. It didn't make a move to overtake.

A cold dread crept through her body. Her heart rate quickened, beating louder in her chest, adrenalin surging through her veins. As panic took hold her throat constricted. Her T-shirt dampened from the involuntary lactation of her breasts as she thought of her infant child waiting for her return.

The cruiser's engine growled as it sped up, closing the gap. The sun in the mirror blinded Songola momentarily, blocking the vehicle from view. A moment later it was undertaking them, drawing level on the nearside as she and her driver looked across into the blacked-out windows. The sound of scraping metal as the cruiser turned into them, the motorbike driver intuitively swerving to correct their position. Again, the cruiser hit them, this time more violently, and the bike flew wide across the carriageway.

The car had perfectly timed its deadly manoeuvre; the oncoming truck, heavily laden, had no way to avoid them. As the motorbike slewed under the wheels there was an agonising crunch, a tortured scream of metal on metal, and Songola was airborne, bouncing off the cab, flying in slow motion across the dusty shoulder of the road, the sun a burning yellow disc above, the screeching brakes and blare of horns distant as her body reeled and landed on the hard red earth.

Crumpled and still, she lay in the dirt her heart beating violently, loud in her head, demanding attention, thumping the blood through her brain in an instinctive reaction to her body's need.

She felt hands lift her, remove her rucksack, then carelessly drop her to the ground. Voices fading away. All became still. Far off, unknown birds sang brightly. In the quiet, her breath became slow and gasping, and her heartbeat quietened, slowing. She had no breath or strength, even to feed the fear. She looked up at the sky, so blue, and stared at the small accumulation of cirrus, like fine rippled gauze. A single line of jet contrails lay in the stratosphere, south to north. Helpless. Now she heard no heartbeat, as life ebbed from her, slipping quietly away on the hard-baked earth by the side of the road.

TWO
LUNGI

The airbus sunk closer to the ground. And an irregular patchwork of lamps and braziers emerged from the night to define contours of activity around the airport. I stared passed my reflection in the glass. Vehicle headlights could now be seen moving along the bush tracks. Fragmentary illumination in the dense landscape. Then the white runway lights, racing along the ground in their uniform pattern, pointing the way. And the new terminal building with its elegant curved steel roof, smooth and undulating, standing like a beacon in the shadow of the forest.

It was nothing like the concrete shack that I recalled. But that had been thirty years ago and events of great magnitude had occurred since then. Military coups, failed peace accords, the ravages of war and the collapse of the state. Ebola.

But some things, I knew, remained the same. Like the circumstances of the nation's people, living as they always had with poverty, disease, and bad government. The constant scourge of corrupt politicians.

On that day, as I returned to Freetown, I believed I was on a mission to change all that. To discover what had happened to the missing aid. To find out who'd stolen all those millions.

And to understand how the people felt, continuously governed as they were by the predatory and greedy pilferers of their state.

I was returning to the beloved land of my childhood, believing that I could make a difference.

———

A DISORDERLY MASS of sweaty passengers clogged immigration. Blue-shirted officials roamed among them collecting passports, stacking them haphazardly at the booths. Behind stood more uniformed personnel, ready to accept a bribe for an escorted short-cut through the terminal. But I'd been warned about the tricks at Lungi airport, so I hung back with the crowd, waiting my turn.

Karen Hamm?

I pushed my way to the front, already feeling the heat, my shirt wet under the weight of the rucksack.

The official sat plump in his booth and studied my passport with intent.

'British,' he said, sagely. Without looking up, he held out his hand. 'Immigration card.'

I passed it over and he studied the detail, comparing it to the visa stamp in my passport. There was an uncomfortable pause.

'Business?' he asked.

'Research,' I answered. He looked at me over wire-framed spectacles that were perched on an enormous nose. His dark skin was as pockmarked as a passion fruit, his small eyes bloodshot with fatigue.

'I've a letter of introduction,' I said, searching my bag for the university's papers, half expecting an interrogation as to my reasons to visit the country. Which were officially, doctoral research. Unofficially, something else.

But the man ignored me, stamping my documents with

vigour and shoving them across the desk. He retrieved another passport from the pile and I moved on.

Waiting officials fought amongst themselves to escort me through security. I ignored them. An older, authoritative type, wearing buttoned epaulettes, walked backwards signalling with both hands for me to follow. I resisted, and stayed in the line of locals lurching their way through to baggage reclaim. The area was packed with passengers, officials in brown and blue uniforms, masses of street lads working as porters, and ancillary staff, all milled around. The noise was alarming. A strong odour of perspiration competed with the Parazone.

Straight away, a number of porters in raggedy clothes descended on me. They shouted in awkward English. One took my arm, another tried to prise the rucksack from my back.

I clung on, panicking, 'Get off!'

'Take bag, take bag!' the lad insisted, and I wrestled with him for a while.

This unfathomable style of service was routine, but I knew the notoriety of the country's pickpockets. Maybe these lads were creating a chance for their mates to do some thieving. The sweat flowed down my face, my confidence disappearing like a drop of rain on parched African soil. Then I noticed them staring at the ring. An ostentatious diamond, flashing on my hand with tantalising allure. I'd meant to take it off before we landed.

We moved along; my rucksack with my paperwork, laptop, and all my valuables, now on the back of a lad in flip-flops, his Man U T-shirt grubby with sweat. Grouped awkwardly, we made our way toward baggage reclaim where bodies stood at the consoles several deep. For each passenger there were three porters trying to grab a bag. I was shoved to the front to identify mine – a red, hard-shell spinner – being lifted from the other side by different lads in tatty T-shirts.

'Oi!' I shouted.

A sudden ruckus, and one of my porters hurdled the console, grabbed the case and heaved it to our side. Another came up behind, dividing the crowd with his trolley. They secured the red spinner and we moved *en masse* toward customs, the lads clinging on like magnets to a fridge.

We approached uniformed personnel who wore solemn expressions and manned low steel tables. A short officious woman in a smooth black wig called us to her spot.

'On the table,' she said, in the authoritative manner of petty officialdom.

My entourage positioned the case for inspection.

'Open it.' She looked at me hard.

In the secret pocket of my rucksack, which was still on the back of Man U lad, I found the purse that held the key to the locks on my red suitcase. I handed them over. Security was paramount; I took it very seriously. I was prepared, knowing how difficult it was to replace a lost passport or credit card, or anything else in these environs. I waited whilst my handlers exchanged meaningful looks with the official. We all waited. Later I was to realise that a bribe had been expected. The woman sighed and made a superficial rummage through my neatly-folded clothes. Then everything was zipped up and we moved swiftly through to arrivals where a young, be-suited man held a card with my name.

'Karen Hamm? Welcome to Freetown, ma.' His smile was broad, his teeth gleamed, his skin the smoothest midnight blue. 'I am Abdou. Sam sent me.'

'Abdou!' He gave me the customary three-grip handshake.

The porters waited, keen to get back for the next round. Abdou heaved the spinner off the trolley and waved the lads away, but they loitered, looking stern.

'They need a tip,' Abdou said.

'Yes…of course.' I searched through my bag for US

dollars, much more valuable than their Leone. The lads looked grateful and disappeared.

Abdou led the way out into the African dawn. The humid heat slapped its wet embrace around me. A whiff of incinerating garbage slunk toward us from the dump.

Abdou said, matter of fact, 'The water is heavy today... they is no taxis.'

'No taxis?'

A fleet of speedboats that usually took passengers on a twenty-minute journey across the vast river to the capital, Freetown. Alternative travel from the airport – which was built on an inconvenient and isolated promontory in the Sierra River estuary – involved a five-hour journey through the bush, or a crossing via ancient ferry recently condemned unseaworthy.

Flashing a smile, Abdou said, 'Don't worry, ma. I have ticket for ferry...first class.' He gestured toward a waiting vehicle. 'The car is here. I will take you.'

As we walked toward the Jeep, I contemplated the undignified loss of control that had marked my arrival. A sorry performance, the very opposite of what I'd planned. I had solid Africa credentials, and some authority in these parts. After all, I had form, the daughter of a former High Commissioner. But I was annoyed by the way I'd spoken to the porters, how I'd forgotten their tip, how quickly I'd allowed the emotions to flare.

THE FERRY WAS a rusting heap of scrap resting its ramp on the slipway and already pitching low in the water. Still waiting to board stood eight military surplus trucks with camouflage canopies over flatbeds. Behind, stood a pair of white 4x4 ambulances, USAID printed blue and red across the paintwork, a gift from the US government for the Ebola crisis, which was now in retreat.

Abdou led the way, trolleying the red spinner up the ramp, the sun already high. On board, a noisy cargo of foot passengers, livestock, bicycles, motorbikes and trucks. We followed a group of market women dressed in bright-coloured wrappers balancing enamel bowls on their heads filled with pineapples. The tropical heat bore down, but Abdou hefted my red spinner onto his thin shoulders and carried it up the flight of steps that led to a metal walkway encircling the vehicle holding space. Then up a second, narrower flight to the first class lounge. Sweating profusely, he shook my hand.

'Have a good visit, ma. Watch out for the kids.' He nodded toward a raggedy group of children milling around the steps to first-class.

I said, 'Thanks for your help… maybe I'll see you when I come back through Lungi?'

He waved and smiled and was soon lost in the crowd.

First class meant a panoramic view of the crossing and indoor seating in an air-conditioned space just below the bridge. Well-to-do Sierra Leoneans and scruffy Europeans had already grabbed the seats. Stashing my enormous case, which now felt embarrassingly inappropriate for this kind of travel, I bought a coke from a vending machine and returned to the metal walkway to watch what was happening in the hold. Vendors wove through the crowds selling snacks and drinks head-loaded on trays. The military vehicles were loading and pushing foot passengers toward the bow, their noxious fumes rising up. They parked four abreast, so tightly and precisely packed that the drivers climbed out of the windows to sit on the roofs for the crossing. Creaking and clanking, the ferry edged from the quay, belching fumes as the expanse of water grew bigger and the oil slick by the dock became visible. The vast river estuary lay ahead. The wind was brisk, white horses swelling on the water, and the sky was strewn with fast-moving cumulus dotted like spoonfuls of meringue against the blue. And in the distance, the towering Lion Mountains, a dramatic backdrop to the densely packed city.

Then a commotion rose from the deck. Papaya, mango and tomatoes; all had splattered across the deck and were being trampled underfoot. Standing by, a young woman was shouting, her platter now empty. A tall man, dressed in yellow linen jacket, diamond piercing in his ear, was trying to make the peace. But she refused to quieten, and pointed angrily at the only white man on the deck whose expression was passive; his shock of steel-grey hair shining in the sun like the airport's architectural roof.

The man in the yellow jacket passed the fruit-seller a wad of notes but she stood firm, hands on hips. *Go girl.* He passed her another wad and she inspected it, glancing at the white man who stood disinterested. In a moment, the commotion was over. The woman wandered away, jerking her chin in disgust, the steel-haired man now relaxed in conversation with his minder.

The kids around first class lingered, expert eyes searching for opportunities. I moved the rucksack to the front of my body, propping it against the railings, the wide, windy estuary ahead, Freetown beckoning seductively. A desire to disappear came over me. To slip like a thief into the scene. To slink and fade, to melt into a world of the *other*. At last, an alternative reality lay ahead, so distinct from my suffocating life back home. I'd returned to the land of my childhood. I'd been too long away.

THREE
KANGARI

The elderly porter wore a black suit and high polished shoes and shuffled down the steps to greet me.

'Welcome, ma... this way please.'

I followed him into the lobby, tired but exhilarated, sticky with sweat, grubby with dust from the dirt tracks we'd taken to avoid the downtown rush. It had been a long journey back to this country. Geographically, intellectually, and emotionally.

'Yes, ma'am?' The receptionist's hair was coiffed in an elaborate arrangement of braids. 'Welcome to the Kangari. Please fill the form.' She slid the paper across the desk, examined my passport and smiled, 'British.' I hoped my own expression didn't mirror the smugness of hers.

Behind her an office door was open where a young be-suited man of heavy build leant back in his chair watching me check in. He sat straight-faced when I smiled. An awkward moment. I looked quickly down at my papers. It was true the British had a long controversial history in his country, and the UK was still the main donor to its hard-pressed government. The last thing I wanted was for people to think I was a colonial apologist; the interfering British come to interfere some more. When I looked again, he was still staring, hands in lap and thumbs revolving.

A commotion behind made me turn. A tall, rugged type with a briefcase in one hand and phone in the other, shouldered his way into the lobby, two porters close behind with his luggage. There were several cricket-size holdalls, two rucksacks, and a large titanium suitcase, which they piled untidily on the floor. The man said something to them in *Krio* and they stood to attention by the pile. Straight away the young man from the office up-righted his chair. He came out to attend to the guest; an attractive man, in a sleazy kind of way, with a deep tropical tan and thick, steel-grey hair that was swept back off his face in a wave-like flourish. The man spoke English with a guttural Dutch accent.

The receptionist glanced meaningfully at her colleague. It seemed the Dutchman was a regular at the Kangari Hotel. Keys were handed over swiftly and he disappeared from the lobby with his porters close behind. I watched him go, thinking he was the same man I'd seen causing commotion on the ferry with the fruit seller.

The receptionist handed me a key attached to a palm frond that was intricately woven into the shape of a lizard.

She said, 'Breakfast from seven thirty. Joseph will show you.'

The elderly porter had reappeared and was waiting. Joseph trolleyed my case past a small marble fountain, empty of water, and into a woody-smelling area with a large craft display. African art: paintings, carvings, beaded jewellery, tribal masks. A bored looking woman sat in their midst and eyed me hopefully. We moved on to the bar – all chrome, glass, and red leatherette – and then the restaurant, a hugely spacious and soulless room, with large windows looking out to a concrete swimming pool. Dozens of tables were laid with peach-coloured tablecloths and plastic flowers, and hanging at the windows were heavy drapes in a darker shade of peach. The effect was uninviting.

We emerged through double doors onto a covered walkway that crossed a tropical garden with raffia palms and orange trees. We climbed two flights to an open corridor that overlooked the tops of the palms. Looking down, I could see how the hotel was arranged; constructed pentagon-like around a central garden, which was criss-crossed at ground level by covered walkways running from block to block. Well-worn footpaths weaved shortcuts through the greenery. Across the space, on the corridor opposite, the Dutchman's porters were manoeuvring his luggage into his room.

Joseph unlocked the door to mine and gave some instructions for the operation of the AC, a spluttering device above a desk of dark laminated wood, chipped at the edges.

He asked politely, 'First time in Freetown, ma?'

'No,' I said, enthusiastic to share my credentials. 'I was here as a child, many years ago.'

He looked perplexed.

'My father worked for the British government,' I explained. 'He was stationed here for three years. But Freetown seems very different now.' I beamed at him but all he did was nod, confused and mildly disinterested. Observing him, I wondered whether it was his vast height that cowed his posture or a lifetime of deference. His skin was as smooth and black as engine oil, but his grey hair and shuffling gait gave away his years.

'Well…anyway…thank you, Joseph.' I tipped him five thousand Leones.

Alone in the room, I went straight to the window which was meshed and shuttered against the midday sun. I wrenched open the heavy bars, anticipating a view of the country's legendary coastline, or a glimpse of the sea. The balcony was a bleak concrete rectangle, its only furnishings a glass ashtray and three cigarette butts. The view across the razor wire was of wasteland and a pile of smouldering rubbish. A few palms stood tall in the distance. Rickety shacks were dotted about, and feral dogs groomed themselves, gnawing at the flees. The wind blew offshore, diverting the stench of decay and garbage toward the coast, away from the fortress walls and concrete balconies of the hotel.

I checked the bathroom. Functional enough, as you'd expect in a hotel built by the Chinese. A droopy showerhead hung over the bath behind a pretty flowered curtain. I stripped and stepped under a cool surge of water. At head height was a small window, barred and covered in anti-mosquito mesh. Passing through was a flow of air that was scented with gardenia. From where I stood, I could see directly across to the opposite block where the Dutchman's porters were arguing violently outside his closed door.

LATER, with the mini-bar already pillaged, I lay on the bed and called my local contact on the hotel phone.

'Sam, I'm in the country!'

'My friend!' He sounded pleased to hear my voice. 'Abdou tells me he found you.'

'He did! I was grateful to see him. What a *nightmare* at Lungi.'

He was defensive, 'We are working on it. Things can only get better.'

'No kidding.' I was happy to hear a familiar voice on foreign soil.

Sam said, 'How're you settling in? Do you need anything?'

I launched straight in. 'Yes. A local phone. The iPhone's not working here and I need something reliable to set up meetings. I'm ringing you on the hotel phone just now.'

He sucked his teeth. 'Expensive.'

I thought of the first call I should have made home to Graham. To re-assure him I'd arrived safely. But I didn't want to break the spell of my longed for arrival in Africa, so I'd sent him an email instead.

Sam said, 'Send a hotel porter to get you one. You'll pay top dollar if you go yourself.'

'Good idea. Thanks.' I considered Joseph, the elderly porter. Maybe he could get one for me.

Sam said, 'You need to come into the centre so that we can make plans. What's your interview schedule looking like?'

'Not bad. I've lots in the diary starting with the GHO and then the Ministry of Health. I just need to firm things up now I'm here.'

'Well, tell me if you meet any challenges. I can pull a few strings this end...we have our contacts as you know.' Sam's family had influence in this town.

'Thanks, Sam. I'll let you know when I'm coming in.'

'Sorry, I have to go,' he said, abruptly. 'Hey, my friend! It's good to have you in my country!' He hung up. Typically brusque, always leaving you eager for more.

Sam Gregory was a post-graduate student at York University, like me. We were friends and we were both working on a PhD about democracy in his country. He was a Sierra Leonean himself, and his family was part of the NGO fraternity. Non-governmental organisations were big business here, especially since the end of the war when the World Bank had moved in preoccupied with democratisation to ensure good governance. And Sam was an intern at his mother's organisation, *Democracy for Salone*, which received UK aid. *Salone* was the local vernacular for the country's name.

Millions of dollars of Ebola funds had gone unaccounted for in his country. I was sure Sam's organisation was legitimate, but I didn't want to put him in an awkward position. Officially, I was in his country for PhD research, but my other preoccupation was to find out about corruption, how people got away with it, who knew about it, how pervasive was it, and what impact did it have on human rights and tensions after the war? After all, it was decades of corruption that had led to so much resentment and grievance in the years before the conflict.

Sam Gregory had a good brain and big ambitions for his country. He was charming, and smoother than the silkiest of his silk shirts. Women fell over themselves to get at him. He'd offered to be my fixer when I arrived in Freetown, but I'd learnt to be cautious around him. He could be unreliable and fickle. Self-absorbed and self-serving, that was Sam. But for now, he was my only point of contact in Freetown.

AFTER A LONELY MEAL of barracuda and rice in the peachy surroundings of the restaurant, I was back in my room and down to work reviewing my list of interviews. This included one minister – I was hoping for more if I made the right connections – several international organisations who were delivering aid projects including big players like the World Health Organisation, ActionAid and so on, and of course local organisations who'd worked with donor partners to deliver essential services. I also had plans to speak to my own government at UKDev; the agency that managed development aid and oversaw spending and programme delivery. I wanted more detail on how and why funds go astray. How does the system allow it? Who steals it? And how does corruption impact on ordinary people? To find out, I planned to use Sam Gregory's influence to get me in.

I checked my interview list and questionnaires three times, then messed about organising my clothes and papers. Graham would be waiting for my call. I sat on the bed and looked at the new phone, courtesy of the porter Joseph, lying there charged and ready to go. I ignored it and opened my laptop to check for emails. There was no reply from Graham so I sent one to my supervisor at York University letting her know I'd arrived safely and that everything was set for interviews the next day. Then I experimented with the air conditioning. The room was cold, and I'd never sleep with its continuous racket. I undressed and got ready for bed, taking another whiskey from the mini bar to make sure I'd sleep. The phone lay waiting on the bed, fully charged and operational; incriminating, the way it looked at me. I picked it up and dialled Graham's number.

'Hi, it's me.'

'Hi.'

'Everything ok?' I listened for hesitation in his voice, but all I could hear was Miles Davis in a complicated jazz narrative trumpeting in the background.

'Yes… all well,' he said.

I waited, not really knowing what to say. Graham had Asperger's and struggled with stress. It had been hard to leave him.

He said flatly, 'I got your email. You had a good journey.' The tension was there in his voice. Miles Davis, his comfort blanket, helping him cope.

'Yes, no problems. All went smoothly.'

'That's good.' A pause, then he said, 'I didn't recognise the number.'

'It's a local phone. The iPhone's not working here.'

'Right. I'll check that for you.'

I twisted his ring, now uncomfortably tight, the solitaire sparkling like Venus on the clearest night. He'd never talked of marriage, but he'd sensed a change in me. Maybe he'd felt the need to stake his claim. One morning, without drama, he'd presented the ring over breakfast. Later, when I'd thought it through, I realised it was a substitute for the emotional security he couldn't give. In his own way, he was trying. But for me it was too late.

I asked, 'Have you had any news?'

'Yeah. The deal looks like it's going through. They're happy with the due diligence.'

Graham was selling his business, a deal that should have been sealed months before I'd left for Freetown. For the past twenty years he'd built up his own hugely successful company that developed computer software and specialised in systems for medical facilities. I regretted I wasn't there to support him. More guilt, as though I hadn't given enough. As though I still owed him.

'That's great,' I said. 'Have they given you a date?'

'Not yet.' His voice was tight, and I visualised him gripping the phone.

I said, 'It *will* come, don't worry.'

'I'm not worried,' he lied, but I knew he was anxious about me, not the deal. There was now *the thing* between us. Words spoken, that couldn't be unsaid.

After a pause I said, 'I'm getting stuck in first thing tomorrow. The whole day's full of meetings, and I've hooked up with Sam.'

We exchanged more pleasantries before we hung up.

Just being in Freetown, already I felt the suffocation of my imaginary bell-jar lifting. The bell-jar was a metaphor for my feelings of entrapment, of confinement, of imprisonment. The persistent lack of oxygen in the dry, stale air of my aimless life back home. Stuck in my own head, spinning the same thoughts of worthlessness over and over. A fruitless, privileged, idle life.

Now I'd slipped away to find purpose, far from everything and everyone back home. Now I'd started to breathe. I'd returned to Africa. To save myself from my own madness.

FOUR
GODERICH

Goderich hospital was on the outskirts of Freetown. A series of single storey, flat roofed buildings, surrounded by a white wall with a bold red stripe along its length. In the middle of the site rose a recent addition, a modern surgical unit, its overhanging second floor supported by architectural braces that resembled the branches of a tree. Such a contrast to the faded-colonial-cum-dilapidated-Soviet-cum-ramshackle-slum that was the rest of Freetown.

The clinic was Italian owned and built at the end of the war as a specialist trauma unit. It was an isolation centre during the Ebola crisis; that deadly, creeping epidemic whose scope and character nobody foresaw. As it took hold, the world reacted slowly and, when the magnitude of the emergency became known, a surge of funding flooded in. But a sizeable chunk of the cash had gone missing.

I was visiting the Goderich hospital to find out the attitude of the Global Health Organisation to the missing funds. Manuel Garcia was the GHO's representative in Sierra Leone, a difficult man to pin down, but one who'd eventually agreed to speak to me whilst doing his rounds at the clinic. I wanted ω ask him about the Ebola crisis and how it had been so easy for vast amounts of money to go unaccounted for.

It was already hot when I arrived outside the hospital, the sun a blurry brass disc burning its way through the haze, and the area was congested with traffic and hawkers. People were buying breakfast from roadside braziers, the tantalising aroma of roasting maize and skewered goat.

Near the gates, patients were arriving off the back of pick-ups, oxcarts and wheelbarrows. Some hobbled on foot supported by their relatives. You'd think there'd been a major incident, but this was an average day in Freetown with so many road accidents, machete incidents in fields or work-shops, falls from palms or mango trees, or from rickety scaf-folding on construction sites across the city.

The clinic's waiting area was crammed. Behind the desk overworked staff were processing paperwork amidst the hum of chatter. It was easy to spot Manuel Garcia, the only suited figure among the lab coats and scrubs. Young and good look-ing, his wavy black hair swept with precision off his face. Beside him was a tired looking woman in scrubs, their heads together over a thick padded clipboard.

I was early, so I squeezed onto a bench between a tall man in flowing white djellaba, and a woman in an ochre turban holding a pair of crutches. She nodded at me politely. The stench of perspiration competed successfully with the clinic's powerful disinfectants. People waited calmly for their turn, some clutching prescriptions, others clutching injuries. I tried to imagine what it had been like at the height of Ebola when so many lost their lives.

'Miss Hamm?' I stood to find that Manuel Garcia was inches shorter than me.

'Please call me Karen.' I shook his hand which was limp and sweaty.

Without further formality, we moved off at a pace through light and airy wards and past rows of occupied beds, monitors, hoists, screens and drip stands. In a side ward a woman in a colourful head tie sat beside a child whose leg was wrapped in plaster from groin to ankle. Manuel Garcia talked to her in *Krio*, listening attentively, making notes on his pad.

As we moved away, he said defensively, 'Yes, GHO have been criticised for the way it handled the crisis. To some extent the criticism is legitimate. It was out of its depth, but this was because GHO's role has always been to advise and coordinate, not deliver *services*. There has never been an outbreak such as Ebola before.'

He spoke beautiful English with the soft lispy ts and ds of the native Spanish speaker. We stood back to let a trolley through, then hurried on, Manuel Garcia speeding down the ward, me following closely with my outstretched dictaphone. A strange way to conduct my first interview.

He explained how during the crisis his organisation had to coordinate the activities of all the different partners as well as the government. They had sent coordinators out into the deep field where eventually they found how quickly the virus was being transmitted.

He stopped walking to emphasise a point.

'Our people became disease *detectives*. What was different apart from the scale and spread was that we had to assist with *clinical* care.'

His speech seemed well-rehearsed, a similar narrative to the one I'd found on the GHO's official website.

We passed through double doors into a short corridor with gleaming white tiles, and peered through an observation window where local surgeons were finishing off a leg amputation. Manuel Garcia spoke more to the air around him than to me.

'The logistics of tackling the crisis were enormous. How were we to get all that heavy complex equipment to the right places where it was needed? You've seen for yourself the infrastructure here. Everything had to be airlifted. For sure we were not equal to the task.'

For sure.

We moved away through another set of doors to a recovery room where local medics in blue scrubs were waiting for their next patient. Manuel Garcia chatted to them while I stood to the side, waiting like an incumbrance. Time passed. We moved on.

He said, 'GHO was never designed to be a *field-based* organisation, but things are changing. There's talk of a rapid response unit so we'll cope better next time, but really the only sustainable solution is with the government itself.'

He was trying to anticipate my questions, none of which I'd actually asked. Being on the move like this, it was difficult for me to speak at all.

I forced in a question: 'What about the missing aid? Do you think there's something wrong with GHO's oversight when so much gets stolen? I mean, can the government be trusted with the money?'

He bristled slightly.

'You will find that much of our disbursement is in the form of staff, equipment, medicine. And of course research. Also, we do have a strong local presence to closely monitor what's going on. A few transactions are overseen by local offices, that is true, but we have a robust system to manage payments. This provides assured accountability.'

Assured accountability?

'But the money does go missing. Many millions of dollars.'

'Yes, but you cannot categorically say that it is GHO's money that's gone missing. You can't say that. Things are not perfect.'

'But can you see that people must feel cheated if aid doesn't go where it's supposed to go, I mean in this case to the health sector?'

'Maybe. But I'm not authorised or qualified to know where your missing funds are.'

'Yes, but if a similar outbreak happens again, something like Ebola, the outcome would be the same, don't you think? Unless the government can be trusted to build a health system that can cope with another emergency, and that could take years. Or decades. Meanwhile people die unnecessarily.'

He paused and looked at me, his dark eyes quizzical.

'Yes exactly,' he said. I must have stated the blindingly obvious.

'Do you know how that might happen?' I asked.

'How might what happen?'

'How do people get the health service they deserve when the funds for it go missing?'

We set off again, my dictaphone under his chin, 'Mr Garcia, you work for the United Nations. You demand democratic transition in fragile states like Sierra Leone. But you seem to condone corruption of aid. How can local people reconcile the two? Can you understand their anger?'

We'd arrived at a pharmaceutical counter surrounded by patients holding prescriptions. Catching the eye of someone behind the counter Manuel Garcia nodded at her and I thought he was going to ignore me, but he turned back,

'We're working with the government to strengthen its health system. They need laboratories so they can detect diseases that could cause an epidemic. We're equipping them to handle high-risk samples. I'll show you.'

He took my elbow and steered me with unexpected firmness through another door into a long corridor with opaque windows illuminating the position of several laboratories marked Lab 1, Lab 2, and so on. We reached Lab 4 which housed banks of modern computers, microscopes, blocks of test tubes, incubators, fridges and centrifuge equipment for specimen processing. Everything you would expect in a modern clinical laboratory. It was impressive. And he continued to press the case that hundreds of thousands of people had been treated through the Goderich facility. But I wondered how this foreign-owned, foreign-run hospital had anything to do with government-run effective public health.

At that point the tour had finished, and I wandered outside into the fierce morning sun thinking it had not gone well. Manuel Garcia had regurgitated all the official statements that anyone could find online. I'd got nothing new out of him. Maybe I was naïve to think that everyone was free to speak their mind. To speak the truth. Resigned I switched off the dictaphone wondering whether they'd all be as dry and unfruitful as this. Anxiety nibbled at the edge of my consciousness. Next I had a meeting with the minister.

THE DRIVER AMADU had been recommended by the hotel. Tall of stature and skeletal of frame he was handsome in a lean and angular way with a white and sudden smile, teeth that gleamed with pearly iridescence. A red air-freshener dangled from the mirror of his red Toyota cruiser, a mark of his passion for Liverpool football club. His head was shaved close, his eyes permanently hidden behind his cool, mirrored shades.

The Ministry of Health was on the other side of town across the Aberdeen Bridge that linked the beachy tourist area to the Freetown peninsular.

Aberdeen Bridge itself spanned a broad tidal creek that flowed into the Atlantic Ocean. It was infamous, used as an execution site during the last days of the war when those accused of being rebels were brought in trucks, stripped, hands tied and shot, their bodies flung over the railings into the wide creek below. But the bridge had also been used as a refuge and a bunker, in which people had hidden from the automatic fire and the raining mortar. A trapdoor in the side led to a void in the concrete where dozens of people sheltered from the fighting. Others tried to escape in overloaded boats that sank in the bay.

As we crossed the bridge I looked into the water. The war had been right here. People shot right here, others hiding just below. What a scene: a fusion of mania and bloodshed, strength and resilience. It humbled me.

Down the creek a number of bulldozers appeared to be demolishing a settlement.

'What's happening there?' I asked Amadu.

'Crab Town', he replied assuming that was all I wanted to know. His English was patchy, but I knew he could say more.

Buildings were being reduced to rubble all along the coastline.

'Why are they pulling it down?' I asked.

'Government says they stinkin' the creek and makin' flood.'

'What will happen to the people? Are they being relocated somewhere?'

Amadu shrugged. 'They go no place.'

'Can we go see?'

We parked on a patch of wasteland close to a crowd of angry residents being marshalled by armed police wearing helmets and visors. The area used to be a fishing town but was now being laid to rubble – concrete, corrugated iron, splintered wood and rusted tin – the remains of peoples' homes and businesses lying all around beside piles of burning rubbish. A determined breeze blew the smoke across the creek.

The atmosphere was tense. It seemed the residents were unaware their town was to be razed. The bulldozers just turned up and started levelling the ground that day. People had rescued their belongings as best they could – mattresses, plastic chairs, cooking pots and crockery, shelving and tables – and had piled them on the side of the road. It was a heart-breaking sight; children clinging to their mothers' legs among the dust and din, alarmed babies suspended on their mothers' backs, the elderly resting on upturned crates, heads in hands. And angry men everywhere searching for answers. All the while the metal arms of the 'dozers turned and spun destroying all in their reach. Fragile homes cracked and splintered.

I moved around the edges of the crowd. A crew from the local broadcaster roamed the area interviewing Crab Town residents.

'Nobody called we to meeting,' a man shouted above the racket, spittle flying. 'Government say they relocate we. But we have no information about this situation! They no inform we!'

At the scene was the Deputy Minister for Tourism who was being interviewed by a TV crew, a fleecy sound boom in her face.

'Actually, if there's going to be any demolition', she said amid the chaos all around, 'resettlement is going to be a priority.' She was calm behind her Prada shades.

An outraged man responded, 'They say this land is the property of National Tourist Board! But we no be illegal squatters!'

He brandished a piece of paper as evidence of his ownership, but the minister explained to the crowd that an historic treaty – the Wetlands Convention – meant that land around the creek was now of immense value to the government and was currently being polluted by the activities of Crab Town residents. The anger was intense, and the mood turned dark. I was grateful my driver Amadu was out of the car and walking with me.

Someone shouted at the minister, 'You want this for yourself! You want be *rich* people!'

People stood around as, unruffled, the Deputy Minister explained, 'Actually, this area is now a tourist attraction,' stating that the swamps and mangroves of the creek were a biodiversity hotspot, important for migratory birds and breeding fish.

Residents stood agape at her mystifying vocabulary. But she went on, saying the creek supported mangrove forests that acted as carbon sinks and were a natural barrier to flooding and rising sea levels. Looking around at the splintered shanty and rubbish-strewn shallows, her description seemed otherworldly.

Amadu appeared to be looking for someone, his head turning this way and that, straining his full height above the crowds. But a growing unease prompted me to return to the cruiser, and we drove slowly back towards the bridge. The car slowed and Amadu pulled up beside a woman, three young children and an elderly man, walking in the dust in the direction of the bridge, overladen with carrier bags and belongings. Amadu jumped out and spoke to them in a language I later learned was Temne, the language of the northern people.

Out on the mudflats, women and children were stooped, searching for shellfish. Near a wooden dinghy half-beached in the rubbish, was a local man in a baseball cap talking to a European dressed in pale jeans and white shirt. He had an orangey tan and steel-grey hair slicked back. It was the Dutchman I'd met during check in. *Was he also doing research here?* I thought it was an odd place to be doing business, and he didn't seem like an aid worker, not the way I'd seen him treat the hotel porters and the fruit seller on the ferry. But I felt slightly covetous of his close local contacts. I would find out what he was up to. He looked at ease in the chaotic environment of Crab Town. He seemed half local himself. Except he wasn't. And there was something distinctly disagreeable about him.

Amadu returned to the car, and the small group he'd been talking to moved off.

'Do you know those people?' I asked him, mindlessly.

'Yes, ma.'

I looked behind at the bedraggled group trudging in the dust, laden under the weight of their belongings.

'Are they your people?'

'She my cousin wife.'

'Do they have a place to go?' I looked across at him wondering what would become of this family. He was impassive behind his shades. A nerve in his jaw twitched slightly.

'Kroo Bay. They have people there.'

Kroo Bay. A slum dwelling of ten thousand souls in the valley bottom of the toxic Crocodile River, and built on a dump. As we drove, I looked across at Aberdeen Bridge, at its underbelly and the activity going on there. It seemed people were still making that concrete womb their home.

FIVE

MINISTER FOR HEALTH

The Minister for Health sat behind a mahogany desk in the chill of his air-conditioned office. In fact, the Right Honourable Momodu Arthur Bangura was the *Acting* Minister, his predecessor sacked for her mismanagement of the Ebola crisis. Now it was he who had the task of clearing up the mess and restoring credibility to the maligned ministry.

The glare of righteous outsiders was upon him, obsessed as they were with the missing funds. Their persistence had him irritated. Why were they surprised? The money had gone the same way as any other missing aid; there was nothing special about the Ebola funds. It had gone to personal bank accounts and down the labyrinth of patrimonial chains that made up the 'government' in his country. Hah! The Ebola funds were small fry in the business of international aid. He sighed heavily reflecting that, even at that moment, a crush of hopefuls sat in his waiting room, every one of them with the conviction they were entitled to a slice of his pie.

The minister leaned back in his chair, polished shoes on the desk, fingertips steeple like, awaiting the arrival of the PhD from England. No doubt she'd be armed with the usual tedious questions about corruption and transparency. Oh yes...and accountability.

He yearned for a Scotch, but that would have to wait.

A respectful knock on the door interrupted his thoughts and he swung his legs off the desk. A slow-moving receptionist entered, eyed him sympathetically, and introduced his next visitor with formality. The minister rose and moved his short slight frame around the desk to greet her, his hand lax and unenthusiastic.

He was tired of these outsiders and their tedious questions; foreigners who thought they knew his country better than he. He was tired of the games he had to play just to prove "ministerial openness".

Smiling weakly, he said to his visitor, 'Welcome to the Ministry of Health, Miss Hamm. Please...' He indicated a chair whilst returning to his own executive swivel behind the desk. 'How are you finding Freetown?'

She looked uncomfortable, smoothing her dress, trying to pull it down over her knees, rambling on about how much she liked his country. Pretty, he thought. Dark hair neatly tied. Eyes – green or grey? Quite striking. Pale porcelain skin that always made these people seem permanently ill. But she looked nervous. Perhaps it was her first time with a government minister. He attempted a kindly smile as he observed her over his wire-framed spectacles. She opened her bag and brought out a sheaf of papers, notebook, and her dictaphone, placing it precisely on the desk.

'Thank you for your patience, Minister,' she said. 'I appreciate your time. As you know I'm a researcher looking at how the international community's response to Ebola has affected democracy in Sierra Leone.'

The minister's weariness deepened as she continued.

'As a condition of international aid, democracy promotion is central. It's the preferred political arrangement for developing states, especially those emerging from conflict such as yours.'

The minister thought it was a shame about the inaccuracies of her statement, sitting as they were in a Chinese-built government building. He wondered at what point he might break this news to her. Aid from China was increasing year-on-year and was only conditional upon access to resources, not democracy. He wondered where his secretary had put his bottle of malt.

Miss Hamm said, 'Millions of dollars of aid poured into the country for post-war reconstruction and there was the promise of a peaceful future based on democracy, getting the people involved in their governance.'

Now into her stride, a charming smile was forthcoming. Perhaps she was seeking affirmation. But the minister sat back, expressionless.

She said, 'After the war your government pledged big investments in health care, yet the sector was dreadfully exposed during Ebola. And the misuse of Ebola funds seems to have compounded dissatisfaction among the populace.'

The minister's eyebrows shot up, and her monologue ended abruptly.

There followed an uncomfortable silence. All that could be heard was the AC unit shaking on the wall.

Bravely she continued, 'Minister, how do you think these failures and lack of transparency help or hinder the consolidation of democracy in your country?'

Ahh, transparency. The minister sat back in contemplation, his manicured fingers touching steeple-like again. He turned his head to gaze out the window. The Lion Mountains were quite a spectacle from the seventh floor.

After a pause, during which his visitor crossed and uncrossed her legs, smoothing the dress over her knees, he said, 'You are quite right to link transparency in government to democracy. Transparency and accountability, to be precise. Bold and worthy aims. But tell me, what do they mean?'

The minister's question was rhetorical. He had not directed it at her.

He said, 'I'll tell you what it means. It means quite simply that people should see how the money is spent and if it's not spent properly then heads should roll. That's what it means.'

His visitor mumbled affirmatively, and he continued, 'Miss Hamm, where is there evidence that these bold concepts have ever existed in African development politics? Indeed, where is the evidence that they exist in the aid industry itself?' He didn't pause for an answer. 'I will tell you – nowhere. They're all a set of thieves themselves.'

He gazed for a moment at the motionless ceiling fan.

Then stealthily he said, 'Your own government is one of the worst offenders.'

He observed her bemused expression with glee.

She was searching for words but he went on.

'Did you know that when UKDev comes with large cheques earmarked for whatever project…well…we're lucky if we see twenty-five per cent of that. Yes! *Twenty-five per cent*!'

Her stunned expression delighted him, and his voice rose slightly as he asked her reasonably, 'Did you as a UK taxpayer have any notion of *that*?'

She confirmed that she had not.

'I didn't think so. But not only you. Our own people don't know that either. And when they see small evidence of aid coming through, they think their *own* government has stolen it. You are therefore quite right to assume that this is not good for democracy.'

He was pleased with his masterful manipulation of her question and looked her in the eye expectantly.

'Where does the seventy-five per cent go?' She had regained her composure.

'It stays with *them*. Don't you think that's worse than

corruption? We're not talking a few Leones here and a few Leones there. If you want to help people, why do you have to take the lion's share yourself? I'll tell you, because you assume we're all rogues and thieves and so you put your own people, your own projects, and your own ideas in place. Most of the time you don't even consult the ministry in charge!'

The minister's voice had risen considerably. He was getting into his stride himself. It was a mystery to him how these well-educated westerners were so ignorant of the simple facts of life.

He said, 'So what does this mean in the outcome?' She opened her mouth, but he continued, 'I'll tell you. Everything is slow and sluggish and ineffectual. What are the people to *think*? I'll tell you what they think. *Who has stolen the money*? That's what they think.'

'Are you saying your country would be better off without aid?' She checked her dictaphone was running. 'I mean, if they think you are stealing the aid and at the same time they see little benefit for themselves…'

'Of course, we need support,' he conceded. 'We're still quite a feeble state and struggling to stand on our feet. The Ebola crisis is a case in point. It's not aid *per se* that's a threat to our democracy, but the way it's administered. You can't demand transparency and accountability when you do not exercise it *yourself*.'

He rocked back dangerously, his hands posturing. 'Your country was too slow responding to the crisis, waiting for a prompt from the GHO. By the time you came to build new medical facilities the worst of the crisis was over. You admit *now* that you should have engaged with local organisations. We could have told you that, but you never ask. And every time you evaluate your programming you come up with the amazing "idea" that consulting the community first would have been a better approach.'

She agreed it was ridiculous, and disrespectful. There was a short silence as they eyed each other like combatants.

'Let me offer you some water.' The minister rose and poured them both a glass of water. He was warming to this interview. She was not the usual PhD. She was receptive. He liked the way she tilted her head like a parrot, as though she was actually listening. It seemed she had her own ideas, but she was intelligent enough not to wholly buy into them.

'When you talk about democracy,' he said, returning to his swivel and sipping at his water, 'you talk about something that is a dream for the people. Remember, we have a barely functioning parliament – a judiciary that's weak and not fit for purpose. We have friends of the incumbent employed in the civil service, most of whom have no idea what public service means. And we have a large illiterate population.' He smiled charismatically.

She asked, 'How would you respond to the suggestion that if you'd put your public health systems in order, you'd have coped better with the Ebola outbreak?'

'Well, of course we would.' He was unfazed. 'But you tell me how we go from ground zero after war to functioning health service in just ten years? You tell me how a country on its knees builds its health sector with so few doctors and medical staff, and the constant burden of malaria?' He tapped the desk with his index and middle fingers. 'Do you know how many deaths we had from malaria last year? Ten thousand. Yes! And we have lost many health workers to Ebola.'

'It sounds like aid should be targeted better.'

'Hah!' The minister slapped the desk. 'Development agencies write their missions with no consultation with us. They don't trust us to handle money or know what's best for our country. Now we're starting to refuse these demands from donors – we do have our *pride*. Of course, there are bad apples among us, but we're not *all* rogues and thieves.'

SIX
MURRAY TOWN

Now my plans were wrecked. The minister had turned my hypothesis on its head, accusing my own government and the aid industry itself of corruption. He'd made me feel personally responsible. I *did* feel responsible. *Twenty-five per cent.* The figure stuck in my head. How could anyone know for sure how much had gone missing when there were so many links along the chain where funds could be diverted.

We were headed back to the Kangari hotel in the afternoon heat but were stuck in gridlocked traffic at Congo Cross. Amadu, cool behind his shades, inched the Toyota along, his angular jaw busy with gum. The temperature was unbearable. It would take me days to acclimatise. In front of us was a rusting *poda-poda* minibus with the words *Fear Judgement Day* in childish script across the back. Reggae rhythms blasted out: Bob Marley asking, *Could you be, could you be, could you be loved?* We parked by an old tattered billboard: *Our future is in your hands! Keep Salone AIDS Free.* I sat motionless in the heat.

I was thinking about the detour we'd made to Crab Town earlier that day, when Amadu had stopped to speak to his relatives who were making their way to Kroo after the destruction of their home. An idea had seeded in my head.

Kroo Bay. A slum badly affected by Ebola and every other crisis that hit the country. A place that, on the face of it, seemed barely touched by development. But despite the township's squalid reputation, I'd decided I had to go and talk to the residents. Discover the mood in the settlement post-Ebola. Sam Gregory owed me a favour. I'd decided I would call it in and he could set up a meeting.

The heat in the cruiser was intense as we inched along in the crush. Fumes and dust billowing through the windows, hawkers all around, *okada* motorbike taxis weaving in and out of the line, leaning and swerving in their choreographed manoeuvres. The constant pap-pap of horns, the rumble of diesel engines. Sweat prickled as it ran down my neck like the march of ants.

A rake thin arm slid through the open window, its fingers crooked with arthritis, palm upheld and ready for coins. The woman's eyes were milky with cataracts. *Could she see me?* I put ten thousand Leones in her hand. She smiled and withdrew her arm.

'Amadu, can we have some AC?' I asked, closing the window, slightly annoyed. AC was a luxury for which I'd paid extra. He was taking liberties.

He flicked the switch and said, 'Ma, we take road through Murray Town?'

An alternative route to avoid the congestion. So we turned off and were soon making better progress through a residential part of town. It was a road of compacted red earth that ran parallel to the coast, crossed at regular intervals by minor dirt tracks running downhill to the sea. The area was built by Freetown's first settlers, and some buildings still retained their old grandeur with colonnaded verandas and wrought iron balustrades, bougainvillea spilling over. There were a number of original ageing board houses interspersed with blocks of low apartments that were painted pink and white. Razor wire secured their boundaries, and filling the gaps were corrugated shacks and rough cement dwellings. Huge cotton trees sprawled out.

I rang Sam Gregory to ask about Kroo Bay.

'That shithole? Really?'

'It's an obvious place to go now I think about it. I mean, how did the people cope with Ebola living so packed together? And what do they expect from the government now?' It wouldn't be a good idea to just wander there myself, but it was hard convincing Sam that he should take me.

'It's not the best view of Freetown,' he said.

'Exactly. That's the point. Will people talk to me?'

'You realise we've only just come out of the so-called surveillance phase. There's no guarantee we're a hundred per cent clear.' But it was a weak argument.

'GHO announced the end of the outbreak months ago. I'll take my chances.'

He went quiet.

I cajoled, 'Can you help, Sam? Do you have any contacts that could get me in? Maybe one of your people could take me? Maybe set up a focus group?' I paused, 'Of course, I'll pay considerations.'

I *could* pay, generously, and now the idea was in my head I'd decided I was going whether Sam set it up or not.

He sighed heavily. 'I know someone, but you'll need to meet with the chief first. They're sick of foreigners snooping about then nothing ever changes. I'll get back to you.'

He hung up brusquely in his customary way.

The AC was off again, the windows wound down, the heat stifling. My dress was drenched with sweat, hugging me in a sticky embrace. Pink dust kicked up from the road and settled on my skin. Now my hands had swollen. I tried to loosen Graham's ring that fit so tight I worried it would stop my circulation.

Quick as a swift, there was an unexpected movement and

Amadu braked hard. My seat slid forward and my knees hit the dash. A heavy thud as the child struck the windscreen.

The dust rose in a thick cloud as we came to a halt.

For a moment everything was still but for dancing particles in the afternoon sunlight. Then Amadu leapt from the car, waving his arms and shouting words of admonishment. He strode to where the boy had landed whilst I sat dumb, trying to compute what had happened. We'd hit a child. He could be dead.

After a moment the boy stood in the road shocked and dazed, Amadu anxious, checking for injuries, a small crowd gathering. Sliding back the seat I opened the door and stepped out of the car, my heart thumping.

'Is he alright?' I asked, shock weakening my voice. The boy, about ten, wiped his hands on his school shirt, his bonny face guilty and confused. I moved toward him, but Amadu shooed me away.

'Madam, please get in car,' he said.

'He's cracked the windscreen. He must be injured.' But the boy did seem unharmed.

'Madam, please get in car.'

We both looked up as a young woman, dressed in jeans and yellow T-shirt, came running down the same street as the boy.

'Moses!' she cried. She grabbed the child and knelt down, holding his face in her hands, inspecting his expression, his eyes, his shoulders. Moses stood remorseful, not knowing whether to cry.

Amadu spoke to her in *Krio* and she replied defensively, rising to her full height, a match for his aggression. She looked strong, resilient, her beautiful head shaved close. Amadu motioned to where I stood, awkward, halfway from the car.

'I hope he's all right,' I said to the woman. 'Are you his mother?'

She said nothing and looked down. In a protective gesture she drew the boy against her legs. A trickle of blood ran from his nose. Amadu tapped her number into his phone. Then he shooed away the crowd that had gathered. Knowing I shouldn't interfere, I got back in the car and watched them, anxious for the boy who looked abashed and was leaning against the woman. She was tall and equine looking. The kind of face you'd remember anywhere.

Before long Amadu returned to the car and we moved off, past the woman who stood rooted whilst the child retrieved his school bag from the road. Her gaze slid my way, following the car until the dust concealed us.

'Sorry, sorry,' Amadu said as we sped up, the new crack in the windscreen marginally obscuring his view, the late afternoon sun slanting low.

'Will he be ok? What will happen?'

'She take hospital and call me for bill.'

'You will pay his hospital bill?'

'Yes. It is so. Ah don wan dem scandal me.'

———

BACK AT THE KANGARI, I went for a shower, standing behind the curtain under the strong flow, feeling the cool water slide down my body taking with it the grime of the day. It was dark now, and through the tiny window I saw a security guard patrolling the opposite block under the dim yellow lights. He was dressed in uniform, listening to a walkie talkie held sideways to his ear, and covering the same few metres, back and forth. The Dutchman emerged from his room, exchanged a few words and passed the guard what looked like a fistful of currency.

I felt powerful in my voyeur's spot behind the mesh. Hidden. Watching. The scent of gardenia moving through. The Dutchman slunk back into his room, and the guard walked quickly down the stairs and disappeared. Drugs, maybe? I resolved to find a way of meeting him.

Under the shower, I took a block of soap and worked Graham's ring from my swollen finger. The diamond reflected the harsh bathroom light with spectacular brilliance. Relieved, I slid it off, enjoying the freedom it gave, rubbing at the welt that remained.

SEVEN
DIAMOND

The cockerel's call from the dump next door woke me early. Feeling energised with new plans, I made my way down for breakfast. The table was in the window looking out across dense foliage toward the pool, a splash of lagoon blue amid a sea of concrete. Bright bunting hung from a thatched poolside bar and beside it the green, white and blue of the country's flag sagging low on a pole.

The waitress, voluptuous and smiley, stood heavy in one hip. She stroked the tablecloth shyly, waiting for my order. I asked for eggs and English tea.

'Could I have boiling water in a teapot, please?' I spoke slowly and clearly, in the patronising manner of the English.

'Teapot.' She looked blank, waiting for more information.

'Yes, teapot…and boiling water.'

I nodded encouragement, hoping for an improvement on the day before when she'd brought tepid water in a cup and a tea bag on the side. The concept of a simple pot of tea seemed to be incomprehensible to anyone outside the British Isles. To help, I demonstrated pouring water into a cup from a teapot. Immediately, she smiled and with new confidence disappeared into the kitchen. Before long she was back with a plastic jug of tepid water and a tea bag in a cup.

A man, shaped like a Highland bull with shaggy red forelock, sat at a nearby table. He waved his cutlery at me in greeting. I'd met him in the bar the night before. An over-friendly, arrogant racist. A Scot with a fleet of trawlers off the Sierra Leone coast and now in town to bribe the Minister of Fisheries. This was all I knew about him, and he knew nothing about me, but it was enough for me to know he could be useful. A new resource to tap into. His name was Robbie McIntyre.

Crossing to the buffet, I helped myself to glistening slices of fruit laid out on vast platters: mango, papaya, watermelon. Returning to my table I nodded at Robbie who was keenly breakfasting on a plate of fried food.

Later, he rose stiffly and walked in heavy strides in my direction. He removed the serviette from under his chin and wiped his mouth with the back of his hand.

'Mornin', lassie.' He leaned his weight on the table, his hands massive, fingers like meaty sausage.

'Morning. Good breakfast?' I asked.

'Just the usual crap.' He shook his ginger head and lifted the plastic jug from my table, '*These people,*' he said with disgust. 'Look at this for Chrissake.'

'Just a misunderstanding,' I said, offended by his tone.

'Misunderstanding, my arse. Freaking idiots.' He stifled a belch.

I flinched and looked down at my breakfast. Later, when I recalled what he'd said, I regretted not defending the hotel staff.

He looked at his watch, pink stomach hairs visible through the gaping buttons of his shirt. He pulled out a chair and sat down. I felt embarrassed to be British, tarnished by the monster at my table.

'When's your meeting with the minister?' I asked.

'Not 'til tomorrow,' he said. 'I've got other business today. Port authorities.'

Then he asked with minimal interest, 'This your first time in Freetown?' He pulled out the phone from his breast pocket, checking for messages.

'Er, yes. Well, no. I mean, not for a long time.' I didn't want to share my history with this ghastly oaf.

'Thought so. You on your own?'

'Well, not really. I mean, I'm working with people here in the country. Doing research for the university.'

'Oh, yeah. Right.' He looked at me for a moment, perplexed.

Changing the subject I asked, 'Did you say your trawlers are already here? I mean, in Sierra Leone waters?'

'Yeah, yeah. We're trawling a number of zones around the coast, but I want a new deal for the Sierra River Delta.'

'Why's that?'

'Snapper and barracuda. Worth a fuckin' fortune.'

It seemed that quotas imposed by the European Union had encouraged Robbie to move his fleet from Scotland to places with incompetent government and flexible arrangements, where a bribe here and there, no matter how hefty, would be rewarded with tonnes of quality fish. Robbie preferred post-conflict states, or failed states, where governments were on their knees and opportunities were at their best.

'The stocks are fantastic right now,' he said. 'After a country has war, you know, the fighting and now this disease thing. Nobody's been fishin'.'

He was there to exploit the weakness of the government and its regulatory institutions. But despite his odious character, I decided I was going to stick with him. I was going to use him to find out how you bribe a minister.

My eggs had gone cold when he checked his watch again, then rose to go.

'We'll catch up later, yeah?' He held out a mutton chop hand in an oddly formal way. Then he said, 'We're away to Hill Station tonight if you want to come.' He gestured towards a Middle Eastern looking man who had breakfasted at his table and was now reading a newspaper.

Robbie continued, 'It's a proper restaurant with foreign staff. Best in Freetown. None of this crap.' He gestured at the waitress who'd come to collect my plate. 'Come with us?' He was nodding, confident of my answer.

Hill Station, a former colonial mansion, where foreign businessmen and Freetown ministers dined and closed deals, popular with foreign aid workers, a place to network with Freetown elite. I was in.

'Great. Thanks.'

'Good. See ye at eight.' He got up and walked away satisfied.

It occurred to me that his invitation might be a prelude to something else, but Robbie McIntyre didn't give off that vibe. Nothing alerted me to any sexual interest and I suspected his predilection lay with the local girls. Maybe he wanted my company as a ruse for something else. Maybe he was just being friendly – fellow ex-pats and all that. Thinking about the possibilities I decided to wear the ring, hoping it would give me some protection in the event of a misunderstanding.

ON THE WAY back to my room I picked up a call from Sam.

'I've got you a guide for Kroo.'

'Great!'

'Her name is Memanatu Browne. You call her Mrs Browne. She'll meet us here at the office and will use your transport to get to Kroo.'

'Thanks, Sam.' I knew he'd come good. 'Did you have any luck with the focus group?'

'Talk to her about it when you meet, she's setting something up. She's related to the chief so don't forget considerations.'

'I won't forget. Thanks, Sam.'

'Yeah. You owe me!' But we were even.

A security guard was patrolling the block as I let myself into my room. Feeling energised at the news from Sam I acknowledged the guard with a smile – a mistake, as he turned and came toward me asking if I would like the hotel's massage services. Politely I declined but would let him know if I changed my mind. That would be another mistake. It seemed hotel security had many functions, intermediaries for other goods and services. The Dutchman and his drugs – or so I thought – and now sexual services.

In my room I went to the safe to get the ring and see if I could get it back on my finger, still swollen. But the diamond wasn't there. Guiltily I realised I must have left it on the window shelf by the shower. It was worth a fortune and I chastised myself for being so lax. But on the window shelf the mosquito mesh gaped where wire cutters had done their work. I stood looking at it, trying to make up an alternative story to the one that stared me in the face.

Rushing to the safe I took out everything; then I checked all my belongings searching bags, toiletries, make-up, even the case for my sunglasses. It wasn't there. Nor was it in the pockets of any of my clothes. I went to the bathroom and searched the floor, all shelving, the plug holes, the pockets of my robe. The panic started to rise as several alternative but implausible narratives entered and exited my head. The consequences of what might happen to the thief if they were found. *Should I report it?*

EIGHT
HILL STATION

The cracked macadam surface on Regent Road strained under the heavy evening traffic. *Okada* taxi riders weaving in and out like free-flowing streams of water. The ceaseless pap-pap of tired motor horns a constant soundtrack to the city.

Freetown was otherworldly after dark; a medieval scene where half-lit forms sat in makeshift booths precariously set upon the earth. Here and there, faces were illuminated by the glare of charcoal braziers. Vendors worked under awnings, their tables lit with lanterns, and shadowy figures moved from lamplight to fire, going about their business, barely visible in the dark. Shack shops were still trading and phone booths were busy, street hawkers shouldering trays of cigarettes, sim cards and gum, peering into passing cars as they slowed in the traffic.

I travelled in the back of air-conditioned, leather-uphol-stered luxury. A black Range Rover with uniformed driver that had been hired by Robbie for the night. It was easier to see out than see in through the dark tinted windows and I hoped I was invisible from outside. The persistent tap-tap on the glass was disturbing. It was good to be concealed knowing what people thought of the occupants of this car, travelling in style while the world outside toiled in the heat.

Beside me sat Bernard. Lebanese diamond inspector and acquaintance of Robbie McIntyre. Well dressed, dark haired and olive skinned.

He leaned forward to speak to Robbie whose vast frame crowded the seat in front.

'Yeah, didn't have a problem,' Robbie said. He'd been to bribe people at the Port Authority that day. Expecting them to ignore his illegal fishing fleet. 'Once you get the right guy, it's just a matter of how much.'

'What's the name?' Bernard enquired.

'Guy called Turay. Used to work at the Roads Ministry but now something senior at the docks. He's got people at Lungi who'll look after you.'

Lungi Airport, where millions of dollars' worth of illicit diamonds were smuggled out of the country every year. Robbie handed Bernard the business card of his Lungi contact.

The vehicle lurched down a pothole, and swerved to avoid another, then we turned to accelerate up a densely wooded incline away from gridlocked Regent Road towards Hill Station. Near the top we turned into a secure compound, pulling up under a graceful portico framed with elegant ferns the size of trees. Bougainvillea crept over the shallow roof, and pretty white flowers lit by lamps were attached to the portico's columns.

A deafening cicada chorus met us as we stepped from the car, and we moved from airless humidity through security into the air-conditioned foyer of the club. Furnishings of African art, tiles of terracotta and clay, the low hum of chatter, the stink of privilege.

'Lady, gentlemen, this way please…'

The restaurant was open-sided, Freetown's twinkling lights far below. We were led to a table with linen cloth and napkins, faux silverware, sparkling glasses and an attentive waiter. Soon there were two bottles of red wine and a glass of beer on the table. A few thirsty gulps and Robbie had downed the beer.

'Fuck, that's better.' He waived the waiter away with orders to bring another.

The buttons were straining on his shirt, his armpits already wet.

The restaurant was busy with an eclectic clientele. What they all had in common was money.

Awkwardness descended.

The place reminded me of my childhood, when I had lived in the High Commissioner's residence in the cool hills above the shanties, and the bustling markets, and chaotic docks. A closed community of manicured lawns and elegant palms, of gin and tonics and rowdy socials, of tennis and golf and house boys. Of envious stares and mistrustful encounters. Of swimming pools and international schools, of cinemas and clubs. Of palms and frangipani, and a shop with imported goods – Kellogg's Cornflakes and Rowntree's Fruit Pastilles. An entire community ostentatiously marooned within a landscape of grinding poverty.

Not much had changed.

I reminded myself why I'd come to Hill Station with Robbie. It was because I wanted to know how you got to bribe a government minister. How much it cost, and what was the process. Who was favoured, who was not. Exactly how corruption worked.

The waiter stood patient, anticipating the moment when Robbie and Bernard would finish their conversation before he leaned in to hand us the menus, opening the cards and laying them proudly on the table.

'Chateauneuf. Yeah. Chateauneuf.' Robbie was examining the wine. 'This ok for you?' He was asking Bernard not me.

The waiter stood ready to answer questions about the menu, but Robbie shooed him away.

Privilege weighed on me like an anvil. I hadn't been the usual ex-pat kid; pampered, brattish, entitled. Back then, I'd wanted to escape the secured compound and explore the curious scene outside the razor wire. Assimilate, as though a girl like me had any notion what that might mean. I wanted to be in the noise and the hustle, the woodsmoke and the spices, the rhythms and the colours, and the people, whose skin was so much darker than my own.

Africa. Still rooted in the heart of my soul's imagination.

'Remind me what you're doing here?' Robbie asked, vaguely interested. For a moment I thought he meant there at Hill Station, as a surprise guest, such were my feelings of insignificance.

'I'm doing fieldwork for a PhD.' The men's expressions became vacant. Bernard began tapping into his phone. Robbie looked down and picked his ear.

'It's research. I want to know how the scandal of the missing Ebola funds has impacted on democracy.' That didn't register either, but I continued, 'And the long-term peace, you know, justice and democracy.' I was angry having to justify my existence.

'Hah! Ebola,' said Robbie, waking up, his voice embarrassingly loud where we sat in the centre of the room. 'What do people expect? They pour in millions of dollars but don't care where it goes.' Then he launched into a monologue about the ineptitude of the international community to control how money was spent in a multitude of developing nations. He shook his ginger head condescendingly. 'They don't learn. It's like a different fucking world out here.'

Yes, it's a different world out here.

There we sat, fellow Brits in the tropics. Part of an exclusive club where the rules of polite society got dumped for the exercise of more primordial impulses. Once *in the tropics*, we became disconnected from the restraints of civilised modernity, of the norms to be expected if we were anywhere else. *In the field*, polite inhibitions to be discarded as casually as a reptile sheds its skin. Debauchery *de rigueur* if one was to do one's ex-pat duty. Europeans had been hiding in the tropics for millennia; the British in the hills of Shimla, their centre of power and pleasure in India. And Mr Kurtz in Conrad's *Heart of Darkness*, the debased white man living the hypocritical rules of colonialism in deepest darkest Congo, with horrifying consequences. And the bored British aristocracy of Kenya's Happy Valley.

I drained my glass of Chateauneuf, embarrassed how quickly my mind had wandered to such behaviour among ex-pats, and curious as to how quickly I'd got there in the company of Robbie McIntyre.

Two whole lobsters arrived, and the men tucked in while I toyed with a bean salad. They talked about business in Sierra Leone, and I waited for my chance to pop the question. The wine was good, and I was grateful when the waiter refilled my glass. Robbie took the bottle from him and sloshed a glass for himself. Time went by. Soon the men were wolfing beef tenderloin as I sat studying a plate of Jambalaya.

Robbie was engaged in illegal fishing. That much was clear.

He spoke without shame. 'Yeah, their fisheries law, it bans foreign vessels. No-go within thirty-five miles of the coast. All this crap about depriving local fishermen. We need a permit, but flags of convenience work just the same.'

'Flags of convenience?' I asked.

'Yeah. Armed government guys ride inflatable boats and patrol the waters, you know. In theory the stocks are protected. But when they see the flags of convenience, they leave us alone.'

Bastard.

Protected stocks of snapper, grouper, sardines, mackerel

and shrimp – hauled out by Robbie's nets. The dhows and pirogues of local fishermen harassed by the armed patrols, not Robbie's trawlers. I wondered what it would cost to keep the minister off his back.

'How do you get a flag of convenience?' I asked.

'Ten grand, US,' he said. 'Pennies. The guy just wants school fees for his kids. Seeing him tomorrow.'

'The minister?'

'Yeah. Fisheries.'

It seemed a pretty good deal for Robbie, but poor Bernard had to dig deeper because the government was now restrained by international law on diamond exports. There was a new scheme in place to check the provenance of diamonds. It was called the Kimberley Process and prevented so-called conflict diamonds entering the mainstream trade. Breaking international law came at a higher price.

'Fifty! Fifty grand?' Robbie snorted. 'He's robbing you mate.'

'It's all relative,' replied Bernard, chewing rhythmically on his beefsteak.

They talked about the labour laws. Foreign vessels had to, by law, employ local workers.

'Nah, we only have one on board,' said Robbie, stuffing a bloodied forkful in his mouth. 'They talk about quotas, but nobody wants to enforce them.' He chomped noisily, the pulp visible. 'It's only the flags of convenience that need negotiating. We don't get any trouble.'

Gulping down draughts of water, I regretted ordering piri-piri with the Jambalaya.

So that's all it took, I thought. Wander into the minister's office and deliver some cash. Job done. Maybe do some deals with the Port Authorities. To hell with local laws. It all seemed so casual.

My attention began to wander, taking in the carefully preserved colonial setting and the diverse bunch of diners. A couple in a quiet booth nearby sat head-to-head like pigeons. I recognised the man as the Minister for Agriculture and Lands, Robertson Abu Thomas. The woman looked European, a ghostly white complexion and Titian curls lying around her head like a Louis XV picture frame. The minister was being wooed. He sat captivated as she attended to his wine, ignoring the watchful waiter whose job she undermined. She wore an emerald silk shift on her skinny frame and a striking amber pendant that lay flat against her chest.

Close by, members of a large group were finishing their meal at a circular table. Among them Ann Wilson – the country manager for UKDev – an auspicious woman, powerful in aid circles and someone who'd already confirmed an interview with me. Her department had delivered the funding for Ebola support, and there was plenty I thought she could help me understand. Dining with her were a bunch of young and jovial types. Maybe they were colleagues from UKDev. Interns perhaps. Their camaraderie made me envious.

They got up to leave, divvying up some Leones for the staff, laughing among themselves as they moved toward the exit. But Ann Wilson stopped as she passed the table of the Minister for Agriculture. At once he stood to acknowledge her, wiping crumbs from his mouth, and placing his napkin on the table. Shaking hands, they exchanged pleasantries. Ann Wilson nodded curtly at the minister's Titian companion whose gaze remained transfixed on her dessert. There was something distinctly awkward about the encounter; an indeterminate tension between the two. It was obvious from their reactions that the women were acquainted.

NINE

DOROTHY

I lie on my mat by the foul mattress and wait for him to come. The earth floor beneath me is hard, but it is comfortable. The mat, it is important to me. I can shake it and brush it and wash it, and know that it is clean. The mattress, that is never clean.

Sweat moistens my brow, fear quickens my heart. It is dark now and soon he will come. He always comes, unless the rains have flooded our hut. Every day I wake, knowing the dark will come, and so will he. For now, this is my life. But it does not define me.

Where I lie is a private space, my place behind the curtain that is torn and tattered and divides slim portions of our hut. It is the place where I dream the nightmares and plot the dreams and hide my precious things – books, money, contraceptive pills. No one is invited here. But *he* comes invited or not.

Our home is five square metres of tin and cement and dirt. We are lucky. Some shacks are built on the dump. Three walls are rusted iron. They are supported, insufficiently, by timber posts. The fourth is crumbling concrete with a slatted door that does not fit. Outside, we have a porch made of sturdy sticks and UNICEF tarpaulin, the place my mother sits to smoke. Our home is in a precarious place. Some years it is swept away by the floodwater that overwhelms our settlement.

One day soon we will leave this place.

At night, my mother sleeps bundled in her rocking chair. But when *he* comes, she moves her aching bones into the night. Where she goes, I do not know. Maybe nowhere. Hanging around in the dark.

Every night he parks his Benz by the bridge on Kroo Town Road. He makes his way in his shiny shoes through the alleys, between the shacks, skipping the gutters and garbage to spare those polished shoes. I wait, my books put away, the lamp extinguished, hoping he won't come because he's dead.

The door creaks and tells me he's not dead. The crack of wood against iron, and the slap of slippers against heels, tell me my mother has woke and gone. There are murmurings, nothing more. The swish of the curtain, then the slash of his zipper, but I lie still and curled on my mat. No good reason why I should make it easy. My father is dead. Now I no longer have his protection, so my abuser comes and takes what he wants. His stench fills the space.

He stands behind expecting me to rise. He is angry, but I am strong, and used to beatings. He wants it easy.

Before, he would use a knife to stop the screams. But now that is not necessary. I know he will cut me if I make the slightest sound. The threat is real. He has that mind.

I fear pregnancy; a child does not fit with my grand plans. Poor women of *Salone* are tied with hungry *pikin*, dependent on a man, powerless, no hope of anything outside the slum. But those are not my plans. I am an educated woman. So, I steal his money – go visit the clinic at the edge of town – and hide those pills in a tiny space inside the mattress.

Before Ebola took his life, my father had plans for me, his clever daughter. I would learn and serve our country, do better than he. Himself, he was a soldier in our war; nothing he had done had ever served our country. Maybe his shame would have killed him if Ebola had not, sickened as he was with remorse inside his soul. When the violence began in '91, he was a child. Abducted from his village. He and his brother, taken by the fighters, dragged from their home when the terror came to town. But everything the rebels did led to disaster, and when the violence stopped, another madness took its place. Many who survived were tormented by the terrors they had wrought. Men like my father. But his brother, recruited by a different gang, shows no remorse. And this is the man who stands behind me now.

───────

HE KICKS my spine with his shiny shoe. I do not respond. He grabs my arm, wrenches it vengefully, and I wonder if it will break this time. His hand cracks my head and there is dullness in my ear. Dizziness. Roughly he picks me up, drags me over the mattress, filthy and stained. Ridden with fleas and maggots, and his stench. He squeezes my throat to a fraction of life, and positions himself awkwardly, his legs bound together by the belt of his pants. Lack of oxygen to my brain, it reminds me of the damage he might do. I lie still and move my mind elsewhere. Switch off my intellect, my emotions, my body. I am no longer here.

Yes, I think of killing him. But what happens to women in our prisons? Far worse than he could do to me.

The sounds. The slash of his zipper, the swish of the curtain, and he leaves without a word. Then the slap of slippers against heels, and the crack of wood against iron, that tell me my mother has returned. The weight of her frame is heavy in the rocker. She sucks palm wine from the bottle, and falls asleep.

This is my life for now, but it does not define me.

One day soon we will leave this place.

TEN

DOROTHY

My mother is sleeping when I wake and light the lamp. The dawn has yet to come. I fill the bowl with water from the bucket and wash. I step outside and toss the contents in the gutter. Residents are about their business, the settlement is busy at this hour. People moving water from the public tap, clanking the cooking pots, filling their baskets for the market, setting off early to secure their spot.

Lighting the cooking fires.

The stench of kerosene starts panic in my mind. But I control it. I step back inside the hut, I dress, wipe my feet and push them into sneakers. I move quietly, extinguish the lamp, pass my sleeping mother and step into the street.

In the dim dawn, a neighbour across the gully sits outside her hut. She is nursing her child. Her *lappa* droops across her breasts. Behind stands her husband, anxious. The two look at me with hopeless eyes. Their child has diarrhoea. Two brothers and a sister died this way.

I tell my neighbour, 'Ma, I will bring salts from the clinic for your child.'

'May God bless you my daughter,' she replies.

I steal money from my employer. I have enough. I hide it in the mattress with my pills.

I LEAVE Kroo Town and climb the road to Tower Hill, an affluent place where crude displays of stolen wealth stand out. I am on my way to my abuser's house, where I work and clean. Take care of his kids. My abuser used to work at the Ministry for Transport. Now he is boss of the Port Authorities. Like a fool, he aspires to be a *big man*.

His house on Circular Road is large and comfortable, and bought for three hundred thousand dollars stolen from the EU aid for roads. The place is low and pink. It has barred windows and a deep, shady veranda.

Dumb security guards sit by the gates and watch me pass with hungry eyes.

'Hey sister! *How di bodi?*'

Rags of fools. Halfwits drawn from his scraps of former fighters.

I move through the gates into the compound. The aged mango casts a shadow on his Benz. It is polished to a shine, just like his shoes.

The child, Moses, sits on the veranda, legs dangling. He is dressed ready for school and occupying his usual moody self, sitting with his elbows on his knees, chin propped in his hands.

'What's up?' I ask, wondering if he has pain from yesterday. Thinking the hospital may have missed a broken bone since the accident with the car.

The child replies, 'They fightin'.'

His parents are always fighting. Uncle Turay beating on his wife, just like he beats on me. He is a violent man.

'Where are your sisters?' I ask, concerned the little girls see the anger in their home.

'They in they room with Bertha.'

Bertha is the household cook.

I sit with Moses, dangle my legs, put an arm around his shoulders. Fear seeps from the house like a bad wound.

We wait. Watch sparrows pecking in the dirt, hopping to and fro, little plumes of dust around their feet. The sun is up, and warmth is on our bodies, but Moses sits beside me stiff and quiet. The house is silent. We wait for him to emerge, never knowing what might ensue.

The door opens and he strides out, straightens his tie, steps into his car. He does not look my way. Coward. Afraid to connect me to the night before. His son's head is down, glancing from beneath his brow, feared of his father. The fools at the gate react in panic. Like imbeciles their feet are up. They raise the gate and the Benz pulls away.

I TAKE MOSES' hand and we set off for school. Walking swift to Siakka Stevens where the *poda-poda* stop. We wait in the queue and the bus to Aberdeen soon arrives. It will drop at Congo Cross where we walk the rest of the way to the Grammar School in Murray Town. It is a good school but, the boy, he is not that bright.

People crowd around, edging for the bus, using many tactics to make sure they get inside. The *poda-poda* boy, he rides the bumper so he can sell his seat. I pay him and we step into the bus. People shuffle up and we move to a spot on the second bench. Reggae music is blasting. Moses sits and stares out of the window.

Some days my cousin rides the same bus as we. His name is Charles. He travels to work at the big hotel in Aberdeen from his home in Tengbeh Town. Today is one of those days. When the bus slows I see him waiting in the street. The boy jumps off the bumper, collects the fair, the door slides open and Charles steps in. His bright smile flashes when he sees me.

'Sister!' He squeezes in and we embrace in an awkward fashion. He pats Moses' head, and the boy smiles up, showing the toothy gap where he likes to twiddle a stick.

My cousin says to me, 'How is my sister on dis good mornin'!' He has enthusiasm for life.

'I am well,' I lie. 'Tell me your news.'

He hesitates for a moment. Then he says, 'Dey has bin *palave*r at hotel.' He looks around and lowers his voice, 'Diamond gone *wey*...big price.'

Charles works at the Kangari hotel. It is a good job. The place is full of westerners and the tips are high. But a stolen ring is terrible news. Someone will get sacked and beaten. That person will never work again in the western area. Their family will be destituted.

My cousin looks down at his hands.

I ask, 'Will you be safe?'

'Maybe,' his usual smile trembles a little. 'Dey say it was taken from her bathroom. Some body cut di wire. I was not workin' in that area, but I worry for my friend, Saidu.'

'Is he accused?'

'Not yet, sister.'

The whole bus is tuned in to our talk. The driver has lowered the reggae on the radio.

I ask in a hush, 'Who took it?'

He looks over his shoulder to see how many listen in.

He says, 'We don know for sure. It big diamond ring. I saw it when she checked in.' He looked at me with worried eyes. 'She from England.'

Fear would now be spreading through our people at the Kangari. Who would be so foolish to risk their job? If management can't find the one who took it, they will sack someone anyway. It is important for rich people to have justice. Something we never see for ourselves.

'Why do you worry for Saidu,' I ask my cousin.

His voice lowers further, 'He was patrolling di block. Maybe he look di other way.'

My cousin's smile has gone now, it is replaced by fear. Something we are used to in our country.

I RETURN to the compound of my abuser.

The poor women of *Salone*, we have few choices. No matter how clever we might be. We suffer at the hands of men. Women and girls, violated every day. Rape normalised in our society. Our mothers, our daughters, our sisters. A life of fear and humiliation for so many. They say it is a legacy from the war. I say that is a man's excuse. We have laws to protect us, but no one is interested in enforcing them. There is impunity for men. Subjugation for women.

But I am not a subjugated woman. I have calculated my abuser's worth to me.

I enter the house quietly, never knowing what to expect. There is no sign of auntie, the kids' mother, who drinks. In the kitchen, Moses' sisters sit at the counter looking pretty in their lemony dresses. They are twins, five years old. Bertha, stirs a heavy pot on the flame. She turns and we exchange our glances. Bertha cares for the kids. The girls are young and she arrives early to make their breakfast. But her real plan is to protect them. She believes the girls should not be witness to their father's violence. She believes that to see violence is to normalise violence, to condone it and perpetuate it. Bertha is like me. She believes in change.

I ask, 'How is she?' I am referring to my Auntie Turay.

Bertha says, 'She in her room.'

I nod. Then ask, 'Does she need anything?'

'Maybe,' Bertha says, straightening the lemony ribbons in the cornrows of the twins. 'It look bad today.'

'I'll pick up at the clinic,' I say, knowing there are plenty Leones to pay for arnica oil to heal the bruises. And for the salts to help the sick child of my neighbour.

My Auntie Turay leaves money unattended, even though there is a safe bolted to the basement floor. She is a weak and wretched woman. Spends her days recovering from the beatings, getting sober, or getting drunk. There is always money for the clinic, but also it is easy for me to steal from her. Cash and food, and other useful items such as phone credit. With the money I buy books and internet time, and pills, and plan the future. A future where he can't get me. A future when I will serve the people of my country, and not him.

Bertha asks me, 'How is ma?'

She asks about my mother's mind, because it is never well.

'Things are still the same,' I answer.

Violent flashbacks keep my mother prisoner of her own self-loathing. There is terror in our past, and sometimes in her fear and madness, my mother destroys the hut. She has many needs, but *diamba* helps her cope. So, I work for my abuser to pay for what she needs. He knows this. Thinks we are trapped. It is a risk, but I take his money and I steal much more.

Poor women of *Salone*, they have no choices. But me, I've made my choice.

ELEVEN

DEMOCRACY FOR SALONE

Amadu dropped me in the Brookfields district, close to the Youyi Building where I'd met the Minister for Health. I was early for my meeting with Sam and his contact, Mrs Browne, so I wandered the roadside among the market women. This was an area where fruit sellers lined the way selling produce they'd brought from their village, long distances away. Bananas, oranges, papaya and pineapple, all arranged in bowls balanced on stools that stood among the kerbside rubble. Rickety tables were laden with tomato paste, okra, onions, magi cubes and cassava leaf. Staple ingredients for the rich sauces favoured in their cuisine.

A woman in a tangerine headscarf stood proud beside her fruit. I greeted her and bought a pineapple.

'*Tenki ma.* You take mango? Is nice.'

I stashed the fruit in my rucksack and crossed to the offices of *Democracy for Salone*, two floors of a modern white-washed building. There was orange bougainvillea cascading from a first-floor veranda. The flags of Sierra Leone, the EU, UK and US, blew together affectionately at the compound's gate. Parked up were two spanking new Land Cruisers and a high-powered motorbike. A sign above the door read: *Expect More From Your Government.*

Sam emerged buoyant and tripped down the steps to greet me. Tall and confident in a traditional shirt of cobalt blue, black trousers with a permanent crease, and super-lustrous crocodile shoes. He looked relaxed in his home town, and pulled back to appraise me, underdressed in chinos and white shirt. Ready for Kroo.

'*How di bodi*, my friend?' He stepped in to embrace me with hard, muscled arms. It was easy to warm to Sam; reassuringly confident, always in control.

'*De bodi fine*,' I answered, 'Good to see you, Sam.' I was hopeful about his contacts in Kroo Bay. There was something to be discovered there, I knew it.

'Welcome to *Democracy for Salone*,' he said in a theatrical manner, arms wide, 'Come. I will show you round before our guest arrives.' He moved sideways up the steps, careful not to scuff his shoes.

I followed him into the building past a pretty receptionist and down a bright corridor into an open office. One by one he introduced me to the staff – young, smart, working at Apple computers. They looked up and greeted me warmly. A lively ceiling fan rotated above our heads. Venetian blinds closed against the vicious morning sun. Modern furniture and equipment. This organisation had funding. The United Nations itself had used *DfS* to monitor the post-war elections. Aid was pumping in from all quarters, the UK government being the most generous donor.

We moved to the coffee machine, 'Milk and sugar?'

'No thanks.'

He handed me a paper cup and we worked our way upstairs, Sam carrying his drink with the tips of his manicured fingers. I followed his long legs and lustrous shoes up to the first floor, into a training room with open windows. A group of young people mingled there in anticipation of a presentation.

Sam explained, 'We're currently training staff for sensitisation on voter registration.'

This was surprising because the international community had spent huge sums on this at the end of the war over a decade ago.

'Do people still need sensitisation after all this time?' I asked.

'Yes, yes, they do.' He nodded his shaved head, immaculately razored across the hairline. 'Especially up-country around the plantations. People there are still misinformed.'

'Right.'

'Don't forget there are still rogues in our country who try their utmost to *de-sensitise* people. You know, persuading them to register their family twice, encouraging electoral officers to stuff the ballots. Things like that. And,' he added without irony, 'cash for votes is still common. A lot of donor money goes that way.'

Twenty five percent. I looked down at his crocodile shoes.

He said, 'It's one thing sensitising the public, quite another sensitising political parties to do *their* bit. We need to move from educating voters to educating parliamentarians.' Sam was an impressive orator. 'They need to understand what their responsibilities *are* and what the democratic process *means.* I'm pushing for that. This is part of my research also.' He nodded, impressed by his own ideas.

Sam continued, 'Until people start to see real change from elections and believe their lives will get better, they'll continue to think cash for votes is to the benefit of democracy. It's an on-going battle.'

I was thinking about the money chain: western taxpayers, international aid, national government, corrupt politicians, voting populace. We'd do just as well sending our money to a local farmer to buy some goats.

I lowered my voice and asked, 'Then how d'you know sensitisation is working with all that going on? I mean, the duplicity of it. Makes no sense at all, does it?'

'Well we don't,' he said flatly. 'But we have to keep pushing.'

The trainees were now seated in a semi-circle with notepads at the ready, and I considered what a pointless exercise this must be. Reading my mind – after all, we'd been in the same study group for three years – Sam led me out of the room saying quietly,

'There *is* no culture of democracy here. You know that as well as I do. As far as the donors are concerned it's all a bit of a game, for them as well as for us. But if we play the game, the donors are happy because they're spending their funding, then the money trickles down and people get to send their kids to school. That can only be good for our country and that's ok with me. In and amongst, we *do* get things done.'

This was an enormous admission. Cash for votes. Aid for votes.

I asked, 'But how does that affect you as a scholar, Sam? Isn't there a conflict going on in your head?'

'Not at all! Don't forget my work is about political culture among the people, how long it might take to change it, or even if that's possible at all. We're working at ground level. It's the only way to influence the people.'

At York, we all agreed that Sam would be President one day, such were his masterful skills in debate. I was envious; grass roots studies held the utmost legitimacy. People would talk more freely to Sam than they ever would to an outsider like me.

Sweat began to bead above my lip. I tried to settle, dispelling the doubts, controlling the anger. It seemed acceptable to Sam for politicians to buy votes with UK aid, and I started wondering about his own organisation.

MRS BROWNE WAS a large woman with a manly physique whose frightening baritone filled the space. She was thirty minutes late but making her impatience known.

She snapped at the cowering receptionist, 'Come along. I busy. Go fine him...'

We approached the desk and the girl looked up with a thankful expression.

'Samuel,' Mrs Browne cooed as he took her hand, her wrist heavy with bangles.

'Memu.' Sam's voice was soft and flirtatious, his almond eyes doing their work. Then they launched into a mutual appreciation in *Krio.*

Mrs Browne was quite a spectacle. Her head dressed in a dazzling lilac cloth that was wrapped in a complicated style; it was stuck with feathers that moved excitedly under the overhead fan and her clashing pink ensemble parcelled her body like a birthday gift.

The two chatted away and I stood by waiting for an introduction, like a faded sepia at the edge of the scene. She studied me slyly from the corner of her eye. Mrs Browne was principally a business woman with a trading company in the suffocating downtown Big Market where she employed many staff to toil in the heat. Meanwhile she preoccupied herself with lucrative NGO work, and today she was working for Sam escorting *the English* to a meeting with the residents of Kroo Bay. I had a lot invested in this woman. She was to be my translator. If the people trusted her, perhaps they would talk more freely to me.

She took my hand limply, hers barely brushing my skin, like she was checking for dust.

'First, we go for visit to di chief,' she said.

This was the local chief in Kroo Town, a man with whom she had a complex familial relationship. Before I could enter the settlement I needed his permission to visit his chiefdom. A common practice sometimes involving substantial bribes. Once the chief had agreed, we would move on to a meeting she'd arranged in the community building at the heart of the township.

'Come along. Don keep him waitin',' she said, as though it was me who'd turned up late.

TWELVE
KROO

Amadu dropped us at the intersection of Waterloo Street and Lightfoot Boston Street, close to the bridge over the Samba gutter. Mrs Browne began her monologue describing the history of the settlement. She moved from one side of the bridge to the other, waving her jangling hands to illustrate the geography. Kroo lacked all public services. Clean water, and sanitation, housing, electricity. Everything. None of that distinguished it from any other slum except its direct access to the Atlantic Ocean, its foundation on a rubbish dump, and its position at the end of the Samba gutter.

Every year the settlement flooded and was almost washed away. Livestock was lost and homes swept to the sea. People died. Samba was the town's main drain, and took surface water that surged from the Lion Mountains through the city to the sea. It was also a dumping ground for rubbish. So, come the worst of the rains, water had nowhere to go but to overflow down the valley and submerge the shanty below. Once submerged, effluent from open sewers floated like curds in whey along with debris lifted from the dump. It became a toxic lake with archipelagos of dilapidated homes. The stench intensified and cholera stepped in.

'This is where di *watta* comes in,' said Mrs Browne, gesturing. 'When di heavy rain come, it rise up and flood every ting. Homes, business. Every ting.'

From where we stood on the bridge, I could see the crawling river of garbage beneath. Plastic bottles, clothing, broken electrical goods, all manner of human detritus on the journey uptown to downtown where it met the Crocodile River in Kroo.

Mrs Browne led the way past a line of girls armed with yellow jerry cans waiting at a public tap. She walked in a slow-moving fashion down a steep concrete track that led into the settlement itself, a spreading landscape of rusted tin and tattered tarpaulin. Dusty-faced kids moved in behind us, whistling, chanting, selling nuts and matches. They called after me in English *'Good mornin' ma! How are you!'*

Mrs Browne wafted them away and we edged through a labyrinth of waste-filled alleys, picking our way across open sewers and clogged gutters, past lads fixing bicycles and an elderly gentleman whittling antelope from scraps of mahogany. Walking swiftly in the opposite direction were suited men carrying briefcases on their way to the business district, and a graceful woman trailing two laughing girls in flamingo pink dresses.

The kids who were following our progress had grown in number, giggling, shouting *'Oporto! How are you!'* Hands covered grubby faces when I turned to chat, reaching in my bag for my stash of sweets.

Mrs Browne looked at me disapproving.

'Don do dat.'

'What?'

'Do you want di whole town upon us?'

'Sorry,' I smiled at the kids and we moved on, but they followed even closer, singing and chanting.

The Community Centre was near the town's football pitch – a wide expanse of beaten red earth where teams from every part of the slum took part in tournaments. The building had a blue roof and whitewashed walls, its windows glassless with vertical bars cemented at close intervals for security.

The meeting room was already crammed with people seated in rows of plastic chairs as though waiting for a lecture. I asked Mrs Browne if the chairs could be rearranged in a circle. She gave the order in *Krio*, waving her bangles in circular motions. The chairs moved noisily, scraping on the concrete floor. Then two lads entered carrying crates that rattled with bottles of refreshment: Fanta, Coke, Sprite. They removed the metal tops and handed them out with thin serviettes.

'Yes, pass dem round,' ordered Mrs. Browne.

Ashamed, I realised this was supposed to be a gift from me. These people were giving up precious time. I hadn't thought of it, hadn't paid for it, and was indebted to her for her thoughtfulness.

THE GROUP LOOKED EXPECTANT. I retrieved my papers from the rucksack, got my notebook ready, and placed the recorder on the table. They looked at it suspiciously.

'I hope it's ok if I record this meeting,' I said lightly, nodding my head, oblivious to what I was asking.

Mrs Browne translated. There was tension in the room, and she eyed me, waiting. A whisper of breeze passed through the windows, the heat intense, the air thick. My shirt already sticking to my skin.

I addressed the group, 'Kroo residents had a terrible time during Ebola and you lost many people. Please accept my condolences for your suffering.' The mood in the room softened slightly. 'The government has issued a report investigating how aid money for Ebola was spent,' I continued. 'It seems a lot was not accounted for. Almost one third of the money, in fact.'

Mrs Browne translated but the group remained passive. She looked at me, impatient.

'Tell dem some ting dey *don* know.'

I said, 'I believe this unaccountability is bad for democracy, the democracy you fought so hard for.'

There was a reaction from a group of men sitting near the back. They settled, waiting for me to go on.

'What I'm trying to understand is how you *feel* about all this graft. Does it affect the way you see your politicians? Maybe it affects your desire to vote?'

An elderly woman wearing a flowered *lappa* with small a child on her knee spoke up.

Mrs Browne translated, 'She says she will vote for di man who brings medicines for di clinic.' Then harshly. 'Of *course* she will vote. It is her democratic *right.*'

Then everyone started talking at once. Mrs Browne listened closely before turning to me.

'Dey need development only government can deliver, not dese people from outside who don know what dey are talkin' about, but strut around as if dey do. Drivin' fancy four be fours all over town, lookin' down on di people. Dey come here talking about poverty and child labour and unemployment. What do *dey* know about it?'

Mrs Brown's baritone had risen to a tenor. I knew she was talking about people like me. Trying to be offensive in an unsubtle way.

'Dis talk about unemployment,' she went on. '*No-one* is unemployed here. How can dey afford not to work! People work doing all kind of tings, whatever dey can get.'

She continued, not waiting for the group's response. 'Dese people from outside talk about grand issues like *poverty*, as if it can be different tomorrow, just like dat. People who live here want *watta* and sanitation. Dey are interested in *waste removal* from dey town. We *know* it takes time, but it isn't complicated! You don't have to write a thesis on it. Look around! Our government needs to *respect* its people.'

The same elderly woman who had spoken before explained her story. She had persuaded her daughter to go the clinic to give birth with the midwife rather than a traditional birth attendant. But the baby had a difficult time and was stillborn. There was no delivery kit at the clinic, no drugs, clean sheets, soap or towels. Then her daughter started haemorrhaging. They couldn't stop the bleeding and she died. Another woman told how her daughter had died at the same clinic after being rushed there during a complicated delivery in her shack.

A young woman with braids then spoke. She was suckling her child, rocking to and fro, patting the infant all the while.

'She says her child before dis one, he die with diarrhoea,' said Mrs Browne. 'Dey is a poor family. Dey sell oranges to feed dey kids. She says di doctor came but asked ninety thousand Leones for di medicine. She only had twenty-five thousand, so di doctor got in his car and drove away! She went to di clinic, but dey don't have medicine for her child. Dey say di medicines are with *di doctor*!'

The young woman spoke again, still rocking, trying to make her point in English, 'Ma child die because of poverty. Because his parents, dey can no pay for di medicine.'

Still rocking, she drew the flat of her hand across her face, wiping away the tears.

'Diarrhoea!' Mrs Browne looked at me accusing. 'Do any child die of dat in *your* country?'

I thought it wasn't poverty that had killed the child. The government had enough money to protect mothers and children. It seemed to me it was graft that killed her child. If the doctor had the medicine to sell, then he had stolen it from the government or from international donors. It should have been free to her. I said nothing.

The group started talking about the floods. A different woman had given birth to five children, but only one survived. The rest had succumbed to conditions in the settlement during the rains.

'The last one,' she said quietly. 'Three month – he sick – he die.'

The room went quiet with respect for her.

I sat listening to these accounts with no words. These women would lose more children in the next rainy season. As they spoke I sat mute and listened to their pain, the tape running, my pen still, the anger rising. I wondered what relevance my research had in the midst of such enormous suffering. Ebola had been a short, unimaginable nightmare, in a long and continuous nightmare.

The men at the back sat quietly. I sensed tension among them, wondering what they were ready to say.

I asked, 'Why won't your government help?'

The room went black with silence. We listened to the noises outside: dogs barking, children playing, women chanting. Sounds coming in on the light breeze that drifted through the barred windows. Sweat ran from my temples. The atmosphere had thickened.

Mrs Browne said, 'If you wan ask questions like *dat*, you'd better turn it *off*.' She nodded at the recorder.

'Yes,' I said, reaching for the machine and fumbling with the switch. 'Of course, I'm sorry. It's off now.'

A man at the back rose from his chair and came forward. He took the recorder gently from my hands, removed the batteries and handed it back.

He spoke good English. 'Our government is not accountable to its people. It is accountable to *your* people.' This was exactly what the minister had said. 'They only care about themselves.' The other men were nodding. 'Take this place – Kroo Bay.' He waved an arm in the general direction of everything outside. 'I have been here three years. Ever since investors stole the land up country for their plantations. That land was given to us to farm after the war. There is no work for me now in my village.'

More nodding from the men.

I thought these must be former fighters who'd been given land to farm as part of the reintegration deal.

He continued, 'Next month this place will flood, children will die, people will suffer. It is getting worse. Government says it is the garbage coming down the gutter. Hah! Yes! We know that, but what about all the land being deforested on our hills to make houses for the big men – *your* big men and *our* big men – getting rich on our country? Taking our land. Chop, chop. Those trees come down. Now there are no trees and no soil to stop that *watta* coming down the hill to drown us!'

Something he'd said registered.

'What was this land up country that was stolen from you?' I asked.

'After the war we went back to the land to farm,' he explained. 'We rented swampland from the chief to rehabilitate for rice. After three years we had to give it back and move on but we had our skills, so we got more land to farm. Rehabilitate the land for rice, then move on, that's what we did. We want our country to be self-sufficient in rice. This was the history of the war.'

His compatriots murmured their agreement.

He said, 'Communities donated their swampland for rehabilitation, we all worked together. It was hard work, but we did it. In the end we had many, many hectares cultivated. Not just rice but beans, cassava, potato, banana.'

All in the room listened closely to his testimony. It felt like a tinderbox, just waiting to be ignited.

I asked, 'What happened to your land?'

'One day a bulldozer came and felled all the trees. We did not know it was going to happen, we were not consulted!'

I thought about the people in Crab Town.

I asked, 'Was this the government?'

'No. It was the company. The chief did a deal with the government to lease 20,000 hectares of land to Arranoil. The place is now a plantation.'

'Arranoil? Is this a palm oil plantation?'

'Yes.'

'Doesn't your paramount chief have custody of the land?'

'Nobody consulted us!' He was shouting now. 'Our elders want to *profit* from the land, but we don't want that. What else have we? People have been shot at and arrested for protesting. I ask you, ma. Where is democracy here?'

FORMER SOLDIERS WERE BECOMING restless anew during peacetime. No access to land. No access to work. Resentments like these had boiled for decades before igniting the horror that followed. New corporations coming in, doing deals with the government, grabbing land and resources. Destroying local livelihoods, just like Robbie McIntyre and his flotilla of ruinous trawlers dragging their nets along the coast. Maybe this palm oil company, Arranoil, maybe it too had fixers resident at the Kangari.

The meeting had ended. As the last of the group exited the centre, I thanked Mrs Browne, spontaneously touching her arm. 'Thank you. For getting them to talk to me.'

She looked at my hand derisively and reached for her bag. 'Maybe now you learn some ting.' Her stout bosom swelled indignantly. She took the wad of notes I gave her and stuffed it in her bag. She looked at me properly for the first time.

'Sam says you smart, you rich, you British.'

I looked down, embarrassed, 'Oh...I...er...'

'Your government is powerful here.' She eyed me for a moment, but I didn't know what she wanted me to say.

'I'd like to see more of the settlement. Would that be ok?' I asked.

'You want a tour?' she said, surprised but interested. 'I will tek you.'

I followed her out of the centre grateful that people had been so open with me, so willing to share their lives and their suffering. I knew it was because Mrs Browne had been there, someone they trusted. I was intrigued about the plantations. Big corporations muscling in on people's land.

Chickens scattered as we crossed the dusty ground outside the centre. We headed past an internet café with a makeshift aerial hanging crooked from the roof, and down a labyrinth of passages that sucked us in, and then a narrow and muddy rut of an alley that ran between concrete shacks. The stench got me as we stepped from side to side avoiding the sludge of sewage that ran down the middle.

Mrs Browne said, 'Europeans used to come here all di time. You may think *for what!* But it was *poverty* tourism. People come to see di destitution of others, have dey photo taken with cute black kids outside dey dilapidated homes. Guides brought dem here. Yes, our *own* people!' She paused as we pressed ourselves flat against the wall to allow a man through in the narrow space, his bicycle laden with bundles of firewood.

We continued, and I asked, 'Has that stopped now? The poverty tourism?'

'Yes. Dose guides were persuaded to desist. Dey don come here now.' I knew then why she'd offered to escort me. People were sick of Western voyeurs.

We emerged from the stinking alley into a sunlit space where beans were drying spread out on a tarpaulin. A woman was bent double at a washboard, others stood behind large cooking pots set upon charcoal fires. There was a tantalising aroma of sheesh kebab that momentarily disguised the omnipresent and fetid stench.

Mrs Browne said suddenly, 'I hungry. Let we eat.'

We moved toward a square-shaped woman wearing a saffron headscarf frying bananas in a pan of boiling bright red oil.

Mrs Browne asked the woman, '*Aw di chop*?'

The vendor smiled showing even white teeth, '*Di chop swit, swit*!'

We watched as the woman used long tongs to lift the fruit from the seething oil, draining it on sheets of newspaper, adding a sprinkling of sugar. I paid with a grubby note.

'*Tenki ya.*'

We moved away with our precious parcels, unwrapping them and biting gingerly, walking past greenish pools of waste and a massive pig resting in the dirt.

We visited the settlement's clinic where I saw for myself the lack of everything needed to care for people's health. Then we visited the *We Yon* primary school whose small structure was crammed with smiling pupils in canary yellow uniforms.

People were hawking the slum itself, head-loading all manner of merchandise. This was a town within a town. Many shacks served as businesses: barbers, hairdressers, cafés, phone repairs, shoe repairs, clothes retailers, fish processers, dentists. Women pounding grain in wooden mortars, and young lads barrowing heavy coconuts weaving across the uneven ground their muscled bodies gleaming with sweat. A mosaic of shacks, huts, crumbling concrete structures, churches, chapels and mosques. The occasional minaret breaking the low skyline of buckled and rusting tin roofs.

We passed a shack with an illuminated green cross sign.

'Yes, di drug seller,' said Mrs Browne.

'The drug seller? You mean…' There was a strong smell of ganja about the place.

'No, I don mean dat. Dey is stolen drugs from di Ministry

of Health.' My mouth dropped, but she shrugged. 'It how tings work round here.'

It seemed that, in the middle of the slum, there was a central shack selling looted drugs that should have been given to people free.

I asked Mrs Browne if I could go inside.

'What you want do dat for?'

'I want to know where the drugs came from?'

'An what you expect him to say?'

I pushed past her and went in anyway. The man couldn't speak any English. I went back outside and coaxed her in.

'He say he bought dese medicines legitimately from di Ministry.' Mrs Browne looked at me in a *told you so* kind of way. The man looked suspicious.

'But they're supposed to be free,' I said.

'Not dese ones,' she replied, and shooed me back out the door.

We moved on and I veered out of the way as a tall man head-loading a bed frame eyed me viciously. I was beginning to feel uncomfortable.

Mrs Browne said, 'Come, I take you to di river. After dat, we go.'

We headed in the direction of the Crocodile River, tiptoeing around the flow of streams-cum-sewers and out towards the beach past piles of garbage and windblown shelters teetering on stilts that served as the women's toilets. Some homes were built of nothing but garbage and mud.

'We have extreme sanitation issues,' said Mrs Browne, unnecessarily. 'Six flush toilets serving ten thousand residents. People don use dem because dey have to pay. Is it a surprise di place is breeding ground for disease! Malaria, cholera, diarrhoea, Ebola. Every ting!' The stench was testament to her claim.

When I asked about fresh water, she said, 'Di price of

water rises tree times in di dry season, so people cut di pipes What can dey do?'

We wandered further toward the river.

'Dis area has always been a trading hotspot,' she contin-ued, and I looked around in surprise seeing nothing but garbage, snuffling pigs and precarious shacks, all standing incongruous against the tall, elegant palms. A vicious mist of mosquitos lay across the stagnant water, a smell of burning rubber stank the air.

'Di river gives access to di estuary,' she waved her hand toward the sea. 'Goods are brought here from di islands for onward sale to di city or up country.'

I looked across the river to the opposite bank. Standing in a shack yard was a group of men in conversation. Three locals in shorts and flip-flops, one tanned European with thick grey hair, swept back. What was *he* doing here? The Dutchman stood hands on hips, head tilted, listening to what the other men were saying. What sort of business could bring him to the banks of the Crocodile River, with its direct access to the sea? Drugs definitely. Or arms, maybe.

I asked, 'Mrs Browne, do you know that man?'

She looked in the direction I was pointing.

'No. I don know dat man.'

I stared at him, trying to work him out. His manner too covert to be an aid worker, or a corporation fixer, skulking about as he did in slums and shallows and congested ferries.

'You coming?'

It was now late afternoon, the shadows lengthening, the stirring sound of women chanting prayers in another part of the settlement. I turned to follow Mrs Browne as she tiptoed her way through the rubbish and back through the complex corridors of Kroo.

She asked, 'Di driver is waitin'?'

I confirmed that he would meet us near the bridge.

'Ok, he can drop me,' she said, wanting a detour past her

house. By this time a group of industrious kids was behind us again whistling, cheering, calling out *oporto*! I was conscious of my whiteness. The kids were vendors themselves carrying basins of fruit, pouches of water, plantain. *Good day ma, how are you?* Then a group of young men carrying T-shirts in every hue swarmed in, pressing on me, elbowing each other for my attention. Claustrophobia closed in.

We approached the steep concrete road by which we had entered the settlement, busy with all kinds of traders and smart suited people returning from work. A tall woman, equine looking, hurried down the ramp toward us. I smiled at her but she lowered her eyes and was gone in the crowd. It was the woman from Murray Town. The mother of the boy who'd been hit by the car.

THIRTEEN

HASSAN

Main Motor Road was busy as we searched for the offices of the Sierra Leone People's Health Association, SLAPHA. It was on my list to visit because it had received Ebola funding. The woman who'd answered the phone had diarised a meeting for me at their office and had given me the address. But, as we slowed outside the building, there was no sign that the organisation resided there.

Amadu turned the cruiser into the deserted compound and parked in the shade of a densely foliaged mango. I got out to investigate. At the entrance, a red door was securely locked with several devices. I followed a weedy path that led round the back where another door was covered by a padlocked grill. The premises seemed to have been abandoned. No vehicles in the compound. No-one around. I stood in the lifeless air, the sound of traffic on the main road muted by the building's wide expanse. It was eerily quiet.

The sun bore down with great intensity, and I stood motionless, taking in the scene of neglect and abandonment, wondering where the NGO had moved, worried I'd be late for my appointment.

I stepped in to take a closer look through smeared windows that were heavily barred. Papers and files were strewn about the floor, a broken desk fan and empty Fanta bottles. Evidence of people having operated there. I made my way to the rear gate to see if there was a notice or something to indicate where SLAPHA had relocated. The gate hung off its hinges. No-one had passed through here in months.

On the track behind the compound, a man of small stature was walking my way, moving along with short, determined strides.

I smiled as he approached, 'Hi.'

'Good morning!' he replied.

He was carrying a briefcase and wearing a tribal tunic. His smile was wide and cheery beneath a thin moustache.

'How can I help you?' His stance was upright and open. There was something about him I immediately liked.

I told him I was looking for the organisation SLAPHA. 'Have they moved?' I asked. 'Maybe I've got the wrong address.'

He said, 'It is not here.' Then happily, 'You are English!' and he extended his hand, energetically grabbing mine.

'Yes.' I knew this man would help me. 'Can you tell me where they've moved?'

'Please,' he let go my hand and gestured for me to follow. 'Come to the office.'

He led me out the back of the compound, explaining all the various attributes he loved most about the English. 'I *love* the English! You always do what you say you're going to do. That is rare here.' He chatted like an old friend, 'I was in Birmingham only last month.'

A small building came into view, no bigger than a garage and situated on a rough track running parallel to the busy main road.

'I hope you had a good trip,' I said, knowing I wasn't going to find SLAPHA but feeling confident in the man's company.

'I did, I did! I was speaking at a conference on behalf of the Association of Global Activists. Perhaps you've heard of us?' He was expectant, but I just smiled.

'Come into the office', he said, and led me into a small chaotic room that was freshly painted white. Metal filing cabinets, a photocopier, a substantial desk with an archaic looking computer linked to a rusting stack on the floor. Wires everywhere. Under the window a wooden table piled with books, files, journals and pamphlets. In a corner on a laptop, a slightly built woman in a fancy wig. She lifted her head to acknowledge me but continued working. The ceiling fan rotated at a brisk pace lifting the edges of the paperwork.

The man introduced himself as Hassan Denbah, a local activist, lobbying government on behalf of the poor. He was a former trade unionist who now spent all his time trying to make democracy work for the ordinary people of his country.

'Sit, sit,' he pulled up a chair, brushing crumbs off the seat. 'Tell me what brings a beautiful English lady to our country?'

I tried again. 'I was looking for the organisation SLAPHA. Do you know where they've moved?'

'You won't find them,' he said, matter of fact. 'They've closed down their operations.' He pulled a cloth from his pocket and polished a pair of glasses, which he placed on his perfectly round and smiley face.

I was confused, and consulted my notes. I knew they'd been active during the Ebola crisis.

He looked at me kindly, watching my confusion.

Then he said gently, 'They took the money, and ran.'

He poured water into glasses whilst I explained to him that I'd hoped to interview a local health organisation about the misuse of Ebola funds.

When I'd finished, he said, unexpectedly passionate,

'Thank you for taking an interest in our country. We need outsiders to support us, because you can say things to our government that we can never say ourselves.'

I felt momentarily uncomfortable.

Hassan went on, 'You are looking for our NGOs, but you will find these organisations are as unaccountable as our government. This one you seek, SLAPHA, it sets up in the middle of a crisis, pockets the cash, then shuts up shop.'

'I'm sorry,' I said lamely.

He continued, 'When people complain about the stolen money, we set up another organisation that calls itself *Accountability Alert*, or some such, which gets more funding to monitor the rest and turns out just as unaccountable itself.' He was still smiling, but I could feel his frustration.

By accident I'd stumbled upon a man entrenched in the risky world of political activism. Confronting his country's *big men*. Powerful individuals with no scruples. This was a dangerous occupation.

'People mobilise to take advantage of funds coming in,' he said. Then shrugged, 'What do you expect? Maybe a cousin of the Health Minister sets up an NGO. The minister endorses the work because she knows them, and that is enough for the donors.'

'Are you saying SLAPHA was never here?' I asked.

'No, they were here, but not for long.' His phone starting ringing with a funky hip hop beat, but he ignored it and carried on talking.

'Did you know our government had 600 million dollars to build hospitals, clinics and schools? But they don't do things well. I have a matrix here.' He rummaged through the piles of papers on his desk, determined to find what it was he sought. 'You will discover that a lot of the money they chopped them-selves.' His head was down as he searched. 'Ah yes, this is the pie chart. See! Only twenty-four per cent of projects completed, forty-three per cent not completed, twenty-six per cent waiting for supplies, and seven per cent waiting for implementation!' He was pleased he'd found his pie chart to quote at me. I could feel his passion. 'Corruption is a *human rights* issue here! Do you see?'

I nodded whilst he continued, 'You need to ask your government: where does your money go?'

He paused and turned to admonish his pretty secretary for chatting on her phone. There was impatience about him. He got up to turn off the fan that was causing havoc with the un-weighted paperwork. He was right, I did need to find out where my government thought its money had gone. Hassan had been a unionist and I wondered if he knew anything about the promises made to former fighters about working the land up country.

I said, 'Someone told me yesterday there is no culture of democracy in your country.'

He chuckled, revealing pearly teeth, unevenly spaced. Then seriously, 'Who told you we have no culture of democracy in our country?'

I felt awkward then, wanting to protect the people I'd met in Kroo, and Sam for that matter, so I said vaguely, 'Oh just a meeting. Part of the research, y'know.'

He said, 'I would say that is a bold and correct statement from an educated person. The democracy we have here is a *sham*!' He leant forward to make his point, 'But at the same time our people believe they should have their fair share of whatever it is they are entitled to. But right now, justice and democracy, they are like a haze on some unreachable horizon.' He zig-zagged a hand in the air, then sat back in his chair abruptly, hands together, thumbs revolving.

I wanted to ask him about the corporation Arranoil, the one that had stolen land from former fighters. So I asked, 'Has foreign investment brought jobs for the poor?'

'Yes, of course! It is a condition put upon them by our government. We have job creation here, of course, of course.

But where else would these investors find such cheap labour? Take palm oil. It is a very labour-intensive. It is in the vested interests of these people to keep a supply of cheap labour, to keep vast swathes of the countryside poor. It's part of the business plan.'

'How do big corporations acquisition the land for the palm oil industry?' I asked. 'I mean, I've heard of a corporation called Arranoil. Some people say they've stolen land from the farmers. Do you know about that?'

Hassan thought for a moment, then smiled and rose quickly from his chair, 'Come, let's do lunch at the canteen. There's someone you need to meet.'

———

WE ARRIVED at the Youyi canteen through an entrance at the back of the building. It was large and airy with rows of wooden tables, and a long counter down one side. The lunchtime rush had gone. Hassan, my new best friend, led me to a table where we sat on benches opposite each other. He gestured to a passing girl carrying a tray of cans and dirty plates, and ordered two Fantas and rice.

'Please,' he said, patting my arm conspiratorially. 'I'll be back.'

He headed toward a table under a broken AC unit where a group of men were huddled with their heads together. I watched as one of them stood and took Hassan's hand in the customary three grasp gesture. When they both turned my way, I looked down, embarrassed. I waited, wondering why the man was so important and what he knew about the corporation Arranoil.

The waitress came back with two cans of Fanta. She laid a plastic cup in Hassan's place and a glass in front of me and said, 'Rice coming,' before drifting off to clear tables.

Hassan returned and sat down. 'He will come and meet

you when he finishes his meal.' Noticing the plastic cup his expression changed. He turned and shouted at the waitress in *Krio*. She stopped collecting plates and slunk off to the kitchen.

He said momentarily enraged, 'This is what we have in our country! You are white therefore you must have a glass, but I myself can go to hell!'

The girl came back with a glass for Hassan and two bowls of steaming rice covered in a sauce of sweet peppers. We tucked in, the mild spices moving comfortably down my throat. Salty, sweet and delicious. We talked about Hassan's work which, from time to time, had him incarcerated in the city's Pademba Road prison. A jail with a malevolent reputation; famed for its overcrowding and poor conditions, violence and rioting, and many deaths. Like doing time in hell.

'In my country,' I said, 'pressure groups and lobby groups are part of political life. Nobody gets locked up for challenging the government.'

'What we have here is *hate* politics constructed on deliberately falsified ethnic barriers, but there are no ethnic or religious issues here. Never! It is a deliberate manipulation to keep our people down.'

'It's a religiously tolerant place.' I knew this.

'Of course! Our incumbent is Muslim and his wife is Roman Catholic. What is more tolerant than that?'

Hassan's comrade came across to join us, stepping over the bench, awkwardly tall and thin. His eyes were deep set and bloodshot. This was Sheku Bai Marah, socialist, vocal critic of the government, and running for office in the upcoming elections. He too had been imprisoned for lengthy stretches in Pademba Road prison. These men were fearless campaigners.

I asked Sheku how he thought socialism could work when Western donors discredited it as a political system. He launched scathingly into his manifesto.

'The "Western donors" as you call them, must no longer speak on behalf of the impoverished of the world. Imperialist capitalists like yourselves have stigmatised every independent effort made by oppressed people to overturn the relationship we have with them. That of exploitation through the extraction of wealth and resources from our country.' The words tripped out like he'd spoken them many times.

'When I talk about socialism in the context of our struggle,' he continued, 'let me say, only a handful of individuals live off our resources, and the rest live in poverty without the services required for even existing.'

Unlike Hassan, there was no humour in his features. Everything about Sheku was dark and edgy.

He said, 'We have a rogue oligarchy that has misused state power for its own benefit, and for the benefit of its partner donors, capitalist corporations, and financial institutions.'

And here I was, the privileged white from England with preconceived notions of what was what in his country. Hassan was hanging on his every word. And so was I. Sheku looked exhausted, but he carried on.

'Our people only want what they are entitled to, basics so they can live. Why does that have to be socialism? Why can't that be popular democracy? Don't be afraid of the word socialism. Maybe it is not what you think.'

'Is there a socialist party in Sierra Leone?' I asked.

'We have been to the registration council to form our socialist party, but they demand a large sum for registration. We can't afford that. The people in power have made it so that they can resist all challenges. They bribe the opposition and corrupt the media. They have *contaminated* the political landscape. We are working with other progressive parties that are already registered.'

Sheku paused, earnestness and weariness branded into his

features, but I could feel the power in him, the fearlessness. It cowed me.

'I'm interested in the palm oil industry,' I said. Do you know of a corporation called Arranoil? I've been told they have a fifty-five year concession and that they've taken farmers' land and jobs.'

'Yes, that is the case,' said Sheku.

'The thing is,' I went on slowly, grasping at my thoughts, trying to make sense of them, not wanting to miss this opportunity, 'your country's status as a post-war state, you know, and the concessions made to the fighters in the peace deal. Well, it's not that long since the end of the war...' I was headed into highly sensitive territory, and my question trailed off.

Hassan and Sheku looked expectant, challenging with their eyes.

I said quietly, 'I mean, the grievances are still there, aren't they?'

Sheku sat back and left it to Hassan, who was wiping his glasses, passive, thoughtful. He said carefully, 'Poverty remains. Injustice remains. But we have no more appetite for war.'

There was a difficult silence, then Sheku said, 'You must speak with my wife. She is working with people on the plantations. Come to our home, she will talk to you.' He got up to leave, apologising and saying he had to go. He offered his hand before striding over the bench to re-join his comrades.

FOURTEEN
SONGOLA

Amadu turned the Toyota off Kissy Road into Hope Hill Street, manoeuvring expertly round the deep potholes that littered the steep incline and slowed our pace. It was eight thirty in the evening on a moonless night, and lights in the East End were out. We bumped along past scab-eared dogs grooming each other in the dirt, and lads perched on crates smoking ganja. The glow of their reefers pierced the blackness. Its sickly scent seeped through the vents.

'I know is here,' said Amadu, peering hopefully through the windscreen.

'Keep going,' I urged. 'Hassan said it's near the top.'

We lurched from side to side as we worked our way up the hill. The Liverpool air-freshener swinging in wide arcs, and bundles of firewood sliding this way and that in the boot.

'Stop,' I said. 'Is this it?'

We examined a pair of solid metal gates set in a graffiti-covered wall. Behind the wall rose a block of crumbling apartments. Kerosene lamps glowed from the windows.

'Amadu, I think this is it. D'you want to pull in?'

'No, I go,' he said. 'Call me.'

I was let into the compound by a teenage boy acting as security and holding a flashlight.

'Dey is no light,' he said. 'Come dis way.'

He held the torch to illuminate the path and I followed him toward the building, up an external staircase, the rattle and drone of standby generators loud on people's balconies. Then into the building and down a dark corridor. The heat was sweltering. The boy opened the door into a small, cramped apartment where a diminutive woman was busy at the stove. Sheku was seated on a shabby, upholstered sofa, conversing with two men.

He rose to greet me. 'Karen, welcome. Please take a seat.' He indicated a wooden stool by the counter where unframed photos of smiling children were propped against a pile of worn out books. He explained something to his wife in Temne. She looked my way and nodded.

'She won't be long,' said Sheku. 'Please excuse me.'

Awkwardly I perched on the stool close to the men who were talking about forming an alliance with another political party. It felt uncomfortable listening to them, so I busied myself staring at my phone. Then at my notebook. The recorder I had left behind this time. The heat in the flat was unbearable and I dragged a cloth from my sack to wipe the sweat from my face.

Sheku's wife, Songola, wore a printed *lappa* and green T-shirt, and stood by the stove stirring a pot. A baby was strapped to her back and a child in pink pyjamas whined by her side. The room smelt of spices and sweet pepper stew. The space was lit by a fluorescent strip rigged up to a generator. At the window were half drawn curtains in a geometric design, and a local batik hung askew along one wall. It was a homely place.

The men's voices were low and I listened, head down, wondering at their courage in a political landscape that overtly threatened dissent. What event in the past had spurred Sheku to harness the burden of his people in the way he had with such self-disregard? Agitators who challenged the status quo were intimidated, beaten, arrested and imprisoned. Some disappeared. Fear and exhaustion were settled in his face, but the power was in him. He courted danger. His little flat was filled with the mood of blind resistance.

The child in pink pyjamas was put to bed and everyone served with pepper stew.

Songola said to me, 'Come, we sit outside.'

We moved to the small balcony, placing our bowls on a low table, sitting on plastic chairs. The view across the East End was black, lamplights dotted about the neighbourhood, traffic noise and the pap-pap of horns rising from the Kissy Road below. The air was thick and hot.

Songola was slight of build, slim hipped, slim waisted. Like her husband she looked exhausted – delicate and weak – like someone recovering from illness. She had a pretty heart shaped face, tight cornrows, and smooth, silky skin. A distinctive scar lay along her jawline, and I wondered about her story.

She swung the baby from the wrapper into her lap, and lifting her shirt began to suckle him. His cherubic lips attached like a limpet to her nipple.

The rich scent of pepper stew rose from the bowls, enticing. But I felt like an intruder, pilfering this family's scant resources.

When she'd settled her child, I thanked her for agreeing to talk to me.

'It's ok. What can I tell you?'

'I want to learn about foreign investment and how it's affecting people,' I said. 'I met some men, they were former fighters, whose land had been taken for a palm oil plantation. Your husband told me that you're working with people who are employed on the Arranoil estate?'

She nodded, her voice was low and calm. 'Yes, I am

working with villagers in Gorahun district. They work for
Arranoil. Let me tell you what is happening there.' She took a
spoonful of stew whilst adjusting the baby in her lap. 'Our
people are not against investment. They want progress for
their communities. But government is so slow at bringing
development, the people think foreign investment will bring
it quicker.' She raised her eyes, black as coals, wide set and
droopy lids.

'We have laws,' she continued. 'All foreign investment
involving land concessions has to bring social development to
improve the people's lives. They expect that.'

'I've read about the legals,' I said.

Songola's gentle manner affected me in a humbling way.

'Also we have international law and human rights law,'
she said. 'In theory that too protects our people's rights. The
government has signed up for that.'

'So officially they are protected from this land grabbing
that corporations do?' I asked.

'Officially, yes. But investors are told by our government
that the labour laws are "flexible". Investment where land is
the issue – like in mining, agro-business, and in biofuels –
there have been human rights abuses. Palm oil is only one
example.' She scooped more beans to her pretty mouth.

'So why are you investigating the palm oil business in
particular?' I asked.

'The land issue is bad. Huge swathes of agricultural land
are involved. It's how the people feel, very disenfranchised.
Land in this country is owned by families and communities.
Not the government or chiefs. It is not *theirs* to give away.
Chiefs are only custodians of the land, they must always
defer to the people. It is our custom and our traditional
law.'

'Is there any registry of land or official law about it?'

'We don't need that. It has always worked this way.
Someone approaches the chief for maybe fifty hectares of land

and the chief negotiates a deal that will benefit the community. Nothing can go ahead without that.'

'So, what's gone wrong?'

Her eyes were pools of impenetrable blackness, half-concealed behind the tired, drooping lids.

'Chiefs – they *lie* to the people.' She spoke slowly, emphasising every word. 'They are doing the *government*'s bidding. It is in their interests to do so. And the government has its own promises to fulfil, like to the World Bank who want to see increased foreign investment.'

I knew that. But nothing was as it seemed in this country.

I asked, 'But, the corporations pay compensation to people for the loss of their land, don't they? I mean, they've built schools and clinics and *have* created jobs. Why don't the people think of this as progress?'

Songola had an unnerving passivity in her stare. There was something dark about her, something consequential hidden in her shrouded eyes. Everything external to her suggested calm – her slow deliberate movements, her voice – husky and unhurried, her accommodating, polite demeanour. But inwardly I sensed a steely core, something dangerous and uncompromising.

She scooped the remnants of stew onto her spoon and tipped them into her mouth, then returned it to the bowl with a deliberate action.

Again, she said slowly, as though speaking to a child, 'People…they *lie*.'

There was a long pause as I waited for her to go on.

Eventually she said, 'Yes, people are paid compensation for the loss of their land and their homes. But it is not adequate to cover the *actual* loss. Nothing is more precious than their land. What happens to the next generations when the land is lost? It is their only means of security.' I nodded. Of course it made sense. 'The land provides diverse means of income, whether it rains too much, too little, at the right time, the wrong time. There is always some way to survive off the land. Think of it. They had access to fish, bush meat, water. They kept livestock, poultry, vegetables, fruit and medicinal herbs.'

She detached the baby from one breast and settled it to suckle on the other. 'Investors never pay the real productive value of the trees they chop down and the land they clear of crops. What they put in its place is a single crop of no use to anyone except for low waged work. They can only survive as labourers. What sort of deal is that?'

I could think of no answer.

'If you are going to compensate someone, you compensate at least as much as you have taken away. The so-called schools and clinics you talk about, yes, they build schools and clinics, sometimes they might even supply desks or beds. But what use are they without teachers, doctors, medical staff? Or medicine or schoolbooks? We have only two hundred doctors in this country. These facilities are no more than empty shells.'

She wanted to tell me about the education of the villagers' children. Those who live remotely, far away from the cities.

'There are not enough teachers for the schools we have already. People in our country, mostly they remain uneducated because our so-called high enrolment figures say nothing about the *quality* of education. Do the teachers turn up? Are they educated themselves? Are they being paid by the government, or do they demand payment from parents who expect education to be free for their kids? Do the kids turn up? Or do their families have other ideas come harvest or planting time?'

She was impressive, this diminutive woman. With her slow calm delivery she was equally as skilful as her husband. There was power in her small frame.

I asked, 'What other ideas? Are you saying Arranoil employ children on their plantations?'

'Of course. But I wouldn't say they officially employ them.

No. There is no payment involved. They work to help their parents.'

'Wait! Are you saying Arranoil are building schools for the children and at the same time working them on the plantations?'

She gave me that patient look again.

'You must *challenge* everything you hear,' she said. 'Look around. What do you see? What is *really* happening? Don't believe the lies. That makes you no better than them.'

I looked down for a moment and fiddled with my pen. These big corporations come in, bringing so-called development in the way of primary schools, knowing there are no teachers, knowing that they'll work the kids on their plantations.

There was a screech of tyres and blare of horns from the Kissy Road below. Then all went quiet again.

I asked, 'So how are you tackling this hypocrisy and breach of international law?'

'The people want to form a union,' she said, 'to improve their working conditions. We call it the Plantation Workers Union. We have a union here but it works for the government. Once we have an official platform of our own, we can tackle all these issues, workers' rights, land, child rights, everything.'

'Wait,' I said again, 'did you say there is a trades union that works for the government?'

She said nothing; waiting for me to catch up.

'Then how do you think the government will respond to your new union for the plantation workers?' I asked.

A premonition of doom joined us on the balcony.

The baby had fallen asleep, its mouth detached from its mother's nipple, watery milk dribbling across a chubby cheek. We sat in silence for a moment. Songola drew her hand lightly across the child's face.

She said, 'I will take you. Then you will see for yourself.'

FIFTEEN
FRANCIS

The next day I was back at Sam Gregory's office to find out what he had to say about phantom NGOs such as SLAPHA. A discussion of that nature might be difficult for him – a conflict of interests perhaps – after all, his own organisation received huge amounts of donor funding. But I wanted him to be accountable for graft in the sector. I was on a mission to find the missing aid, but it seemed that funds flowed down so many channels; high level, low level and everywhere in between. It appeared that graft infected the beating heart of the country, polluting its soul. Every aspect of life seemed dependent on favours.

He was defensive, 'Of course people take advantage. What d'you expect?' He sat behind a desk with paperwork strewn about. Maddeningly he changed the subject, asking about my research.

'Who are your next respondents?' His head was down as he scrolled through the emails on his phone.

I replied to the top of his manicured head, 'Well, I was

hoping to interview NGO's on the health side of things.' He wasn't taking me seriously, still scrolling.

I continued, 'I've got appointments with the likes of CARE and World Vision, but they're not exactly local. I expect they won't tell me anything I don't already know.'

'Forget *them,'* Sam replied.

'So, what about local organisations?'

'Such as?' He'd stopped scrolling and was now reading an email. Instinctively, I'd decided not to tell Sam about my meetings with Hassan, with Sheku and Songola, or the fact I was going up country to visit the plantations in Gorahun. I didn't want to share those things with him. There was something in his demeanour now he was back in Freetown that made me feel uneasy.

I said, 'Maybe Coalition of Health for the Child. Do they still exist?'

'Hah!' he looked up briefly. 'You won't get anything from *them* seeing as they have the interest of the ACC.'

There was a list of individuals and organisations due to appear before the Anti-Corruption Commission, and the director of Coalition of Health for the Child was on that list. He'd received $65,000, undocumented, made out in personal cheques direct from the Ministry of Health who was at the same time denying Ebola existed. When I'd called the ACC itself, a threatening voice had told me to back off and stick to conversations with NGOs.

'And I'm talking to people directly affected by the loss of a relative to Ebola,' I said.

'We were *all* affected. Who you talking to?'

'One of them is Francis Caulker, he's a pastor.'

Sam looked up, impressed. 'Pastor Francis! Good call. He lost his wife. Terrible, terrible. You should go to one of his sermons.'

THE STEPS of the Wellington Street Baptist Church led to huge wooden doors under a castellated portico. The entrance was flanked by gothic windows with complicated criss-crossing ironwork painted white. Dominating the roof was an enormous white cross. Inside a choir was singing. I wondered if I'd done the right thing, being deliberately late. Baptist services could go on for hours, so my plan was to slip in unnoticed during the singing, stay for the pastor's sermon, then slip out again.

My whiteness was weighing me down a bit, especially after the visit to Kroo. I didn't want to justify myself at this church, my faith, or non-faith or anything awkward like that. I worried that the expectations I had for myself were beginning to align with local expectations of *white*, and I hated it.

The choir was getting into its stride and clapping had started. I pushed open the heavy doors and stepped into a small vestibule with windows on all sides looking down on the congregation. The church was crammed. People stood several deep at the back behind rows of tightly packed pews and plastic chairs. At the windows, polyester curtains in a violet hue blew voluminously in the breeze. But the temperature in the church was stifling. Sweat ran down my spine.

I loitered at the periphery, but friendly hands took mine and guided me through the standing bodies to a better position behind the chairs. I felt an emotional response to their warmth, feeling unspecial in every way, my whiteness discoloured in a congregation of every hue.

The choir stood behind microphones on a red carpeted dais, dressed in blue checked robes and matching head ties. They were responding gustily to their caller, swaying *en masse*, a vision of blue and white moving like the tide. A low hum and an irregular clap emitted from the crowd, then unexpectedly everyone rose and responded to the call with a cacophonous upsurge of voices.

'Praise the Lord!'

'We praise Him!'

'He gives us life!'

'We praise Him.'

Bodies swayed, eyes closed, hands uplifted, the congrega-tion mirroring the choir in their simple choreography of open palms and upturned faces. As the singing ended, a place was found for me and I was encouraged to sit.

'Welcome, sister,' a large bespectacled woman in an intri-cate woven wig smiled as I sat beside her. A friendly man with Downs leant across and stroked my skin. Anticipation filled the room. There was energy in it.

Someone from the back of the room spoke loudly, 'Give thanks to the the Lord for He is *good*!'

We all replied, 'Amen.'

The atmosphere suddenly shifted like a weathervane. A deep timbred voice, a preacher kind of voice, came boldly from the dais, and five hundred heads dipped in veneration.

'Loving God, creator of all. You made us human and gave us hearts to love and follow you.'

There was a low hum as people raised their heads and shifted in their seats. When I looked up, I saw a broad shoul-dered, sharp-suited man, standing quite still at the lectern, head bowed, holding a battered bible in one hand. His afro was short, and his crisp white collar stood stark against his skin.

Pastor Francis Caulker.

He opened his bible and drew spectacles from his pocket. He read:

Jesus said to the crowds and his disciples, the Scribes and the Pharisees sit on Moses' seat; so practice and observe whatever they tell you, but not what they do; for they preach but they do not prac-tice. They bind heavy burdens, hard to bear, and lay them on men's shoulders; but they themselves will not move them with their finger.

They do all their deeds to be seen by men; for they make their phylacteries broad and their fringes long, and they love the place of

honour at feasts and the best seats in the synagogues, and saluta-
tions in the marketplaces, and being called rabbi by men.

There was a short pause. Then he brought the palm of his hand down on the lectern with a startling crash.

Woe to you scribes and Pharisees, hypocrites! For you tythe mint, and dill and cumin, and have neglected the weightier matters of the law, justice, mercy and faith.

Woe to you scribes and Pharisees, hypocrites; for you cleanse the outside of the cup and of the plate, but inside you are full of extortion and rapacity.

The pastor paused dramatically. Then he said loud, with authority,

'This is the word of our Lord!'

'Amen!'

The minister closed his bible and placed it on the lectern. Crossing the dais, his eyes down, he moved slowly, the hint of a limp, cleverly disguised.

We waited in silence, tense and expectant. The accusation from Matthew's gospel hanging in the air. Like provocation.

'Brothers and sisters,' said the pastor in a voice that resonated in the deepest range.

He stopped pacing and faced his congregation. 'Do we all know who I am talking *about*!!'

'Yes, sir!'

'Amen!'

'We hear you brother.'

When the ruckus died down, Pastor Francis said solemnly, 'My friends, of course we all know who I am talking about. In this gospel passage, Jesus is teaching us about hypocrisy, about injustice, about the misuse of power. About *bad leadership*.'

Like the crowd, I sat mesmerised. The pastor's point was obvious. The behaviour of the scribes and Pharisees, their extortion, their duplicity, their craving for power and admiration, a clear metaphor for their government.

The pastor said, 'What does Jesus teach us to do when we are faced with leaders who don't do their jobs? Who refuse to lead us in paths of righteousness and justice? Does he teach us to follow their lead?'

'No, sir!'

'Does he teach us to practise what they do?'

'No, brother!'

'Does he teach us to admire them? To *copy* them?'

'No!'

He waited for their zeal to die down, calculating in his delivery. His voice dropped to a whisper, 'Then tell me why, my brothers and sisters, do we *persist* in our desire for their riches, for their power, to be their friends, to use their methods?'

The room went silent. An atmosphere of shock and guilt pervaded, everyone hanging for his next words. He pointed at them combatively.

'You know it! Who among you can say they have never taken a bribe? Or offered a bribe? Who among you does not covet the riches of public office? Who among you is confident to challenge bad leadership knowing in your heart that your only teacher is your Father, who is in heaven?'

No-one spoke.

'I tell you, my friends. Until we, as a people, clean our own hearts and minds from the corruption of mortal things, we will have failed. Corrupt governance and all the suffering that brings for our people will continue. We forget. Our future is ours! We must break out of the chains of greed and indifference, and embrace the life that Jesus taught us. Only then can we stand up to those who lead us with a clear conscience, with the *right* to better leadership. One that we *deserve*. Leadership cemented in the foundations of righteousness – as our Father has taught us.'

The church erupted.

'Amen!'

'Lord have mercy!'

'Hallelujah!'

The choir struck up again in a stirring four-part harmony.

THE NEXT DAY I visited the Mission School to meet the pastor. It was situated to the rear of the Wellington Street Church, in a large dusty compound, where the buttresses of a cotton tree stood along the ground like pews. The school had a deep ironwork veranda with dwarf tree palms that framed the entrance. Inside, I found a woman in a spangled robe and violet turban sitting alone on a bench. She ignored me when I sat down and greeted her. The room was stuffy and woody smelling. The air solid. The only way to survive in heat of that magnitude was to sit motionless, slow the heart rate, breathe shallow. The turbaned woman slunk a glance my way.

The door opened in a timely fashion and Pastor Francis stood be-suited, smiling, a hand resting on the handle, gesturing with the other for me to enter.

'Miss Hamm! Welcome. Please come in and take a seat.' The deep timbre of his voice reminded me of his sermon the day before, and I entered feeling awed.

The room appeared to be the library, shelves bulging, a desk stacked with papers, books and bibles neatly piled. Francis Caulker was not just a preacher but also the director of development projects, and head of the Wellington Street Mission School. He'd studied in the UK, had a doctorate from Durham, and for some reason wanted to talk about the country's civil war.

'People come here asking about the war. What were the terrible grievances that made people commit horror upon horror against their countrymen? What was it that incited the violence that brought such an abomination in this small and insignificant West African nation?'

It sounded like a well-rehearsed introduction to a lecture. I was minded to look behind me, to see if some other person in the room had asked a question about the war. But I switched on my recorder and placed it on the desk, my notebook ready, listening politely, wondering how much time he would grant me for this interview.

'Of course, there were countless different grievances. Mostly against authority; the government, the chiefs. Grievances born of unremitting poverty and lack of justice. We still have that. People always hope things will change, but even after all we've been through, in many ways things stay the same.'

He got up and hung his jacket with precision over the back of the chair, picking a fleck of dust from the collar. He unbuttoned his cuffs and rolled up his sleeves, workmanlike, then sat down and smiled straight at me with soft eyes that shone with warmth. 'You see for yourself that there are no miracle cures for poverty.'

He clasped his hands on the desk – long fingers, wide palms – and continued talking about the psychology of the war. There was power in him. I hung on every utterance, the recorder running, convinced he would reveal untold mysteries about the war. After a while, he paused and looked out of the window at a group of children arriving in the compound. There were flecks of grey in his manicured beard, his Nubian nose regal in profile. It was unsettling, the attractiveness of the man.

'Of course, the war was moved along with a little help from our friend next door,' he said.

'You mean Charles Taylor in Liberia?' I asked, following his gaze to the children outside in a game of tag, their feet picking up clouds of dust.

'He got what he had coming. Thank God, for that.' The pastor turned, 'He's serving his sentence in your country. Did you know that?'

I confirmed that I did, and asked, 'Did his conviction bring a sense of justice for people here?'

'It helped,' he said, 'but let's not waste our time on him. Tell me about your research.'

But I didn't want to talk about corruption and Ebola. I wanted to pick up on his comments about the war. About aggrieved young men. About the tinderbox that had lain for years just waiting to ignite.

I asked, 'Pastor, you mentioned the deeply held grievances that led to the outbreak of the war. Do you think they are still there. I mean, are they harboured by those who still feel locked out?'

'What do you mean by locked out?' He leaned in, smooth forearms on the desk. I was thinking about the men I'd spoken to who felt their land had been stolen by new investors.

'People don't seem to have benefitted much from the post-war investment,' I said. 'You know, the country has so many natural resources.'

Later, when I looked back at that first meeting, I knew the lecture he'd given on his country's civil war was Francis' way of stalling. Of taking time to appraise me, judge my reactions, know who it was he was dealing with. But what he'd done was deepen my interest in a new line of enquiry. I wanted to find questions more relevant to local people than an investigation into the whereabouts of stolen aid.

'Our country is blessed with a fortune in natural resources,' he said. 'Only one of them is diamonds. They called them *blood* diamonds, but I don't like that expression myself. There has been much post-war investment, in iron ore, minerals and agribusiness, especially palm oil. Our soil is rich.' He shrugged his substantial shoulders. 'But the exploitation of our natural resources means acquisition by foreign corporations of our ancestral land. Yes, most people have not directly benefitted from foreign investment, but they have also lost their land to it.'

Former fighters had lost their land to it.

He looked at me studiedly, and I shifted in my seat, conscious of my appearance, my skin slick with perspiration.

'Is land reform the subject of your research?' he asked.

'No,' I confessed, and then went on to explain with practised vigour the aims and objectives of my research, to get it out of the way. I wanted to move on to more interesting things. He listened and nodded at regular intervals.

He seemed disappointed, and there was an embarrassing pause before he said, 'I see.'

The sound of children's voices floated in through the window.

He asked, 'What is your theoretical framework?'

'Democratisation theory,' I hurried on. 'So, how can a fragile state successfully democratise the body politic, or the local political culture, when decisions affecting the prosperity of the voters are being taken from outside?'

'Indeed,' he conceded, 'and Ebola?'

'Well, the Ebola crisis is a useful starting point in terms of decision-making on the disbursement of aid.' Annoyingly, the pastor wanted to engage with my thesis.

'What makes you think outside influences in what you describe as a "fragile state" are any different to the influences on your *own* government, or any government in the international system for that matter? We are all dependent. Think of the EU or IMF, and the control those institutions have on your own country.'

'Well, a fragile state emerging from civil war is more dependent,' I said. 'In your case, your government collapsed and the army ran away to join the rebels. *Of course,* you needed the international system but you had little leverage or negotiating power.'

The pastor's expression had brightened a little.

I continued, 'Well, much less than a stable and highly developed country like my own. You are much more susceptible to conditionalities from outside which *must* affect local democracy.'

'Quite so! I'll give you that. But don't think those conditionalities just came because we had a war. No. They've always been there, ever since our earliest independence days. Perhaps dependency theory would be a better framework for your research.'

He got up and wandered over to the door, which he opened, popped his head outside, and requested tea from someone.

'I considered it,' I said, watching him return to his desk, wondering about the limp. 'But I'm interested in the *participation* of local people. Have they really any power? And do these concepts of accountability and transparency make any sense to people who seem perpetually to be *locked out*?'

I didn't mean to raise my voice. My face flushed beetroot in the claustrophobic heat. The silk scarf, soaked in perspiration, clung to my shoulders. It was my turn to stare out of the window.

He said kindly, 'It is a noble and insightful hypothesis.'

'Thank you.'

'You seem passionate about my country.'

There was a desperate moment when I wondered whether to explain my personal history in Sierra Leone. But this man was no fool. I wanted to impress without grasping at inconsequential credentials from my past.

'Yes,' I replied. 'I'm passionate about your country.'

'We appreciate genuine interest,' he said. Whatever his motives for combat, I felt we had made a connection. His tone was serious, 'Outsiders can be very powerful. I would ask you to be careful what you choose to say in your reports. You are very convincing, Miss Hamm, and you can say things to our government we could never say ourselves.'

I'd heard this before. From the activist, Hassan Denbah.

The pastor asked, 'Will you be speaking to our government?'

'I've already spoken to the Acting Minister for Health,' and I thought what a betrayal of local people that interview had been. But still at the back of my mind – *twenty five per cent.*

'A good man!' said the pastor. 'But he won't do. Anyone else?'

I said impulsively, remembering the evening I'd spent at Hill Station, 'I'd like to interview the Minister for Agriculture and Lands.'

There was something new in the pastor's expression. 'May I ask why?'

I hesitated. I felt protective of Songola. But he listened closely when I explained my up-coming trip to Gorahun.

'I know of Songola Bai Marah,' he said. 'Is it she who is taking you?'

'Yes.'

'She is an exceptional and courageous woman'.

'Yes.'

'Our government doesn't like the idea of the working people of *Salone* having a voice. It likes them "locked out". This *participation* you talk about, it doesn't really exist here in any meaningful fashion.'

'No, I realise that but…'

'There are risks involved in the work she does for our people.'

'I'm going to see for myself what goes on at the Arranoil plantation.'

He nodded, approving. 'Do you have the minister's contacts?'

'Not yet.'

He moved some papers on his desk and said, 'I will locate his details for you. Can you leave me your card?'

'Thank you.' I fumbled in my wallet for a university card and wrote my local number on the back.

He asked, 'Where are you staying in town?'

When I told him about the Kangari he looked surprised but made no comment.

Then he said, 'I'll get the minister's details to you. It's been a pleasure meeting you, Miss Hamm.' He shook my hand with a firm, dry grip, 'God bless you and your research.'

The pastor crossed the room, his limp barely perceptible at a strolling pace, and opened the door.

'Thank you for your time, pastor.'

'Francis.'

'Er, yes…um, thanks.' He backed away charmingly, beckoning for the violet-turbaned lady to follow him back into the room.

SIXTEEN
GORAHUN

Songola slipped her small frame into the back of the Toyota and dragged in the heavy rucksack behind her. It was six thirty in the morning and still dark in the East End.

I leaned over my seat, 'Songola, thanks so much for this.'

She nodded, 'It's ok,' but I couldn't see her expression, only the glint of her gold-hooped earrings and the glow from her cell phone. Today, she would travel in air-conditioned comfort all the 350 kilometres to Gorahun, a journey she'd usually make by minibus *poda-poda* and *okada*, a motorbike taxi. I was weak with gratitude for the opportunity she'd given me.

'I have to check with the village,' she said indicating the phone. I got the message, and settled back as we set off in silence down the rutted track, the Toyota lurching unpredictably in the darkness.

We left Freetown on the road to Port Loko, straight into the breaking dawn and the brooding Okra Hills that cast purple shadows in the early light. We were headed for a distant corner of the hinterland, bound for the oil palm plantations. It was a journey that would take us southeast towards Bo, then to Kenema, then on through bush and paddy fields toward the Gola rainforest and Liberian border. My expectations were high.

Songola made her connection and I heard her soft raspy voice speaking quietly in Mende, the language of the southern people. The journey would take us five hours, leaving only two hours for me to talk to the villagers before I'd have to return to Freetown before sunset. Songola would stay overnight in Gorahun, making her own way back to Freetown the next day.

Amadu was indignant about night driving up country.

'Ah no drivin' in di dark.'

There was no lighting on the highways in the countryside, and travel after dark was suicidal. A quick internet check revealed the sobering figures on fatalities.

He went on, 'If di accident don kill you, you bled for hours afore ambulance come.'

The Bo highway was a two-lane strip of tarmac with wide dusty verges and heavy traffic, the side of the road crowded with pedestrians, bicycles, motorcycles and carts. It was a caravan of industry, moving goods and services from far flung villages to the markets. At every junction on the highway the connecting tracks were red and rutted and meandered off into dense scrubby bush.

The scantily forested Makondo Hills came and went, replaced by a spreading landscape of stumpy bush dotted with bananas trees and isolated palms. Along the route were thatched settlements and shambolic shacks that had been pitched to service passing trade. Roadside stalls piled with watermelons, mangoes, pineapples and papaya, bright red tomatoes and chilli peppers. Mechanics operated from ramshackle huts, and lads worked on bicycles under tattered awnings. At a sharp bend a small bus was lying on its roof in a ditch.

'What happened there?' I asked Amadu.

'Dey hit with lorry from come Liberia.'

'It looks bad'.

'Dey all ok,' he said quickly.

I checked Songola. She was asleep, curled up neatly, her head resting on the bulging sack.

Eventually we stopped at a main intersection by the regional capital Bo. It was congested with heavy trucks carrying agricultural products and all manner of manufactured goods from the Liberian border.

Amadu parked under a spreading acacia in an area of cafés and stores, and we stepped out into the sweltering heat. A pedlar hawking CDs from a wheelbarrow approached keenly, but Amada shooed him away. In a shack café we sat on benches sweltering under the lazy rotation of an overhead fan, and ordered Sprite, rice and cassava leaf. We ate hungrily, the cassava stew a seething mass of pounded leaf spiced with chilli and thickened with glutinous okra. Amadu sat proud and skeletal, still wearing his shades, and I wondered if I'd ever see his eyes.

Back in the car we swung back onto the road behind a rusting *poda-poda* with its sliding door wedged open. A boy was hanging on the side and African beat-bop was blaring out. We passed a sign to Sumbuya and the mangrove swamps of the coastal plain, and drove onwards east toward Kenema. Soon the landscape changed to savannah, small copses of short trees scattered amongst the tall tussocky grasses, the distinctive outline of oil palms in the distance. The plantation was coming closer.

Songola was now awake so I asked her about the oil palms.

'They grow only ten degrees north or south of the equator. They need prime rainforest.' Her voice was quiet, I had to strain to hear over the Toyota's engine. 'You can see why the land is valuable,' she said. 'Our people have always produced palm oil on a subsistence level. If they have small farms they sell it at market. It's a staple ingredient for cooking every-thing we eat.'

A multi-coloured wooden necklace lay flat against her chest, and beads were twisted into the tight cornrows that were woven across her head. There was physical fragility about Songola.

'Arranoil don't sell to the local market, though? I mean like replacing the local supply?'

She looked at me deadpan, as though I were an idiot.

'They're producing mostly biofuels,' she said. But I knew the government was pretending biofuels could be sold on the local market to help reduce the carbon footprint of the country. And I told her this.

'Have you seen the condition of our vehicles?' she replied. Her tone wasn't scathing but there was an undercurrent. 'You can see they don't run on biofuels.'

I persisted, 'What about the working conditions? You said the people feel strongly.'

'They do. Conditions are very poor and exploitative. The men do the heavy work clearing land, removing the trees. They harvest, bringing the fruits down with sickles and long poles or machetes. They have to climb high with only leather belts to hold them and the fruits are heavy. One big fruit can fill a barrow. Sometimes they fall from great heights. When the workers get sick, they don't get paid. Sometimes the whole family has to work the harvest.'

'And what about the children? It must be a dangerous place for them to work?'

'Of course. But our people have few choices.'

She was staring out the window now, so I leaned further in to listen.

'The women work in different parts of the plantation. They spray pesticides in the nurseries and spread chemical fertilisers. There is no protective clothing for them. They only have a headscarf round their face, so they suffer with their breathing and rashes on their skin. Pregnant women are scared for their babies.'

'Pesticides? What happens to their babies?'

Before she could answer, her phone rang and she took the call.

We'd turned off the highway and were now heading south toward Gorahun, bouncing over potholes. The landscape was changing with vegetation becoming sparse into open scrub and a few scattered huts where women stooped low over cooking fires. The track was hard and rutted, and a number of military vehicles lay abandoned, rusting in ditches. Ahead, a small boy herded goats with a bendy stick. Unhurried, he moved to the side as we approached. Soon the vegetation became more ordered with regimented rows of stately palms, their lines disappearing into the distance. They were quite a spectacle across the southern landscape.

We slowed for a 'checkpoint' that was manned by half a dozen giggling boys who'd strung a rope across the track and were half hidden in the bushes. Amadu tapped his horn impatiently and they came out grinning behind their hands, making the rope go slack. The kids' faces were dusty and smiling. They had bare feet, tattered shorts, and bright eyes. Laughing, I wound down the window and handed the tallest boy some coins and small value notes before the younger ones fell upon him bringing him down in the dust, scrambling for the booty.

AT LAST, the Toyota slowed to a crawl weaving round potholes on the approach to the village of Saraybu in the Binji chiefdom of Gorahun. A woman in batik cotton dress stood by her hut pounding maize with a long pole, watching us pass. Children playing on a rusty vehicle scrambled to follow us, running behind shouting *oporto, oporto*. Colourful washing hung on lines strung out between the dwellings and piles of mud bricks lay drying in the sun. The settlement was situated on the edge of the plantation, a tight community of mud and thatch huts, and concrete homes with narrow verandas.

We came to a halt in front of a low bungalow, the house of the headman. Introductions were made and I paid the man the usual consideration. Amadu settled to sleep in the car and I was taken to the meeting place where I was presented with a plate of slippery papaya. This was the *barrie*, a space with open sides and tin roof supported by wooden posts cemented into a low concrete wall that formed its boundary.

A dozen or so people were waiting, the rest at work on the plantation. They'd gathered to learn why their trusted friend Songola had brought this *oporto* to their village. Elderly men and women sat on benches, wide-eyed grubby kids cross-legged at the front. The children were young, under five years old, too young to be working on the plantation.

Songola introduced Yusuf, a light-skinned man with close-set eyes in a peach polo shirt. He was the only English speaker in the village. There was tension in the air. High expectation. Like I was the sole *oporto* representing the west, an interlocutor between these noble people and the outside world that abused their rights. I listened while people talked about working for Arranoil, and how agri-business had affected their lives. They explained how any form of protest was suppressed by the police – beatings, imprisonment, threats. They used tear gas and live ammunition. Two men had died, and officials had come to the village to arrest anyone they considered to be part of the protests, dragging them from their homes, holding them in custody for days without food.

I asked what compensation they'd received for their land.

Yusuf spoke for them, 'When the land was taken away, we were given money. But this money wasn't even enough to take care of one person. This woman here,' he pointed at a curvy woman in a pink dress, 'she worked to raise young trees in the nursery and the money was 250,000 Leones.' Only fifty US dollars each month. 'There are health problems for these women. Chemicals are used but they are risky for these pregnant women. They have told the company but the company ignores them.'

I was eager to understand about the risks for pregnant women, 'Can you tell me what the risks are for the unborn child?'

But the woman in the pink dress wanted to talk about the protest rally.

'She say the women try a peaceful protest, marching along the road to the authority to demand action against the company. But the police set up roadblocks and ordered them to return to their villages. But they stayed put and the police arrested them and now the company have dismissed all the women who took part in the protest.'

The woman in the pink dress now had no work.

Songola explained how things used to be for the villagers, before the land was planted up purely for oil palm and I thought about the meeting in Kroo and the promises made to former fighters, that they could work the land and live off it, that they could be masters of their own destiny.

I asked, 'What about the public consultations with Arranoil?'

There was a ruckus in the *barrie* and an ugly mood descended. Gestures were made toward the headman, sitting in isolation on a tall wooden chair, now looking down and studying his shoes.

Yusuf said, 'Nobody here saw any of the lease documents. It was all agreed over their heads at paramount chief level. The government made sure the chiefs agreed.' He pointed to the head man staring at his shoes, 'Their own man here was even locked out, and they are very angry about that.'

At that point the head man stood up to defend himself.

'He says he tried to influence the deal, but he believes it was government that bribed the paramount chiefs, incentivised them to accept the deals, however bad they were.'

Songola turned to me, speaking with the speed and clarity owed to what she considered my limited intelligence. 'People have no choice but to work for the company, or they don't eat.' She gazed at me under hooded lids. 'The development this company promised is just a sham. The company medic used to work at the clinic and treated people injured on the plantations, but he's gone because of Ebola. Now that clinic stands empty with only the goats in residence.'

The villagers talked about the working conditions, why they were desperate for Songola's new union that they thought would protect them. When they complained to their supervisors about their lack of work clothes, even rainwear and rain boots, they just got their hours increased not their wages. They described the trees' palm fronds, like blades cutting their arms and feet, and that they they got infections, but that nobody would listen to their appeals.

Tensions started to flare in the afternoon heat. The air was baking, intense, breathless. I felt their frustration. No-one there had any leverage or power over these big corporate investors and their friends in government. If the authorities had criminalised the workers' association, how would they feel about Songola's national union? Her strength and courage humbled me.

'Can you tell me about the risks to babies if their mothers are working with chemicals?' I asked again, wondering why no-one wanted to explain about this.

Songola spoke in a low voice. 'The pesticides affect pregnant women. The mothers get sick and dizzy. They vomit. Sometimes their babies aren't right.'

'Aren't *right*?'

'The chemicals impact the foetus – there can be miscarriage and pre-term births, or low birth weight, maybe defects.'

'*Defects*?'

Songola's expression was inscrutable, 'Now you've heard for yourself what our people are living with. Where are the international standards here?'

There was quiet in the *barrie* as people shuffled their feet and waited for someone to say something. The heat was unrelenting, the humidity grasping. My body was soaked in sweat. Songola looked at me with those half-moon black eyes, expecting something.

Then she said, 'Come. I will show you.'

———

LATER I RETURNED THE TOYOTA. Amadu was keen to reach Freetown before dark and was standing by the car, arms folded, the outline of the village *barrie* reflected in his mirrored shades. I went to Songola, took her hands and thanked her for bringing me to the village. She withdrew them, embarrassed, looking away with her eyes cast down.

'It was good you came,' she said.

We were soon on the track that led back to the highway, the cruiser bumping and swerving, Amadu with his foot to the floor, tall palms rushing by. It was later than planned but still mid-afternoon, the sun at its hottest coming straight in through the windows.

We joined the main highway to Kenema hurtling through the dirt sections, blanketing pedestrians on the verge with dust. Women carrying the world on their heads: a demijohn of milky palm wine, a foam mattress, tall bundles of firewood held together with elephant grass topped with bowls of plantains, girls with yellow jerry cans. We shrouded them in a mist of fine red dirt as they laboured on, disappearing into the choking cloud behind us.

My heart pounded in my chest as I tried to understand what I'd seen.

After the meeting, Songola had taken me to an isolated hut close to the village. Inside the space, thick with the odour of firewood, was an elderly woman sitting crumpled on a stool, a colourful shawl around her shoulders. Beside her a small boy with huge brown eyes and toothy smile who fitted twice in the short time I was there, convulsing on the floor, the elderly woman attentive and soothing. Then Songola revealed to me a blanket-lined box on the floor in which a new born girl lay quiet, her breathing difficult, intermittent, rasping. When I looked, the tears stung like soap behind my eyes, my heart hammered reckless against my ribs. My mind trying to compute what I saw.

Songola said, 'It's called HPE. Soon she will die.'

Now the blistering heat of the late afternoon swept by in a blur of bush and scrub, the shimmering tarmacadam beckoning in the distance up ahead, and I was lost in a labyrinth of half-formed ideas, trying to bring order to my thoughts. To make sense of what I'd learnt, what I'd seen. I tried without success to get signal on my phone so I could Google HPE and discover a link with the pesticides used on the plantation.

My notebook now dusty and smudged, I scribbled furiously as thoughts came to mind: illegal land grabs, abuse of human rights, abuse of labour rights, food insecurity, virtual slavery, the effects of pesticides on unborn children, the dangers of chemicals for pregnant women (and there were so many pregnant women in Sierra Leone).

How was Arranoil getting away with it?

'Amadu, please pull over.'

He looked surprised but slowed the car and swerved onto the verge. I got out, ran to a patch of scrub, and threw up. I stood in the heat, watching the copper ball of sun dipping, inching its way. Like it had all the time in the world. The heat closed in. The anger and distress, pumping through my blood.

I got back in the car.

Amadu sat placid behind his shades, his angular jaw grinding gum, 'Let we go?'

'Yes…let's go.'

We resumed, and for a moment visibility became zero as we ploughed through smoke from burning elephant grass. The traffic then slowed and Amadu sucked his teeth

'What is it?'

'Police,' he said with disgust. It was a checkpoint that hadn't been there earlier in the day.

As we pulled up two armed officers took their time circling the vehicle, Amadu tense and quiet. He wound down his window when one of them tapped and the officer ducked in his head, surveying the interior. There was a silver crest insignia on his dark blue beret. Amadu handed over some bank notes which he had ready in his hand. The officer took them but shook his head, speaking loudly and indicating something at the rear of the cruiser. The tyre? Amadu reached into the pocket of his door and produced more money. The officer took the notes, pocketed them, then looked across at me.

I eyed him confidently and asked Amadu, 'What does this officer want?'

With a broad smile, the policeman replied in English, 'Good day ma. This is highways offence. The vehicle is not fit.' And with that he stood up and waved us through.

We soon picked up speed.

'What's this traffic offence?'

'Dey thieves,' he said. He sat, jaw clenched, eyes hidden behind his shades.

We travelled in the growing dusk toward Freetown and the Atlantic Ocean, the hills mottled with patchy sunlight and deep blue-purple forest. Mile upon mile of chaotic highway lay ahead, vast trucks silhouetted and shrouded in dust, the canopy of forest framing their progress. The honeyed sun seemed suspended on the horizon, dipping imperceptibly into the familiar lilac haze, the sky shot with aubergine and amethyst.

Darkness tiptoed over the scrub, the tall palms, the thick grasses. Soon there was nothing to see but the lights of the vehicle ahead. Our speed had slowed, but not that obviously, and we were still an hour's drive from Freetown. Amadu sat stone-faced, concentrating. Large sections of the highway in complete darkness. Headlights speeding in the opposite direction were the only indication we were on the right side. We hurtled through the darkness. Then out of the black came the taillights of a truck jacked up, men on the ground fixing its underbelly with spotlights set up on the tarmac. Involuntarily I screamed, but Amadu calmly swerved and overtook.

SEVENTEEN
UKDEV

Ann Wilson covered the mouthpiece of her phone. 'Karen. Come in and take a seat. I'll be with you in a mo.'

She indicated a chair beside a coffee table littered with the detritus of an earlier meeting: coffee cups, water bottles, a full and malodorous ashtray.

This was UKDev's senior representative in Sierra Leone, a perfectly square woman with a small head and precision-cropped natural blonde hair. She spoke in plummy tones, her vowels so long and enunciated it was difficult to understand what she was saying. But her disposition was chummy, and the mood was relaxed. On her desk, a collection of photographs suggested a passion for Great Danes and women's rugby, and included a frame of her wedding, where both women were dressed in white linen suits carrying bouquets of blue and yellow iris. I sat where instructed, notepad on lap, dictaphone in hand.

She spoke into the phone, 'Yes, yes, indeed, no problem, we're ok with that. Fabulous. Yes, yes, yes.' She looked at me and raised her eyes, *what can I do?* The call ended and Ann Wilson came to sit opposite, pouring water into stumpy glasses and smiling in a manner that suggested it was her professional expression. Her skin was heavily freckled with large patches of hyperpigmentation that implied overseas postings in hot places.

'Karen, how can I help?' She sat back, crossing sturdy legs. So I explained my research and the reasons for requesting an interview. I was careful to keep up the pretence of the PhD, otherwise she would never have agreed to the interview and might yet eject me from the room before it got started. She listened politely, tilting her head judiciously. She looked like she had a genuine interest even though my research was the tetchy subject of international aid and corruption.

When I'd finished my introduction she said, 'Oh yes, I see your point.' She uncrossed and re-crossed her legs with alarming speed. 'You are quite right. People have spent millions on democracy promotion in this country – ourselves included – so *of course* it's important to us that citizens have a good relationship with their government. But getting people to actually *engage* is really not that easy. In fact it's quite problematic. You travel to the north east of the country, for example, where people have to trudge for hours to get to any services and then you only have a tiny little ramshackle school, and goodness knows what government input is to that. There is no infrastructure, no clinic, nothing. To a lot of people government is a bit irrelevant really. They tend to rely on themselves.'

They tend to rely on themselves. I wrote it down in my notebook.

She smiled engagingly, seeming to overlook the enormity of her statement. I had to admit I thought she was right. After what I'd seen and heard in Gorahun, government was pretty much irrelevant to people in the countryside except for the absolute havoc it wrought on their lives by the concessions it made to rogue corporations. But why wasn't the biggest donor and democracy promoter to this beleaguered country not sticking up for the rights of local people?

How were companies like Arranoil getting away with such abuse?

Ann Wilson rattled on. 'We'd love to do more but we're massively overstretched in terms of human resources in the office. I would *love* to be out there every day talking to people about their needs and expectations. Gosh, yes. But it's simply not possible. That is not my role. Absolutely, for any major programme we do a consultation process. We go all over the country, and the analysis feeds in. We want to hear the voices of poor men and women right out there.' She waved both hands overhead. 'Of *course*, we want all that feeding into our development programme. On all general water and health campaigns, part of the design phase includes at least *something* that enables that to happen. For people to *engage*.'

'Could I ask you about the structure of UK aid?' I said. 'And the fact that it seems to be designed to accommodate thirty per cent graft, and then forty per cent gets used up by the aid industry itself? I mean by NGOs and INGOs.'

'Ahh. Well, I don't know where you get your figures from, but it's certainly the case that the delivery of aid is a costly business. We need good people on the ground who know what they're doing and who can train locals to eventually do it themselves.'

'I've always been proud of my government,' I said, 'being the first Western nation to meet the obligation of 0.7% GDP for overseas development. A huge commitment that others didn't want to make. But isn't it a bit cynical given the fact that such a large proportion goes nowhere near the poor?'

There was no hope Ann Wilson would give away secrets or personal opinions on the use of taxpayers' money. Instead she preferred to explain the difficulty of her job and the challenges of international development, her blonde bob swaying as she shook her head wearily, emphasising the good that had been achieved in small pockets of programming all over the country.

She concluded, 'You are right to be proud. Our government has made a huge impression on the lives of locals here.'

She was a consummate professional in full control of the situation. She answered my questions with masterful sangfroid.

'So,' I asked, 'do you feel that democracy is working for them?'

'In what way, specifically?'

'Well, for example, do you know about the protests people have been making about the acquisition of land for palm oil?'

'Oh yes, that is such a hot potato.'

I was careful how to phrase the next questions.

'It seems that peaceful protests have been violently suppressed by the authorities. I did wonder how that conflated with UKDev's commitment to democratisation?'

She stiffened slightly.

'You must realise that these issues are very complicated,' she said. 'Protests are not always peaceful and the government does have to maintain law and order.'

'Do you know about the conditions in which they work? The plantations workers, I mean? There's a company called Arranoil, in the Gorahun district...'

She bristled then. Her eyes icy blue. And I felt the shutters coming down.

She said carefully, 'Of course things aren't perfect, but you must know foreign investment is very important for the future stability and prosperity of the country.'

I wasn't for backing down. 'Did you know that UKDev itself, quite recently, commissioned a report about land and conflict here? And the report concluded there are still simmering tensions around land issues, in particular land grabbing by big corporations.'

'These accusations about so called *land grabbing*...they cannot easily be verified due to the lack of any accurate land use records held by government or indeed any of the local authorities. I'm sure you know that. You will have done your research.'

We eyed each other for a moment.

'Karen, I realise what it is you're trying to get at, but you must remember that we are really no more than bystanders. We can only encourage governments to do the right thing, and of course we have very little input into the behaviour of corporations. That is not in our remit to interfere. We can't go around demanding this and that. We can only encourage.'

But of course that's exactly what UKDev was expected to do, demanding at least an impression of democracy.

Ann Wilson was a seasoned operator, a member of that exclusive club of diplomat hierarchy intensely schooled in the impenetrable doctrine of the British Foreign Service. Her job was to reveal nothing, to follow the official line. Which she then proceeded to do, dictating UK policy verbatim. I knew this because I had accumulated my own thick file of policy documents and could recite it verbatim myself.

When she'd finished I asked, a little violently, 'How much did it cost the UK to help bring about peace in this country?'

She smiled at me in a threatening way. 'Karen, I can't see this line of questioning is in any way helpful for the pursuance of your research.' Her mood had darkened. I was reminded of the look she gave the Titian-haired woman who was dining with the Agriculture Minister the night I'd gone to Hill Station with Robbie McIntyre.

I changed tack. 'Of course, but it's so easy to get distracted by what's actually going on when you get out to do the field-work. I *have* felt the frustration.'

She checked her watch and lifted her brows in an air of surprise.

'Karen, I must make a call. I do apologise, but I'll have to let you go.'

We shook hands courteously and I was ushered out.

IN THE DUSTY compound the unforgiving sun bore down. The offices of UKDev were situated on one of the few remaining forested hills overlooking Freetown, high above the choking fumes and acrid smoke of the city. A modern two-storey block with large gleaming windows, solid wood doors and a wide shady veranda. At this altitude the air was cleaner, the heat less oppressive and I could look down over the palms across the extent of the city where the vast canopies of cotton trees made the town look much greener than you'd think when you were actually passing through.

Freetown sprawled from the coast, first in an ordered grid format, then up the deforested hills with their irregular pockets of development scarring the landscape. Beyond the balding foothills stood the breath-taking Lion Mountains.

The slums and raggedy settlements weren't visible from this point, only the National Stadium standing like an empty fruit bowl in the centre of a chequered cloth, the iconic Youyi building, and the modern business blocks stood out in any detail. The expanse of the Leone River glistened in the distance, sliding effortlessly into the Atlantic. The huge white warehouses of the port were visible, and I watched the ferry from Tagrin approaching Government Wharf where I'd alighted only three weeks before.

I thought about Ann Wilson. She really hadn't liked the name, *Arranoil,* and I wondered how much she knew.

The sun burned like a naked flame against my skin. I moved to the shade of a sprawling breadfruit tree to wait for Amadu who was taking advantage of my meeting to deliver his wife and her tie-dyed cloths to a market on Lumley Beach. The security gates opened and a small white car entered the compound parking under a spindly jacaranda, yet to bloom. A man stepped out, gangly, awkward. He was dressed in crumpled cargoes and white shirt, sleeves rolled up. He leaned in and pulled out a jacket and leather briefcase, slamming the door and dropping his keys. Picking them up, he slung his jacket over one shoulder and wandered to where I stood.

'Good morning,' he said, smiling pleasantly.

English, mid-twenties, wiry. Shoulders that stood out bony through his shirt. He looked familiar, and I realised he was one of the group dining with Ann Wilson that night at Hill Station. He stood pleasantly, half in, half out of the shade, his expression kind. I wondered what he must think of me standing there under the breadfruit, emotions high. I returned his greeting, glad of the dense shade.

'Can I help?' he asked, 'Are you waiting for a car?' He sounded northern. Manchester perhaps.

'My driver should be here in twenty minutes.'

He looked sympathetic and I explained that my meeting had finished early. He offered his hand in greeting, 'David Westbrook.'

His skin was sweaty but his handshake firm.

We chatted. He explained that he'd arrived in Freetown during the Ebola crisis and was working with UKDev as a humanitarian advisor. Previously he'd worked for Save the Children in South Sudan, among all the horrors of that region. David Westbrook had proper, indisputable Africa credentials. South Sudan, the youngest country in Africa, wracked with war and humanitarian disaster, a dangerous and challenging posting. But his style was self-effacing and un-threatening. *Anyone would have done the same in the circumstances*, kind of style.

We moved to wicker chairs set out on the veranda and I launched into a monologue about my research and the reason for my meeting with Ann Wilson, his boss. He listened politely, leaning in. Respectful. I liked his harmless, deferential manner. He was the kind of person you wanted to trust, someone with genuine curiosity. I wondered what I'd get if I asked him about the amount of UKAid that goes to graft.

He said frankly, 'Corruption's costed in. It's treated separately to amounts that get lost on natural wastage or on the sort of incompetence you'd expect to happen as a normal consequence of operating in these settings. If corruption didn't exist, and when hasn't it in the history of mankind, levels of aid would be lower. There is this culture of turning a blind eye.'

He looked at me with an expression that suggested he was stating the obvious. Development money had to be spent, it was enveloped, even though people dared not always ask where it had actually gone.

He got more pointed and serious, a bit conspiratorial, 'Aid does go AWOL. It's known about. Sometimes it's even used as a carrot to get ministers to do our bidding.'

Then I mentioned Gorahun.

'You went to the plantation?' His pale blue eyes struck alight with interest.

'I was invited by a local woman,' I said. 'She's supporting the workers, forming a union, I didn't get any further than the village but it was an enlightening trip. I mean, the way the farmers have been treated. It seems to me that the promises made to former fighters, you know, in the peace treaty, well, something's gone wrong, hasn't it?'

It was good to share it, but I held back from telling him everything. My true confidante should have been Sam Gregory, but in the context of his own country and his own organisation, Sam was changed.

David Westbrook said, 'Things are different up country. I've done work in the plantations myself. Their isolation makes them vulnerable to all sorts of human rights abuse, modern slavery even.'

Modern slavery.

The security gates opened and a familiar dusty red cruiser entered the compound.

'That's my driver,' I said, annoyed that Amadu wasn't late.

David Westbrook stood up and rummaged in his pocket, a bit panicky. He produced a dog-eared business card and asked for mine in return.

'I'd really like to finish this conversation. There's more to say. Can I call you soon?' He seemed over earnest. 'Perhaps we can have a drink this evening?'

At the Kangari I lay on my bed with wet hair strewn across a towel, waiting for a drier to replace the one that had just blown up, electric sparks flying from the death wired socket in the wall. I listened to the AC rattling away, blowing cold air across the room, thinking about David Westbrook and what it was he wanted to share with me. He'd said we should meet in person, that he didn't want a conversation on the phone. There was more to know about Arranoil.

The hotel phone rang close to my ear.

'Good afternoon Ma, how are you?' It was the receptionist's voice, polite and friendly.

Startled by their efficiency, I said, 'I'm well thank you. Is the electrician on his way?'

'No, Ma, you are to come down. The pastor is waitin'.'

'The pastor?' I repeated. 'Waiting?'

'Pastor Francis.'

'Pastor Francis?'

'Yes, Ma. He says he will meet you in the lounge bar now.'

'You mean *now*?' The water dripped from my hair.

'Yes, he says he will meet you in the lounge bar.'

There was a shuffling on the line, and then a different voice.

'Miss Hamm, I'm so glad you're here. I have that information for you. Do come down and I will talk you through it. I don't have long.'

I recognised the timbre of his voice and the adrenalin rose in me like a geyser.

'I'll be right down.'

Roughly I swept wet hair into a knot on my head, hoping it would stay, and cursed the fever of freckles emerging on my face thanks to the African sun. I threw on some clothes and slipped my feet into bejewelled flip-flops. The pastor must have the contacts for the Minister of Agriculture. Half way out of the door, I caught sight of my reflection. Back in the room I searched for the red silk sarong Graham had bought me in the Maldives, and draped it round my waist to cover the tight fitting jeans. I hurried down the concrete steps and along the interconnected walkways through to reception. The receptionist and clerk eyed my flushed cheeks with interest, so I slowed to a dignified pace, walking nervously into the lounge, noticing my quickening pulse, knowing I was more excited than the meeting justified.

He was seated in a red leatherette chair, reading something, a crisp white shirt open at the neck. He looked up and smiled, polite enough not to comment on my appearance.

He stood, 'Miss Hamm!'

'Karen.' My heart was thumping so violent, I wondered if he could hear it.

'Please,' he indicated a chair and we sat. 'I'm sorry for the short notice, but I have the information we discussed.'

He passed me a folded paper, indicating I should put it in my bag without reading it.

'The details are there,' he said. 'The contact will give you access to the minister we talked about. Speak to his PA and mention my name, she will get you an appointment. I know you'll ask the difficult questions that need to be asked.'

He was nodding and I found myself nodding back. I thought he was going to say something more, so I held his gaze, but he didn't, so I said, 'Thank you for this, I won't let you down.' I winced at the gaucheness of the words and felt the colour flush my face. He nodded at my bag where I'd carefully filed the note.

'There's another name there. Speak to him about your *own* government.'

His eyes gave nothing away, crinkling as he smiled, and I found myself nodding though I wondered what he meant.

'Thanks,' I said. 'I appreciate the trouble you've taken to get this to me.'

He'd come all the way across town to Aberdeen in rush hour traffic and it occurred to me how important he must think my work. The pastor was a busy man, local hero, inspirational preacher, and now he was here, at the Kangari, unplanned, to talk to me. I felt a rush of anticipation, and wondered if he'd had lunch.

Then he looked at his watch and said, 'I have a meeting in ten minutes...some people from Canada. I can't be late because I want their money!'

He laughed, his big shoulders jiggling at the thought. A surge of disappointment ran through me.

'They're educationalists,' he said. 'I want them to take some of our people for teacher training in Ottawa, and I have some excellent young people ready for that now. Did you know we have no teacher training college in our country?'

'Yes, I knew that,' I said. 'Is this for your school at the church?'

'Yes initially. But I'm hoping it will evolve into a broader project so we can have qualified teachers all over the country. Really, our education system is in a desperate state. We aim to change that. If I can get them to agree.' He looked at his watch again, and I already felt the loss of his departure.

He glanced through to reception where a man and woman were waiting in sharp suits. He had to go, but hesitated, and for a moment we observed each other in a silent conversation – a muted consensus of private knowing.

'I must go,' he said getting up and thrusting his hand towards me, 'let me know how you get on.'

Then he asked unexpectedly, 'What are you doing staying here?' He looked around the lounge bar where prostitutes were already gathering near a group of Arab businessmen. 'My aunt has a place in Murray Town. She calls it Hibiscus Guest House. Look her up. I'll tell her to expect you.' He patted me on the arm, smiling warmly.

I sat prim, clutching my bag with his precious note inside, watching his tall frame walk unevenly away. The limp was on the left side.

He greeted the Canadians heartily and moved with them through the lobby to a waiting car outside. He looked back, smiling as he caught my eye, then he disappeared into the afternoon heat. But I couldn't take my eyes off the place where he just stood.

———

LATER A TAXI DROPPED me in a potholed car park fringed with palms and a raging scarlet hibiscus hedge. The faded-pink buildings of the Cape Sierra Hotel stood in front of me, an iconic but dilapidated establishment situated on a lush promontory overlooking Lumley Beach. It was destined for demolition, to make way for a five-star Hilton. Ornate retro screens of cut-out pink concrete framed the hotel's entrance with showy hibiscus and flimsy mimosa growing wild among untended flower beds. The glass entrance doors were smeared, and chipped tiles covered the floor to reception.

Rumour had it that the rebels had spared the hotel during the war so that the junta leaders could encamp here. The place did have a subversive feel about it.

I called a greeting and a sleepy woman arrived gesturing for me to follow. The bar was all chipped glass and dull chrome, locals propped up drinking. An exotic girl in a green, fluorescent boob tube lounged in the lap of her companion.

I was early for David Westbrook. Beer in hand I wandered out to the deserted terrace where there was a wide vista of Lumley beach and the rolling Atlantic. From here I could also see the Kangari, a hideous concrete mass, its rows of cell-blocks perched like Alcatraz atop the palm-clad hill. I pulled up a chair and sat at the only table, sipping my drink, admiring the view framed by frangipanis, fig trees and graceful palms in the hotel's gardens. Dusk was coming but people were still in the sea. Black bodies darting in and out of the surf, small heads bobbing further out. Overhead a helicopter approached from Lungi airport, the noise of its powerful rotors filled the bay. But the sound soon died away, and music and voices rose up from the beach.

The humidity was intense, the sun low on the horizon, skeins of crimson running out across the sky. I thought of home and Graham. And of Francis, and the easiness of betrayal. Before I'd left, the possibilities and realities of Free-town seemed as remote and unimaginable as a journey to the moon. But this was a parallel universe, and now it was all very real.

Swimmers gathered their belongings, moving slowly up the beach. The light a smoky blue. Traffic taillights moved along the beach road, and the rhythm of the cicada grew louder as darkness fell. Dim lights illuminated the hotel's terrace. I pulled out the note that Francis had given me. It had handwritten contact details of Patricia Jalloh, Special Assistant to the The Honourable Robertson Abu Thomas, Minister for Agriculture and Lands.

The second name written on the note was David Westbrook.

I STEPPED BACK inside the hotel to avoid the mosquitoes' imminent assault and David Westbrook was waiting in the bar sitting at a table pouring Sprite. He rose to great me, apprehensive I thought. A bit distracted. His quick smile showed a jutting incisor among otherwise even teeth.

'Thanks for coming,' he said, running a hand through his messy brown curls.

'No problem,' I replied, sitting next to him, and indicating to the bar staff to bring another Sprite, but wishing for something stronger. Hip-hop beats throbbed from a loudspeaker on the bar.

He sat on the edge of his seat, legs wide, elbows resting on his knees, wearing the same crumpled clothes from before. One knee was jiggling, his heel tapping the floor. Whatever it was he wanted to say, it must be sensitive. There was no other reason we'd be sitting in a former luxury hotel that was now reduced to seedy bar and hook-up joint. David stared down into his Sprite.

A couple of military types entered the bar and sat together on upright stools close to the ladies. The overhead fans sped up to compensate for the air conditioning that had ground to a halt.

'Would you like something stronger?' I asked sensing the tension in him.

'No thanks, I don't drink alcohol.'

The waitress slunk over with my Sprite then slunk back to her spot behind the bar.

I leaned in, 'Are you ok?'

'Sure yes, I'm fine.' He took a mouthful of lemonade. 'Sorry, this must all seem a bit odd.'

'No need to apologise,' I said. 'It was good to talk to you this morning. Most people think my research is a bit irrelevant, so it was nice to have someone interested and asking questions.' I nodded encouragement, trying to get him to spit out whatever it was he wanted to say. Wondering why his name was on Francis' note.

'Actually, I was interested in your trip to Gorahun,' he said.

I thought so.

He said, 'I think I told you I've been working on humanitarian aid. That's what I came here to do during Ebola. But I'm not a permanent employee of UKDev, just a consultant, in many ways a bit on the periphery. My contract's due to finish soon.'

I was a bit disappointed he might be leaving the country. I poured the Sprite and sipped slowly.

'I'm also working for Human Rights Watch, writing a report for them,' he said. 'They want a follow up on the abuse of Ebola workers and their lack of protection from infection. Y'know clothing, equipment, information.'

I thought about Pastor Francis and the death of his wife who was a nurse and had caught the infection from her patients.

'Officially, that was what I was here to do,' David continued. 'It's the duty of national governments to protect people from known and preventable health threats. Did you know that?'

'Yes. Yes, of course.' I was still wondering what was his point.

'My work for HRW has taken me all over the country, to Gorahun to.' He breathed slowly but the toe of his shoe was tapping on the tiles with a quick rhythm. 'Government here has permitted corporate actions that deliberately violate the rights of local residents. And, well, I think they must have some other incentive.' He ran his hand through his curls.

'What are these corporate actions that you're talking about?' I was thinking about the pesticides used by Arranoil. I wondered how many people knew about it. David paused, and sat back, pale blue eyes staring at the ceiling.

I asked, 'What is it you're not saying, David? What are these corporate actions and what do you mean the government must have some other incentive?'

He leant across, his gaze intense from underneath his hair.

'Actually, I've been looking at the Arranoil concession myself. At the impact on pregnant women of the fertilisers they're using.'

The image of the infant child crashed into my head.

'What is it you've found?'

He hesitated for a moment, and I wondered if he was sure he could trust me.

'David, you've asked me here tonight. You must feel I'm someone you can trust.'

He nodded, then said in a low voice, 'The UK government knows about the fertilisers and the affects they have on pregnant women, and the foetuses that have been exposed to it.'

'They *know*?'

'They say they've raised it with the corporation and the government, and challenged Arranoil directly. Apparently it's common in all their operations worldwide. The company has a reputation. It's no secret.'

'No *secret*!' I hissed. 'David, do you know about the condition known as HPE? I saw for myself what it can do to a child.' I couldn't bring myself to speak it.

'Yes. It's been documented. There are studies, but they're not conclusive.'

'But can't the UK put pressure on the government to withdraw the concession or use its leverage to ban the fertilisers? We do still have *influence* here.'

'That's just the point,' he said. 'I think it's the UK gov itself that's brokered the deal with Arranoil.'

'What!' Stunned, I kept my voice low, but no-one was listening.

'I've no proof. In fact, I've very little detail.'

Our heads were close together.

'Does Ann Wilson know about this?' I asked.

'I've raised it, but she evaded all questioning, not surprising. And now I've been marginalised from their programming. I think she's unwillingly covering up for something.'

David wanted to be clear why he was sharing his concerns with me. 'I'm too close to operations here, and now people know I'm asking awkward questions, I've no chance of learning more. I keep heading down dead ends. You. Well. You're still under the radar.'

He looked at me hopefully, but I was already sold. He explained he'd tried to find out who was behind the Arranoil concession, why a company with such a bad reputation had been allowed to start operations, especially so soon after the end of conflict.

He said, 'Let's not forget, the conflict emerged from exactly this situation, government predation and powerful chiefs, exploitation of the land and its resources.'

'But you can't think this is the same thing?' I said.

'No. No, it isn't. But only because there are different predators in the game now.'

THE RECEPTIONIST WAS WAITING for me on my return to the Kangari.

'Madam, we have found the boy but not the ring.'

I'd reported the theft of my ring. But it wasn't an issue and I'd almost forgotten about it.

'Oh, right thanks,' I said, trying to walk away and get to my room.

'Ma?' She was determined for me to stay and have the

conversation. So I turned and feigned attention. I hadn't expected anyone to give me back my ring. It would be long gone. More use to someone else than to me, and I'd regretted reporting it missing.

'Yes, sorry,' I said. 'Did you find out what happened?'

'Yes. He gone now.'

'He's gone?'

'Yes, gone. And security. There is new staff on the block now.'

'Right,' I hesitated for a moment, slightly alarmed. 'Do you mean you've fired him?'

'The hotel management will make compensation.'

'Compensation?' I didn't want compensation and I wondered about the boy. I said, 'Was it the security guard who stole my ring? What has happened to him?'

'Don't worry, madam. The management send apologies. And compensation.'

The young man in the office was sitting in his usual position, leaning back in his chair, eyeing me through the open door and listening to the conversation. I wondered about his role. It was an uncomfortable feeling, knowing that someone had lost their job. It was only jewellery, replaceable. I hurried up to my room.

NINETEEN

MINISTER FOR AG AND LANDS

I returned to the Youyi Building's suffocating elevator that shuddered and groaned on its way to the fifth floor. Something had radically changed since I last rode this lift to the Ministry of Health a few weeks before. Now my interview had nothing to do with writing a PhD. This time it was human rights activism, journalism even. Thoughts whirled and blended in my head. I was riding a wave. Like some missile travelling toward an indistinct destination. Corruption, missing aid, human rights, Arranoil. I believed there was some link between them all.

Painted in gold lettering on the minister's door: *The Honourable Robertson Abu Thomas, Minister for Agriculture and Lands.* It opened onto a crowded waiting room where a lukewarm receptionist took my name. I found a spot between a large sweaty man texting on an old Nokia, and an elderly woman in *lappa* and blouse with small child on her knee. Sluggishly they made room for me. The minister was running late.

I sat poised, allowing the heat to flow over me. The child, pretty ribbons in her braids, stared open-mouthed at such a close encounter with *oporto*. I smiled and said hello, but she just gawped. After a while, a small hand touched my arm. I smiled encouragement, stroking her hand in return. Her eyes widened and there was a flicker of recognition in her expression. Spurred on, she stood on her grandmother's knee and touched my hair. She squealed at the new texture and laughed when I feigned shock at her boldness.

After an hour my allotted appointment had long passed and no-one in the room had moved. Behind the desk the receptionist chewed gum, painting her nails with studied precision. Several more supplicants had arrived, along with a tiny stooped peanut seller in lacy shawl. People stood checking their phones as the vendor offered brown paper cones filled with pink-skinned nuts.

At last, the minister's door flew open and two besuited men were jettisoned from the room. The door stood wide. The minister, sitting behind an enormous desk, noticed the peanut woman and shouted 'Yes!', gesturing to his receptionist who looked at her nails in panic. But the girl stood and purchased a cone of nuts, counting out coins with the pads of her fingers, carrying the parcel to his desk in her palm. I recognised him from the night I'd dined at Hill Station, and wondered what the Titian-haired woman had been bribing him to do?

The receptionist returned and checked her nails for blemishes. Then she nodded at me and said, 'Go.'

———

THE MINISTER for Agriculture was a thin man with shaved grey hair and gunmetal skin that had lightened in places with age. On his top lip clung a thin grey moustache. A goatee rested on the point of his chin. He wore a grey pinstriped suit, pinstriped shirt, and dark blue tie with yellow dots, and looked relaxed in his leather chair, gazing over thick reading glasses that were attached to a chain, nibbling at the peanuts. I got straight into the main question.

'Miss Hamm,' he replied. 'Are you suggesting that a minister for the government of Sierra Leone is taking bribes for overseas concessions?' He tried to make his tone aggressive, but his heart wasn't in it.

'Of course not, minister,' I replied. 'It's good of you to see me, and I do appreciate how hard you work and how many demands there are on your time.'

'Do you?' he asked, raising a cynical eyebrow. His gaze was steady, his milky eyes unreadable behind the thick glass.

I said, 'Forgive me, but I'm trying to understand the logic behind some of the difficult decisions you have to make.'

'Nicely put,' he said, in a measured tone. 'Actually, let me ask you this. What would *you* do in our position? You're at the end of war and your country's on its knees. There's a Peace Agreement, but will it hold? Your economy is dead. You have no army, no government, a fractured society.' He gestured lazily left and right with his chin, the gold chain swinging round his jaws. 'Your essential services have collapsed. Roads destroyed. Bridges down. No lights. People need work but there isn't any. And then you have Ebola.'

'A terrible situation,' I agreed.

'Who can give your country what it needs?' he asked rhetorically. 'And at what cost?'

I waited.

Then he said forcefully, 'The international community, of course! They have what you need. They can give it to you. But you need to do all these things to get it.' He was motioning in circles with his hands, shoulders hunched, energised. 'So you try to do all the things they want. You make a business-friendly environment so people can invest in your country and steal away your natural wealth. But actually this is ok because GDP is looking good and the aid you are so desperate for starts to flow.' The minister was being sarcastic.

He narrowed his eyes at me. 'Threatening to withdraw aid always gets ministers' attention.'

Threatening to withdraw aid. In the minister's mind there seemed to be some confluence between foreign investment and international aid.

'Of course, people don't like the extractive industries,' he continued. 'But that is all we have. People prefer manufacturing – but that needs infrastructure, skills – and we don't have those things.' He organised the detritus of peanuts on his desk, skilfully sweeping up with the edge of his pen.

'Actually,' he continued. 'It's very easy for people to steal away your country's wealth – some call it GDP – but it is better that other people steal it than we steal it ourselves. Our government has a poor record on that, it is true.' There was heavy irony in his voice.

He looked at me expectantly.

'But the working conditions,' I said, 'what has happened to the human rights legislation that you passed not long ago? Minister, I'm keen to know why you tolerate companies that come in and treat your people so badly. It's like you have no other choice. But surely you do?'

'Working conditions are not good, I agree, and we are working on that.'

I considered my next words carefully. I wanted to know about the control of unions by the government but wanted to protect Songola. I couldn't get involved in local politics, it wasn't right for me to do that, and I didn't want to stir up anything that would make things worse for the villagers. I couldn't mention the name Arranoil.

'Minister, could I ask you about land issues? How can you justify taking people's land away from them, especially after the promises you made at the end of the war. Don't those land concessions to former fighters count anymore?'

He was watching me closely, his cloudy eyes inscrutable, deliberately making me feel uncomfortable. Looking at my body. What could he be thinking? Upper class, rich, privileged Westerner. I stared back confidently. I knew the effect I had on men, but I didn't expect it would work on him. His eyes returned to my face.

'What would you have us do?' he said. 'Our hands are tied. Agriculture is the future for our country. We can be self-sufficient in rice. As you say, farming is what our people know. But we have free trade, and it seems China can produce rice and ship it to us cheaper than we can produce it ourselves.'

He smiled at me benevolently. He was playing me in a clever game, blaming globalisation and the international system for the sale of his people's land. 'You talk about human rights but you must know, Miss Hamm, that human rights are luxuries not everyone can afford.'

'Yes, I know that. But how can you explain giving agricultural concessions to corporations with such bad human rights records. Surely there are better choices?' I couldn't say the name.

'Are you thinking of any particular corporation?' he asked.

Bastard.

'Well no, not particularly. People are demonstrating all over the country.'

'Operations differ,' he said. 'Some are better, some are worse, they are not perfect by any means.'

His rationality was infuriating.

'But these corporations use child labour.'

'Of course they do. Why wouldn't they? Children are cheap.' He leant forward and said in a patronising way, 'You will find, Miss Hamm, that life here can be a matter of survival. If you want your family to eat, everybody works. Comfortable people sitting in comfortable offices who never know a hungry day in their lives write the legislation on

Child Rights. What do they know about it? Child rights are a luxury our people cannot afford. Maybe they will one day.'

'I appreciate that. I do know that children sometimes have to work, but surely they need protection from hazardous working conditions. Why does your government make grand claims about how many children are in school when they are busy working the plantations?'

Time was running out and the minister sat relaxed, unruffled, totally in control. Now he was looking at his watch. Sitting back in his chair, he removed his spectacles and wiped them with a cloth. His eyes looked much smaller now.

'I think it is the case that you came here to accuse me of taking bribes, of corruption,' he said. 'One day it would be nice to hear a more interesting question from outsiders like you.' His voice was calm, almost casual. 'But it might interest you to know that in many cases,' he paused as he examined his spectacles against the light and returned them to his face, 'it doesn't matter whether you want a bribe or not. You get one. Either way, you get accused.'

Dismissed by the minister, I made my way furiously back through the waiting room crush, feeling no guilt that I'd been prioritised over people who might have been waiting months. Most of them were there to extract money, favours, or resources from a minister they'd put in power. I took the stairs down to the lobby.

It doesn't matter whether you want a bribe or not. Either way, you get one.

TWENTY
DOROTHY

I am sitting cross-legged in the dirt, rolling a rusted can along the ground. The can is filled with shards of grit so we can hear the sounds. Metal scraping against flint. Cooking smells are coming from the kitchen hut, bushmeat the wives have caught, now roasting on spits. The smell of kerosene too – strong and pungent – fills my nostrils as the fires are lit. The light is fading. The hum of a mosquito is near to my ear.

Blood seeps from a small wound on my leg. I pay it no attention. I cover it with my *lappa* as it gives no pain. Pain is every day. And casual. It is what we are used to.

Songola is sitting near in her ragged dress. It is red like the blood. Her head is shaved, like mine. We sit like thieves, brows close together. Rolling the cans. Songola and me, we are not womb sisters but we feel that way. Born on the same day, the same hour. We know each other's mind.

From the forest we can hear them coming. We exchange glances, our heads low, the shouting and gunfire getting close to the camp. Songola and me, we are curious, but not alarmed. These are familiar sounds. Soldiers herding the kids, their cries coming nearer, the racketing gunfire meant to terrorise them. They break cover from the forest. The kids, they are staggering into camp, heads loaded with bundles looted from the village. Some of them have heavier loads strapped to their backs. The soldiers push them along with the butts of their rifles. They crack rounds of ammunition in the air to remind the kids who's captured them.

Those kids' worst fears have come true. Abducted now, their parents dead, their villages burned. Everything they know, gone. It is a rebel life for them now. The life of a child soldier. And it won't be long before they are rebels them-selves, the fighters their families and communities had feared for so long.

Songola and me, we are sitting at the edge of the scene. We stop rolling the cans. We can see the kids' faces – bewil-dered, terrified. They have dropped their heavy loads and huddle together. Two boys, maybe brothers, weep and cling. They are young, maybe eight, not much older than we. I look at Songola, but her head is still down. The soldiers surround the kids. The sweet odour of *diamba* floating in, wreaking the air with its stench. I sit watching, dispassionate.

The commander is wearing his combat jacket and tattered shorts, red bandana round his head. He orders the kids to line up, sit down. He is shouting at them, spittle flying. Drug-froth saliva webs the corners of his mouth. The soldier boys start up with their drumming, and the wives, they are chant-ing. They sound like ghosts.

The kids sit in the dirt. They shiver and sob. This is their induction, like all the kids that came before.

The man we call 'doctor' is here. Injecting the kids with drugs that will give them the mind to do what they have to do, because now they are soldier boys and soldier girls. Soon their bodies will get hot, and their eyes will turn red.

The commander is shouting, 'No cryin'! No cryin'! Shut up now, or we kill you.'

His voice is rising in a fever. He is brandishing his

weapons above his head. The kids whimper on. They are fools.

The commander, he says again, 'You are soldiers now. No cryin'!' and he pulls from the line the brothers whose tears still fall. Separates them from the rest. Then the casual up jerk of his head. He is signalling towards a soldier boy standing by, who raises his weapon. Fires two shots. The brothers drop, slump together. The rest of the kids are quiet now.

I feel the weight of their bodies. They are heavy on mine. Warm, seeping blood, bearing down and burying me. Their features stare me close in the face. Tear-stained cheeks, gawking eyes, slack mouths, their last sighing breath rancid in my lungs. The weight gets heavier as the pile grows bigger. Disintegrating corpses overwhelm me where I lie. At the bottom of the pile, still breathing.

I WAKE VIOLENTLY, but silent. Gasp for breath. Like those kids in my dream, I make no sound. Like them, fear and anguish are suppressed. My heart beats madly, pumping fast, and I reach for water. Wipe the sweat from my face with the thin blanket. The dream keeps coming. A rebel life of terror. Hallmarks of the Revolutionary United Front. Every night the little brothers come to me. Small boys abducted and executed together. The merciless way of the RUF.

My mother and my father were abducted that way. The same initiation inflicted on them. If the war had been prolonged, perhaps I too would have learnt to use a weapon and gone to the battlefront to fight.

Sleep won't come again now, so I lie quiet on my mat behind the curtain, calming my mind, making my plans. My mother is snoring in her chair. Dawn has yet to come, but I can hear Kroo wakening around me. The sound of cooking pots and utensils, and fires being lit helped by a touch of kerosene – an everyday odour that triggers the memories. When I ran with the rebels, burning villages. One touch from a raffia mat – rolled up, soaked in kerosene, set alight – it would destroy a whole community. Crackling, spitting, the whoosh of flames seeping up oxygen, thatch disappearing from a single spark. Choking smoke filling the air as we ran, looting what we could carry, gunpowder residue saturating the air, stinging our nostrils.

We were only children ourselves.

My father's name was Joseph Turay, a child soldier with the RUF.

But that did not define him.

One night he told me what had driven him to fight. What had happened to our nation's children during those many years of madness.

I was fourteen years when they came. They were abducting kids everywhere. We all feared for our lives, but we never really thought they would come. When they came to our village they looted and burnt everything. Killed people right in front of us. Yes, our mothers, our fathers. I thought they had killed my brother too, older than me and tall, tall. I didn't want to die so I went with them, not knowing what was in store for me.

The day I was abducted, it was like death had come to collect me.

I carried looted goods from my parents' home. We ran along the bush tracks to the soldiers' camp deep in the forest. They injected me with drugs straight away and trained me to use the AK47. We used civilians as target practice. If you missed your target three times, they killed you. I was a good shot. When I had killed my first civilian, the soldiers accepted me. They were my family now.

They trained us in bush warfare. We ran with heavy weapons, crawled through swamps and bush, and learnt how to avoid enemy fire. We laid low over many hours for ambush. We used drumming and chanting to terrorise ourselves. If we complained or tried to run away, we were punished by beatings lasting hours, or by days of starvation tied to trees.

We took drugs and alcohol all the time, especially before a big offensive when we were given extra rations. We drank beer and palm wine and we smoked marijuana. They injected us with cocaine and hid gunpowder between cassava leaves to ingest while we ate. But I found the gunpowder and threw it away. They said these things would free our minds to do what we needed to do.

They called themselves freedom fighters and when we had killed, we could not show remorse, or sadness or any shame. We no longer identified as community members or as citizens. We had no family except the RUF.

When we were fully trained, we were sent to the front, but the older soldiers held back or manned the checkpoints. I survived many ambushes and offensives and as time went on, they saw me as a good soldier. They promoted me to Captain and then Junior Commander. I was still only fourteen. Commanders had special privileges – access to food, drugs, women. So now I had the power to protect people.

When your mother arrived at the camp she was eleven years old, and when the Senior Commanders had finished with her, I had the right to claim her as my own, as my bush wife. This was a good thing for me because I could care for someone. It reminded me what kindness was. But in front of Senior Command, I still had to abuse her, but at least I had saved her from being everyman's wife. I could show kindness and mercy in small ways.

This saved me.

I was born in the bush, and they named me Dorothy. A miracle child. Malnutrition, disease, the violence – it did not kill me like it killed many others. When the war ended, we fled to Freetown.

But now Ebola has taken my father, and we remain, the bush wife and her *bush pikin*. Stigma that invites abuse.

But the abuse does not define us.

TWENTY-ONE

DOROTHY

The Sunday heat is bearing down and I see the pastor hurrying toward me as I approach the mission schoolroom. When he quickens his step, the limp is accentuated in a comical way.

'Dorothy!'

I feel proud when he calls my name.

In his hand he carries a bible. There is merriment in his expression.

'Dorothy, I am expecting a visitor. Can you take the senior class while I give her the tour?' Small beads of sweat appear on his brow. He looks cheerful, relaxed. He has not much smiled since his wife died. We both lost much to Ebola.

My chest swells at his trust. I am happy to teach our seniors. The pastor brings many visitors to our school. Rich, white visitors, who are welcome. They bring money, and so-called good intentions. We are willing to take their money, but not so much their good intentions. We need finance for our school. Resources that will allow the best of our students to attend the best universities.

Our best student is me.

I say politely, 'Yes, pastor. I can do that.' Trying to hide my pride. He always chooses me. I am the only person he can trust, because the place is full of inadequates and fools.

His eyes are bright when he says, 'She will be here soon. I will give her the usual tour.'

His shirt is smooth across his deltoids.

I cast my eyes away. Try to control my eager heart.

I say 'I know the lesson pastor. It is memorised.'

'Good, good. Excellent.' He nods energetically. Brings his hands together, prayer-like against the bible. Stands there smiling. Something inside me sings.

———

THE SENIOR LESSON ends and the students, they are gathering their things. They know to respect me as their teacher. The lesson has gone well.

Diligently, I return every book to its rightful place on the library shelves. I have documented and ordered every item myself and choose new volumes to take home, because I am a serious student. And clever. I have seen what ignorance and helplessness have done to the women of our nation. I study law, and one day I will practise law. And one day I will emerge from the slum, buy a house, and lock the door.

In my hut, you will find a collection of books on the shelf above the mattress. Philosophical thinking, political ideas, history, law. And my father's tattered bible – a book he carried upon his person 'til the day he died. He pored over its contents in the dimness of the lamp, shared with my mother the sacred texts. The guidance of the gospels, the beauty of the psalms, the wisdom of the proverbs, and the hope of revelation. Many passages underlined on those thin pages. That book was comfort in the dark days of war, when the world around us was saturated with incomprehensible sickness that sank into the pores of our red earth, clutched at the heart of our nation, and spread through the veins of our people. A disease more deadly than Ebola.

Now the students have gathered themselves like goats around the schoolroom door, it is because the pastor is standing there. I push through the crowd, slip unnoticed into the compound. I do not compete for his attention. He can rely on me.

Outside, I am surprised to find his visitor waiting in the shade of the veranda. She stands erect, expectant. She has finished the pastor's tour – made her ooos and aaas.

When she entered the seniors' class where I was teaching, I recognised her straight away. Tall and confident in that Western way. The pastor introducing her like she was the queen herself.

I lower my head. Pretend not to know her.

She makes a move toward me that I do not welcome. The sun is low, slanting rays across the dust. The light penetrates her dress.

The air is hot and still.

She has been waiting for me.

She smiles wide, says hello, and reaches to touch my arm in a familiar way that is not our custom. She excuses herself as though she has the wrong person. But I am the right person. This is the white that was riding in the car that hit the dear boy Moses.

She says, 'How is your boy?' Looks concerned. But all whites look concerned and charitable on African soil.

I reply, 'He is well, thank you.' She makes me feel wary, like all apologists, she has the need to interfere.

'I've been worried. Did you take him to the hospital?'

English. Rich. Privileged. You might say she is beautiful if you were Western yourself. I try to hide my loathing. Others might take advantage but I say straight, 'Yes, I took him to the hospital. His bones are not broken. He did not miss school'.

Her smile is wide again and she removes her hand from

my arm, says how pleased she is. That she has been thinking about him. She reaches in her bag and I watch patiently. I have work to do.

She says, 'Perhaps you could give him these to cheer him up?' As though she knows Moses, what he likes.

She offers a bag of sweets and I want to tell her Moses does not need cheering up. But I take the gift graciously, thanking her. She passes me something else.

'It's Karen. Here's my card. My number's on the back, just in case, you know. I'm glad your boy's ok.'

I look down at the card. I don't want it. But I take it from her outstretched fingers in the courteous way I know.

I say, 'Excuse me, I have to go,' and I leave her standing, looking righteous as they do, expecting you to crown them for the smallest act of kindness.

I make my way along the familiar tracks toward Kroo. My mind is full of the white. But I don't want her on my mind. There will be work waiting for me at home: our hut dusty, the latrine bucket full, the water vessel empty. Maybe my mother has eaten the beans and rice I left for her. Maybe today has been a good day. Perhaps a visitor. Perhaps she has walked to the stall of her friend, bought a mango, or some plantains for me to fry.

I think maybe my abuser won't come, because he's dead.

I get to our hut and find my mother slumped against the post, peaceful, snoring. I adjust her *lappa* for modesty and remove the pan of rice and beans half-finished in her lap. I stash my books behind the curtain. Pick up the switch to sweep the floor.

IT IS DARK, he has not yet come, and I sit on my mat.

Kangari is written on the card she has given me. Kangari Hotel. Now I think this is the same white who reports a stolen ring. Causes the trouble. My cousin, Charles, he said she was English. The worst kind of trouble. The old colonial power disguised as the new.

I reflect why the pastor invites her to the mission and decide she must be from an educational NGO. But he did not say she was from an educational NGO, and I wonder what was her business with our pastor and our school.

TWENTY-TWO

RIVER NO. 2

The Hibiscus Guest House was close to the sea on the edge of Murray Town. It was sheltered behind a white concrete wall that was graffitied with pink flowers. In blue sloping letters was written *Guest House – Welcome*. Separating it from the coast was a red, dusty road, several advertising boards, and a narrow strip of bush. I peered through the iron gate, but lush gardens obscured the view to the house.

Trailing the noisy spinner, I clattered along the path through a cool oasis of overhanging palms and delicate pink blooms dangling from the mimosa. A wraparound veranda encircled the lodge, hibiscus growing rampant along its sky-blue balustrades. Massive fuchsia flowers, their sturdy petals curling back exposing virile probes of stamen. The sweet scent made me heady.

A slow-moving woman emerged from the lodge and approached me with a gap tooth smile.

'Welcome to Ibiscus Guest Ouse, ma.'

Plump as a hen, Francis' aunt was dressed in traditional *lappa* and blouse with a purple-red design. Long earrings quivered where they hung from her fat lobes.

She extended both arms to embrace me – an unusual expression between strangers in *Salone*. I wondered what Francis had told her. Relocation to the the Hibiscus Guest House was a professional recommendation not a personal arrangement.

It was claustrophobic in the woman's iron grip. I mumbled a thank you, and her arms sprung open to release me. She called *Tamba!* over her shoulder, and a young lad appeared from nowhere to porter the heavy spinner to my room.

'Take to lodge five,' she said, indicating the bag and shooing him away.

'Please,' she said, 'let me offer you a drink.' Her manner was over friendly and I didn't want to chat. But I took a lemonade and we sat in cane chairs on the veranda discussing my impressions of her country (all good), and my ambitions for my research (all impressive). But really what she wanted to know was information about my connection to her nephew. I offered her nothing. There was nothing to offer.

Soon she said, 'Let me show you to your room. It is ready.'

I followed her through the cool hallway of the lodge, straight out the back to another garden and a group of small lodges, their verandas dripping with magenta blooms of bougainvillea. Lodge five was furnished in upmarket African style. At the door was a wood carving of a bare-breasted woman with a basket on her head. A low double bed was draped in fine mosquito nets. There was oilcloth artwork hanging from yellow painted walls and an ample mahogany desk stood at the window. Yes, I could work from here. No prostitutes, no pushy staff, no aggressive hawkers lining the approaches. I convinced myself The Hibiscus Guest House was exactly what I needed, away from world of ex-pat and into the world of *other* where I belonged.

I thanked Auntie politely and she took the hint and left.

Quickly I unpacked. That day I was meeting Francis at the Mission School. He'd rung to say he would give me a tour if I could meet him early in the day. He was so earnest about his project at the school, to take the brightest of the country's pupils and prepare them for university or other professional training at home and overseas. He wanted well-schooled, talented, skilful young people to move the country forward. His passion for it burned like the African sun. *Let me show you…you must see…you must meet.* He drew me in.

When I got there I found one of the teachers was the mother of the child we'd hit in the car. I recognised her immediately – there was no-one like her that I'd met in Sierra Leone. Stunning in a way that suggested she wasn't aware of it. Passive beauty that might be distorted by a smile. There was an air of brooding about her – strong, suspicious – slightly threatening and outwardly hostile. Her eyes were watchful, like she was expecting at any moment that I would make a violent move in her direction.

She was taking the senior class when we'd arrived, and she stood respectful when Francis addressed the students and talked about the Canadian project. But she said nothing, her eyes veiled and vigilant, averted from me.

Now I'd seen this woman three times: the accident in Murray Town when we'd hit Moses, then when I'd left Kroo Bay after the tour with Mrs Browne, and now at the Mission School. I wondered what she'd been doing in Kroo Bay. Whether she lived there.

Afterwards, I stood with Francis in the dusty compound waiting for Amadu to return.

'I hope you enjoyed the tour,' he said, his body close, almost touching. And I confirmed that I had, breathing in his scent. My skin alive. Then, unexpectedly he said, 'You have to see our beaches, we are famous for them. Forget Lumley and Aberdeen, they are nothing!'

Amadu's red cruiser arrived in the compound, stunt like, in a cloud of red dust.

Francis went on, 'If you will allow, I'll take you to River Number 2.' I'd heard about its paradisal reputation. And its remoteness. It was then that I knew where our relationship was headed.

'RIVER NO. 2. Not an imaginative name, I grant you!'

We pulled off the Peninsular Road, Francis' green Mazda bumping along a potholed track lined with palms. It was like arriving in paradise. The entrance to the Coconut Palm Resort was framed with stately palms that must have been there a century. Fan and fern palms grew in the garden, and heady scented flowers – mimosa smothered with vast flotsam of cream hearted blossom, and billowing clouds of scarlet bougainvillea that hung from the lodge's thatch. Inside, a smiling receptionist stood behind a desk that was meant to resemble a hut, palm leaves arranged overhead, coconut shell room keys hanging behind her on the wall. A West African Grey parrot stood hunched on a perch on the counter.

We sat at a table right on the sand, Francis in a traditional print tunic looking sublimely tribal, relaxed and conversational. He was quoting literature in a mildly theatrical manner, something I was getting used to.

'*Whatever you are is never enough.*' He looked at me, gleeful that I was paying such close attention. '*You must find a way to accept something from the other, however small, to make you whole and save you from the mortal sin of righteousness.*'

Righteousness. I thought we'd been talking in general terms, but the way he looked at me made me think he was addressing me personally. He smiled at my discomfort as I groped for an adequate response.

'I can't take responsibility for that quote!' he said, 'it's from the genius, Achebe.'

There was a pause before he clarified, 'The Nigerian author, Chinua Achebe.'

'Yes, I know who he is.' I bristled some more. Francis' charisma was distracting. His pull irresistible.

'*Anthills of the Savannah*,' he said.

'Yes, I've read it.' There was a slightly combative approach to everything he said.

'Karen!' He sat back, delighted. 'You impress me more each time we meet.'

I blushed irrationally, still wondering whether he thought me righteous. Wanting to ask about his relationship with David Westbrook. Whether he had any idea that David had suspicions about Arranoil and the UK government. Wanting to share the awful findings from Gorahun, waiting for the right moment to do so.

'I think you should know that the reason I'm here in your country is in fact to *learn* something from *the other*,' I said.

He leant back delighted, 'Quite so! You are right to put me in my place.'

His eyes were full of mischief. The warmth of him magnetic. He drew me in as easy as the moon draws the tide.

We were sitting on the country's most famous beach, sighing waves of the Atlantic breaking metres from our feet. Along the pristine white shoreline palms grew horizontal toward the sea, pirogues upturned at the water's edge. It was unthinkable that twenty miles down the coast lay the environmental disaster of Kroo Bay.

I asked, 'How do you know David Westbrook?'

'I'm glad you met him. Was it a productive meeting?'

'You could say that.'

'Are you going to trust me with your findings?' he teased.

He asked it in a light-hearted manner, but when I didn't

answer he said, 'We met through his work with Ebola survivors in Makeni. It is where my wife died.'

I felt embarrassed at the mention of his wife, at the notion of his pain, and looked down at my hands.

'I got to know David quite well,' he continued. 'He was there on behalf of Human Rights Watch. We had some serious issues around the protection of our medical people. Too many died there. But then the whole country was overwhelmed.' He thanked the waiter who had brought a Diet Coke and Star beer. 'David is a good man. Some of these aid workers are excellent people. Deeply frustrated by what they see and hear in the field.'

He was leaning in with a benevolent smile, trying to catch my eye. He liked to provoke, but was truly discomforted by the genuine mortification of others. He sensed my embarrassment, tempting me back to join the conversation.

Quietly he asked, 'What did he share with you?'

'He told me he's got concerns about the UK government,' I said. 'You know, the goings on at UKDev. He thinks maybe someone's too interested in the Arranoil concession.'

Francis smiled kindly at the staff who had now brought a platter of seafood.

There was no-one else on the beach, but I lowered my voice and leant in. 'He thinks the UK government brokered the deal.'

'Yes. He hinted that to me also.'

'But it's so much worse than that, Francis, I mean, sometimes we think we know what bad working conditions are, you know, low pay, hazardous conditions, poor equipment, all that. But the pesticides.' I felt the nausea rising. 'Do you know what they can do to unborn children?'

'Yes, I do. But have you found the scientific evidence to prove the links?'

'Well, no. Yes. I mean, I've found some studies online. There's more work I need to do, and I know it's a contested thesis, but...' I couldn't bring myself to tell him about the baby in the village, to actually say the words.

Francis said, 'Some of these corporations will get away with whatever they can get away with. It's in their DNA. People have been protesting against the use of pesticides for decades.'

I hissed, 'It's outrageous in the twenty first century. It seemed like a slave plantation to me. Actually forced labour.'

Francis stayed annoyingly calm. 'So, what are you going to do about it?' He placed a piece of barracuda in his mouth with precision.

'I've done some digging into Arranoil.'

'And?'

'It's registered in Panama and is owned by a holding company Arran.Inc., and Arran.Inc is registered on the Panama stock exchange. All its directors are US-based. No names that are obviously connected to the UK or UKGov. All my searches have brought up virtually no detail about the backgrounds and activities of the board executives.'

'So where do you go from here?'

'I'm not put off. When I met with your Minister for Agriculture, I was convinced he was making a point. I mean, he hinted that Africans aren't the only ones capable of corruption.'

'Well of course they're not the only ones.' He was listening closely, outwardly attentive, inwardly itching for the challenge, the gentle correction. The opportunity to enlighten.

'He told me it didn't matter whether ministers wanted a bribe or not, they got one anyway,' I said. 'I think he was saying that corruption in the ministries is motivated by outsiders. Do you think that's what he was saying?'

'Well, partly. He could well have been saying exactly that. Batting the ball to the outfield. But our ministers are perfectly capable of managing their own corruption.'

A waiter stood by awkwardly, lurking on the periphery,

waiting for the moment when Francis' cutlery would clank against his plate. But Francis was still busy with his lobster, prising the meat from its claw, seeking the last morsel with his fork. Deftly popping it in his mouth. He looked up and saw me watching.

I said in a low voice, 'Is it just a coincidence that a government minister hints to me he's forced to take a bribe when an aid worker has already said that my own government may be involved?'

He shrugged. 'Don't be surprised. It's only business by other means.' And then, 'Did you mention Arranoil specifically?'

'Of course not.'

'It would have been interesting to know his reaction.'

'Well, yes! But what about Songola and the villagers. I have to protect them.'

'Forgive me, you must know that I know that,' he said. He wiped his beard with his napkin. 'Karen you are moving into murky waters, but I can tell you that David Westbrook has an instinct for these things. You can trust him. Remember, it's too easy to focus on the obvious – corrupt ministers in Africa. Yes, yes. But what *don't* we know? Who's really pulling the strings?'

I felt better, 'What d'you mean by murky waters?'

'Just be careful. I admire your courage. And you have tenacity, but you could well be treading on some powerful toes.'

His soft eyes were serious now, the merriment gone. There was anxiety in his expression as he smiled at me affectionately. I thought about how weary he must be with the unregulated, morally deficient business environment in his country.

Our hands rested on the table, his long dark fingers close to mine. I attempted to concentrate on what he was saying through the fog of many Star beers. Teetotal himself, he was speaking as eloquently as he would at a morning sermon.

'It's up to you what you want to achieve,' he said. 'It seems to me that you're no post-colonial apologist, like so many who come here from your country. You seem to be seeking some deeper truth.'

The sun was dipping low. Vaguely, I wondered about the return drive to Freetown, knowing that today there wouldn't be one. Crabs were emerging from their sand burrows, shimmying along the beach toward the sea.

The waiter returned and placed some cakes on the table – sesame, peanut, banana.

Without warning Francis scanned the trees.

'Listen!'

I listened.

'Emerald Cuckoo,' he was excited. 'Can you hear it?'

There was a distinctive call, a melodious and rhythmic whistle coming from a tight copse of low palms.

'I can hear it,' I said.

'They're difficult to spot. Rare to see. Come, we must find it.'

He rose from the table and wandered in the sand. I followed him at a short distance, hearing the bird's call, knowing it must be special. A few metres in he stopped and whispered, 'it's here,' and took my arm, a finger against his lips. I followed his gaze toward a brilliant metallic green bird with a canary yellow chest, perched in a mango. It was calling its mate.

'Beautiful, isn't it?' he said, enchanted by the iridescence of the bird's plumage and the magic of its song. I watched his profile as he stood spellbound in the sand, noticing the neat shape of his head, the sharp square jaw and the princely nose, how the close beard accentuated the angle of his bone structure.

'They're sexually dimorphic,' he murmured. 'This is a male. The female is very different. Brown but barred with green and white on her underside. Pretty enough.'

Spellbound in a different way, I stood observing him. The hum of the cicada starting to swell. The wind was picking up, palm fronds overhead beginning to slap against each other. The bird flew off and the spell was broken.

He turned and took my hand. 'Come, we have cake to eat.'

TWENTY-THREE
TRAFFICK

I sat cross-legged on the bed watching him dress, methodical, meticulous, his beautiful skin shining ebony black. A well-maintained body, muscular and lean.

'You ok?' he asked.

'Yes, I am ok,' I said, in a voice that didn't sound like my own.

I asked warily, 'Are *you*?'

But he said, 'I don't do this.'

My heart dropped like an anchor searching for the ocean floor, little throbs of panic in my chest. I looked down at the crumpled sheets with an instant sense of loss.

The morning sun had risen across the estuary and silhouetted his frame where he stood at the window. His gaze was steady on me. Expecting something. Maybe this preacher man regretted his reckless, ungodly night with me. Panic and anger surged like the tide. I could think of nothing to say that wouldn't break the spell.

As though I were some idiot or lacking the power of hearing, he repeated in a slow, grave tone, 'Karen, I don't *do* this.'

Trying to keep the shrill from my own, I said, 'Neither do I!'

What was I charged with? Rampant seduction? I asked him what he meant but he turned away, pretending to search for his socks.

'Is this a one-night stand?' My voice sounded far off. I stared at him, dreading his reply.

After a pause he stopped reshaping his socks, folded them, placed them on the bed. He said, 'Not for me. That was not my plan.'

He looked vulnerable standing there. Hardly daring to look at me. No longer the confident pastor, the exceptional interlocutor, the superior mind. He was waiting for reassurance, and at that moment I saw the weakness in him. Maybe the only weakness among his vast arsenal of talents.

It was loneliness.

As I watched his pain I felt sick with relief.

I said quietly, 'I don't do this either. What d'you think I am?'

He looked at me, remorseful. Immediately I felt responsible for his happiness.

'I'm sorry,' he said, embarrassed. 'I don't know how it works. Forgive me.'

He dropped his head and said to the floor, '*For whom so firm that cannot be seduced.*'

'Anne Frank,' I replied.

He looked up, brighter.

'Did I seduce you?' I asked.

'Maybe we seduced each other,' he was smiling now. Coming to the bed he sat and took my hands. 'Some temptations are not meant to be resisted.' Kissing my palms, he said, 'Karen, I want you to know how special you are to me.' Then patting my knee, he said 'Get dressed. There's something I want to show you.'

WHEN I GOT down to the sea there was a small pirogue beached and Francis was negotiating a price with the oarsman. A pencil-thin woman balancing a basket of pineapples strode down the sand toward us. Her maroon *lappa* swayed with the sashay of her hips. Breakfast, I thought, and beckoned her. Masterfully, she drew her machete from a canvass bag and sliced the ripe fruit in careful strokes toward her body, the yellow juice running across her wrist.

'*Tenki, ya,*' I said, and she wandered gracefully away, her shadow long in the early sun.

The pirogue rocked side to side as we climbed on board and settled with our legs outstretched on the floor. The lean-muscled oarsman heaved the boat from the shore, then out into the shallows alighting weightlessly. He knelt and with practiced expertise paddled left and right with a single oar. The pirogue, not much bigger than a canoe, seemed precarious with its uber low position in the water and shallow sides.

We moved parallel to the beach in the direction of the river estuary, sucking on the sweet pineapple in the silence of the morning, leaning in against each other. From the water, we could see the spectacle of the peninsular landscape. The dense rainforest that crept up the mountains which seemed so close, magnificent with lush vegetation and shrouded at their heights in dark cloud. On the sand below, the sun bore down with its usual ferocity. Up ahead, where River No.2 broke into the sea, a flock of white egrets had settled on the water where fresh water met salty, attracting a feast of shoals. Out to sea, a single dhow was fishing in deeper waters, its sail raised. Francis was silent, my hand in his.

At the estuary, the oarsman turned the pirogue and we made our way through rippling currents upriver at a slower pace, the banks on either side tangled with mangrove and dense vegetation. Soon the oarsman transferred to a pole, standing to navigate the boat through the shallows, turning toward a sandy area where a clearing had been made for boats to land.

We alighted, leaving him texting on his phone, and followed a well-worn track through the vegetation to arrive at a hamlet of huts. Beyond was a clearing where a modern thatched building stood surrounded on all sides by dense forest.

'Where are we?'

'Come, let me show you.' Taking my hand Francis led me up the steps onto a wide veranda with potted palms. We stepped inside where it was cool, vaguely clinical, but without the usual odour of antiseptic. There were no signs giving a clue as to the purpose of the facility or the money behind it, but given the quality of the structure and the resources inside, it was surely private funding that was running it.

I'd already noticed the disproportionate number of amputees and the youthful demographic.

Francis said in a low voice, 'This is a psychological trauma unit. All the residents here were amputated as young children or as babies in the war. They were either orphaned, or lost contact with their families, or they were abandoned.'

We moved through to a large airy room, furnished with rattan chairs, a bulging bookcase, drums and baskets of different shapes and sizes. It overlooked a patch of bush that had been cleared and planted with flowering shrubs and trees: hibiscus, frangipane, mango, fig, avocado. Open doors led out to a quiet section of veranda where a middle-aged woman was chatting to a teenage boy with missing arms. We moved away to a different side of the building where an area of garden had been planted with cassava tended by two young women practising the use of prosthetics.

Francis told me he had built this unit deep in the bush and close to River No.2 as a quiet, safe place for young people to talk about their experiences, their memories of war, and the stigma of amputation.

He said, 'All the staff are local social workers specially trained to encourage people to open up about the past and share their hopes and fears for the future. Sometimes that's all they need to move on. Sometimes it isn't.'

'It's been fifteen years since the war,' I said. 'And people are still here?'

He smiled patiently, 'Some will never leave.'

I wondered how any child could recover from such experiences.

Francis said, 'Many have come here, stayed for a few years and moved on with their lives. I've been privileged to witness that. We mustn't look at these young people as victims. It isn't helpful.' His voice was low, 'The children who came here after the war had very specific needs in terms of their mental health. And we decided the best way to support them was to train community-based nurses and encourage traditional healers to work with them. That way, people build trust.'

We stood watching the women working the cassava garden.

Francis explained, 'The psychological approach is important. We need to break down these attitudes to mental health that we've held for centuries.' He turned to me, 'Do you know we still enforce our 1902 Lunacy Act? It's archaic. People still believe mental health is an evil sent by the ancestors that can only be cured by killing a goat! This is what we are up against.'

'What's your role here?' I asked, but I knew what the answer would be.

He said vaguely, 'I've contacts in the UK. We've been able to bring professionals here to train our people. We're lucky in that we can pick and choose who we want to invite. No-one is imposed upon us.'

I sensed his modesty. He'd funded this himself, with

support from Western charities. He was proud and excited sharing it with me, and I recalled what he'd said when I tried to interview him at our first meeting. That questions were simple, but reality was complicated. That questions simplified what could only be fully understood through a long process of intimacy and experience living in the locale.

This moment felt like the start of something, and I wondered what part I would play in his plans. Who I would be in his life. What he would be to me.

The forest around us looked threatening, feebly held back from its natural impulse to march toward the building and devour it, which one day it would.

'It's a peaceful place,' I said.

He turned to go inside. 'Feel free to look around. I need to speak to some people.'

He disappeared and I wandered through the vegetable garden, a patch of maize growing strong and green at waist height, sage green cassava standing in long straight beds. In another part of the garden, under a spreading mango, there was a group of younger boys, counting out loud in English, their teacher pointing a stick at a blackboard. The children were able-bodied and too young to have experienced the war, and I wondered who they were. I edged toward them, their teacher nodding and smiling, but the lads seemed fixated on the repetition of the counting. They stopped when I approached, heads down, eyes slanting my way. *Oporto.* I backed off, sensing something. Deference, submission? Their teacher was smiling but I indicated that I would go.

When I returned to the building, Francis was waiting with two members of staff. All three looked my way as though I'd been the topic of conversation, and the familiar heat spread across my face. An improbable realisation dawned. *He could be mine. He thinks he's mine.* And a small node of panic rose in my chest.

THE BOATMAN WAS WAITING, and we made our way back to the Coconut Palm Resort, straight to the green Mazda and back along the rough track headed for the Peninsular Highway. I asked Francis about the group of boys I'd seen reciting their numbers in the garden.

'Are they children of the amputees?'

'No. In fact we are not sure yet who their parents are.'

'What d'you mean?'

'The boys are too young and traumatised to know where they come from. We believe that most are from *Salone* but some of the tribal marks suggest Guinea. Most of them haven't spoken yet but for some reason they like counting.' He smiled across at me. 'It's a start.'

'Why are they at the trauma unit? Where've they come from?'

'We have a problem with trafficking gangs in our country,' he said casually, swerving to avoid an oncoming truck that was clattering toward us, shrouded in dust.

'Trafficking gangs!' I wondered what else this shattered country was hiding.

'Yes. Children are bought by gang leaders, sold to others, and forced to work. It's very profitable for them. The children we have currently at the unit have been rescued by our people from the alluvial mines in Koidu. They were working the open pits. We are collaborating with the government, of course, but it may take some time to find their parents. They could be anywhere. What we can offer is a safe place where children can recover and try to remember who they are.'

'Dear God.'

'Yes. He is helping us too.' He looked across and smiled. Put his big hand on my thigh and squeezed gently.

As soon as we picked up some signal, Francis' phone began to ring and he took call after call on our way back to town. He dropped me outside The Hibiscus, saying he'd call me soon, and I wandered in, passing through the lodge on the way out the back.

Auntie was preparing vegetables in the kitchen and her head jerked up as I tiptoed past. I was desperate for a change of clothes, and must have looked like a woman returning from an unplanned rendezvous, which I was. She stopped chopping and looked at me, vaguely judgemental.

'Good morning, Auntie,' I said, before hurrying away to my room.

TWENTY-FOUR
DOROTHY

I am waiting outside the tailor's shack, the midday sun direct upon me, a row of customers patient behind. The proprietor of the establishment has disappeared into his hut, searching for my auntie's order. He returns with the garments carefully folded. Stands proud. Demands from me, 'Forty thousand.'

I reach inside my bag for the roll of tattered notes and hand them over.

'*Tenki ya.*' With two fingers he counts the notes at the speed of a practised dollar boy. The tailor is satisfied. Respect-fully I put the neat, bright bundle in my bag. I turn and weave through tightly packed stalls and the weighty crush of shoppers, place the bag on my head to save space.

It is Tuesday at King Jimmy Market. The place noisy and heavy with traders and their customers. Tourists too. The tourists come to appraise themselves of our market's historic significance. It has been trading on this spot since the Portuguese slavers docked here. That was lifetimes ago.

Now the stalls groan with kaleidoscopes of offerings. Sweet peppers – emerald, red, orange, yellow – and purple beets and eggplant. Medleys of green vegetables – avocado, okra, cabbage, cassava leaf – and herbs: bay, thyme, parsley, coriander, mint. Can you see it? We have pale gnarled roots of ginger, and turmeric, and brimming wooden bowls of fiery chillies. Barrows of plantains, potato, and red, smooth-skinned yams. Orange and yellow pumpkins, large and small. Tomatoes in every shape. Deformed looking calabash, purple and red. And stalls with dried goods, bread, spices, fufu. Neat piles of groundnuts, maize and garlic. Bottles of cloudy palm wine, and vats of red palm oil. Fish too, fresh from the ocean: striped barracuda, snapper and grouper, lobster and shrimp. We have tailors, cobblers, hair salons, household goods, tools, bicycles. Yes, this is our market at King Jimmy.

I push through, crushed vegetables under my feet. Ahead I see her.

'Sister!' I call. Trying to be heard above the noise. Glad to see my friend. She stands packing onions and tomatoes in a sling across her front, her infant son hanging on her back, her daughter clinging to her legs. We exchange greetings. She hitches the baby and takes her daughter's hand. I pat the girl's head and chuck the baby's chin.

Songola says, 'Walk with me.'

Falling in, I walk beside my sister. I ask her how the work is going.

She is fighting for rights on the plantations. Forming a union for agricultural workers. Our brothers and sisters up country, they are exploited and abused by the corporations that employ them. I am proud of my sister's work, her courage. This is the kind of fight that inspires my own ambitions, to make human rights meaningful in our country. To hold people accountable. Songola and me, we share this passion. One day soon I will work with her, myself a qualified lawyer.

We push our way through the crowds and the warmth of many bodies pressed together. There is a stench of discarded food that is decaying in the heat. I ask my sister about the work.

'We are making progress, the bosses have quietened. Now they say they respect the rights of workers to form a union.'

This was news.

'But you don't trust them.' I say.

'No, of course we cannot trust them. But they have said it, made a formal statement. It is something we can work on.' She greets a friend coming the other way, then continues, 'They've even said it on TV.'

'On TV?'

'Yes. French journalists came to film at their plantation in Cameroon. It was for some news channel. The situation is as bad in Cameroon as it is in our country. Of course. That is what we would expect.'

'Why were they filming?' I ask.

'They were looking at the working conditions but, of course, they did not see the worst. What do we expect? But the company has made promises, all lies, but it is a starting point.'

'And our government?' I ask.

'They want considerations. I am working on it.'

This is the situation we have in our country. Our government will oblige if the price is right, but we cannot always rely on cooperation, even if the right price is paid. But my sister is defiant. The people of Gorahun cooperate with her, even though they risk retributions. Much is at stake. She makes me proud.

We leave the market at Government Wharf, holding hands we bid farewell. Songola will make her way to the East End and her home with Sheku, whilst I make my way to Tower Hill and the hateful compound of my abuser.

Songola and me, we survived the war together. We share the same terrible history. We remain *bush pikin*. Sometimes I wonder whether she has the nightmares too. But the past, it is something we never speak about.

I HURRY TOWARD TOWER HILL, concerned about my sister. Something in her has changed. The way she speaks of the work, eyes darting around, not settling. The way her arm protects the child, wedged in close beside her. The thing that is new in Songola's face. It is fear.

I cross the busy street at Siaka Stevens, at the spot where the *poda-podas* park in an untidy way.

'Hey, sister!'

I recognise the voice. It is my cousin Charles purposefully walking towards me along the gutter edge.

'Brother. What is the hurry?' I ask.

'What's happening?' He is breathless, and sweating.

'The usual. Running for Auntie,' I reply.

He looks at me sympathetic.

Then he asks, 'When is yo exam, sister?'

I wonder why the interest, but I reply, 'Four weeks revision. Then I sit. Then I go to university.' I know I will do well. I am the first in my class. The pastor has faith in me.

'We are expectin' from you!' says my cousin.

His smile is bright but not his eyes. I ask him what is happening to his friend at the Kangari, the one who is in trouble. The one who knows about the diamond that was stolen from the English.

He replies, 'Dey chop him. He gone. Now he has no work.'

His smile diminishes, and I become angry, thinking of the English who gives me sweets for Moses.

My cousin says, 'Things are bad for his family now.'

I do not ask if it was his friend Saidu who took the ring. I believe he did not, that he looked the other way when the thief broke in.

My cousin says unexpected, 'The pastor.'

My interest is alerted at the mention of that fine man, and I look at my cousin expectant. 'Yes?'

'My sister. The pastor has new girlfriend.' My cousin looks at me straight.

I stand still. I am mute. I am wondering what this silly boy is talking about.

He repeats himself, 'He has new girlfriend.'

He is my beloved cousin, but he is not that sharp. I have misheard him in the noise of the traffic.

Then he says, 'It is di English. The one who diamond it gone.'

I look at him with blankness on my face. Try to comprehend this incoherent youth.

'Pastor Francis?' I enquire. Maybe he speaks of someone else. Because the only new girlfriend I expect that man to have, is me.

'It is true.' He is nodding with a concerned expression, knowing what this news will do. Then he says in a small voice, 'I saw them.'

Thoughts hurry into my head. Pastor Francis? And the English?

Her with the expensive diamond that tempted our people. The one in the car that hit the child, Moses. The one that was touristing Kroo.

That *white* he brought to the Mission School.

I feel the contents of my stomach rise on their way to the street. I keep them down and say to my cousin, 'I must go.'

He says, 'Ok dat,' and I turn my back, half running toward Tower Hill, my heart tumbling in my breast.

I ignore the lewd calls from the *poda-poda* boys.

TWENTY-FIVE

TENGBEH TOWN

Francis was in the mood for theological debate, but I was in my own head thinking about Arranoil. He lay on the bed staring at the ceiling fan, expounding to himself in sermon mode.

'In the Western world you could say religion has been embarrassed out of existence. So there is a need to change the vocabulary of faith to save secularists from their own squeamishness. Mention the word *God* and everyone runs for cover.'

My head was resting on his chest. Above us the mosquito net billowed in the breeze. It was still early.

'People believe that rationality is the first casualty in a Christian life. But on the contrary. Christianity is perfectly rational.'

I listened patiently. A cockerel crowed in a deranged falsetto drowning out children's voices passing under the window and singing brightly.

I lay pondering, frustrated I hadn't found solid evidence, some incontrovertible scientific proof, that the chemicals Arranoil used could directly cause the condition of the newborn I'd seen in the village – although there was much speculation in published articles. But I had found evidence linking pesticides to the epileptic seizures experienced by the other child I'd seen. In fact, epilepsy was a known side-effect of early exposure to pesticides.

Then there were the children I'd encountered at Francis' trauma unit. The group of little boys counting aloud in English. Trafficked children forced to work in alluvial diamond pits, way up country, far from their homes. Was it possible that trafficked children were also forced to work on the plantations? On Arranoil's plantation?

The noise of early traffic rose from the street and through the open windows flung wide behind the mesh. Beside me, the dear pastor was getting into his stride.

'People think that if you're the kind of person who believes in an intangible force you must be lacking in intelligence. Deranged, in fact. That in the modern world', he patted my hair, 'well, I'm thinking more of your *Western* world, my dear. People regard faith communities as they would regard dead civilisations. Freak shows, outdated, quaint. Irrelevant to the goings on of civilised, intelligent life in a post-industrialised world.'

He sighed in annoyance. 'If people are genuinely open minded, they don't insult the intelligence of others. They could learn that faith *does not* rest on some super-natural awareness of ethereal entities. No! Religion is a path of understanding. It can say little to those who have not set out on the journey.'

He paused for a moment, resting an arm across his forehead, totally relaxed. The timbre of his voice so low it seemed to resonate the glasses on the table.

He said, 'We need a different language to describe our relationship with God and the journey our faith can take us on.'

He nodded to himself, pleased that his thought processes had led him to a satisfactory conclusion. It was this self-interrogation and reflection that preluded his best sermons. I watched the gentle rise and fall of his chest, my hand resting like a ghost, pale against his skin.

Freetown was awakening in the streets below.

'Karen, my dear, you inspire me.' He took my hand. Turning it he kissed the palm, ruminating, 'How to explain that you can't think your way into a new way of living, but that you live your way into a new way of thinking?'

'Just that.'

'Hmm?'

'You have the words, dear pastor. There's deep meaning in your utterances. I believe you are gifted.'

'It's God's gift, my dear. I take no credit.' But secretly, he was satisfied with my response.

'And now it's time for breakfast. Today I will surprise you.'

———

SINCE MY MOVE from the Kangari I'd spent few nights at the Hibiscus Guest House but many at Francis' home in Tengbeh Town, an elevated suburb of Freetown on the rise to Hill Station. During the day I returned to the Hibiscus to write up my notes, listen to my interview tapes, do more digging on Arranoil and its pesticides. Hassan, Songola, Gorahun, David Westbrook, and now Francis. All serendipitously aligned. I wrestled with the prospect of discovering Arranoil's connection to UKDev.

Now I made my way downstairs following the aroma of fried plantains, the tiles cool under foot. Francis stood at the stove, bare foot and square-shouldered, poking a knife into a pan of hot oil, separating the slices of fruit with meticulous care. Grey sweatpants, and a black round-necked tee.

'Smells good,' I said.

The heat from the stove brought droplets of sweat to his brow. They glistened and shone like jewels.

'Breakfast, madam. Take a seat.' He gestured with the knife to a tall chair at the counter but instead I moved toward him, slipping my arms around his waist, resting my cheek against his back, breathing in his scent. Passion and her sisters – love and hope – were taking control.

He lifted the plantains from the simmering oil, perfectly browned and tender, and drained each piece before piling them on a single plate.

'Come, let's eat.'

We sat together, timidly testing the piping food, laughing at each other's impatience. Much had been shared between us. Feelings. Commitments. And privileged intimacy had revealed to me Francis' loneliness and vulnerabilities. That knowledge lay on me heavy as clay, like the guilt I felt when I thought about Graham.

I raised the issue of our cultural differences. But he'd dismissed them: *love has a universal passport to the hearts of everyone. It's an international traveller with no concern for borders. When it finds you, there is no defence.*

This is where I'd always hoped to be. Where I'd always thought I belonged

———

FRANCIS' home was a two-storey house painted blue. A white balustrade wrapped round a wide veranda through which bright bougainvillea flashed crimson. Ornate and rusty iron-work secured the windows on both levels. At the front door, a laden orange tree and to the rear, directly accessed from the kitchen, a private garden with fruit trees – avocado and mango, and a rose apple glowing with clusters of pink bell-shaped fruit.

It was to the garden that we wandered after breakfast,

sitting on plastic chairs, sipping guava juice from thick-based glasses. In the mango tree overhead was a cup shaped nest with a pair of Paradise Flycatchers. Striking chestnut-orange birds with elegant long tails, crested heads and bright blue bills. Around their eyes an iridescent blue ring of flesh. The pair were in a frenzy; feeding scrawny chicks, to-ing and fro-ing with morsels of every kind. Moths, dragonflies, ants, spiders, flies. We leant against each other, watching in silence. Staring up through dark green foliage, fascinated by the everyday parenting of these airborne masters. Quick as light-ening, on and off the nest, stuffing insects down the throats of their insatiable young.

Francis said, 'If you're lucky you'll see them catching flies mid-air.' But the birds were far too quick for me to spot.

I was thinking about the little band of boys.

I asked, 'Do you know if children are trafficked to work the oil palms?'

'That is very conceivable. We find them working in agri-culture. Also fishing, which is very dangerous.'

'Do their parents report them missing?'

He looked at me with the benevolent expression I'd come to expect.

'My dear, very often it is their parents that have sold them to the gangs.'

'Dear, God.'

'Do not judge. Many of our people are destitute.' He was starting a lecture. 'Maybe if they sell one child they can feed the rest. And there are always those who will take advantage of that. Remember you are now in a world where extremes of everything are normal. People have few choices. It it hard for Westerners to comprehend these realities.'

A patronising slur. I simmered.

'Don't forget your heritage, Karen. You are a scholar, but you may still harbour colonial ideas, prejudices, preconcep-tions perhaps. Our country is already flooded with that kind of crusader. You must find a way to be different. You *are* already extraordinary.'

His smile was comforting though his words were harsh. That was his power.

'Well it's nice of you to think that,' I said in a measured tone, feeling livid. 'I'm not here to deliver aid, Francis. Maybe you've forgotten that?'

His voice was soft, 'But you still have your western baggage. You cannot help that.'

'Maybe you have your own prejudices, pastor. You have very clear notions about Westerners.'

A Flycatcher swooped low out of the branches. Francis leant across to kiss me, but I pulled back.

'Whatever so-called baggage I might have doesn't mean I can't be useful. Call it out. There's shit going on here, Francis. I want to know if my government's involved.' The emotion surged. I didn't want to control it.

He stroked my hair in a pacifying way, but I shrugged him off, wondering if he had any notion of what I was capable of. Wondering if I knew myself.

He sat back, 'Dig deep, Karen. You *are* extraordinary. Listen to what your inner voice is telling you.'

———

IT WAS evening and Francis was resting on the sheets eyes closed, his bible open on his chest. I stood by the window and looked out across the city. The landscape below was a sea of rusted roofs stretching far into the distance, terrain broken by scant concrete structures – an ancient board house, a mosque, a church, a cotton tree. Loud cries flowed from minaret to minaret, the call to evening prayer gathering momentum as darkness began to settle on the city. Between the shacks, fires were being lit. Luminous smoke rising up into the sky like rippling gossamer, in vertical plumes, no air to disturb them.

Vaguely I wondered about the risks of investigative journalism. Because this was the territory I was stepping into. Big corporations hired unscrupulous thugs and African states had their own *heavy boys* who carried out threats all over town. Then there was my own government. What methods could it deploy to dissuade people from asking awkward questions? But ignorance and arrogance were my friends, and I believed my whiteness would protect me. How could I stand by after all that I'd discovered?

I thought of home. Of Graham. Of the worry it would cause him if he knew.

The comforting odour of woodsmoke floated in through the window mingled with dull acrid fumes from a smouldering dump. The odour of poverty. The scent of Africa.

Dusk bore down, and lamps were lit at little kiosks on the kerb. Behind the city, dark clouds had gathered over the mountains. A distant rumble. Muggy and humid, the air heavy. No breeze to drift through the rusting ironwork tonight.

I slipped in beside Francis. He turned drowsily and lay his head on my shoulder, the weight deepening as he moved from rest to sleep. I adjusted the shape of my body to accommodate the load and stroked his fine head. Feeling the power of him. His breathing deep and comforting. Rain started to patter on the tiles outside. I settled to sleep, dimly aware of my phone vibrating, the soft glow of the screen fading as I drifted off. If it was Graham, I couldn't trust myself to speak to him tonight.

TWENTY-SIX

HOME

Two days later, I had returned to the UK.

The rain bounced off the tarmac and ran in wide rivulets down the cabin windows as the plane touched down at Leeds/Bradford airport. There was the prospect of Graham waiting in arrivals. But my return was short notice and unplanned, and Graham didn't do unplanned, so I clung to the hope my brother Dan would be waiting for me instead.

On the flights home from Freetown there'd been time for the guilt to stew, and the panic to set in. I'd have to face Graham much sooner than I'd thought. Would have to explain that my betrayal, not wholly unexpected, had taken root in a spectacular way. That I now planned to live in Africa, with Francis. And my work was now perilous, not benign.

The guilt and shame lay as heavy as the skies over the Yorkshire moors.

In arrivals, Dan stood waiting. Tall and blonde, fragile and expectant. I hugged him with relief, so good to feel the familiar sharp lines of his angular frame.

'Thanks for coming back,' he said, the scent of Issey Miyake hanging on his neat blonde stubble. 'She keeps asking for you, but really, she's much improved. I feel guilty now for dragging you back.'

Dan was a decent sort. Always anxious to confess straight away.

'You did the right thing,' I said. 'It's good to see you Danny. Can we go straight there?'

Our mother was in hospital after a stroke. A woman who had never loved me, cared only for herself, resented my very existence, and was now in her hospital bed demanding my attention. I hated the idea she felt entitled to drag me back from Africa.

Dan led the way to his canary yellow Mini in the airport's car park and, as he drove, he talked about our mother's stroke and the plans he'd put in place to get her home. On the phone there'd been fear in his voice. The medics were concerned there'd be a second, more deadly attack. But it hadn't come, and his anxiety had diminished. The reality was I'd come home to support Danny, not my mother.

I asked him about Graham – how he'd been coping without me.

'He seems to be doing ok,' Dan said, pressing the button to drop the roof and let in the Yorkshire sunshine. 'I've had him out for a beer, but he made it clear I shouldn't have bothered. I think he's ok but it's difficult to know.'

It was true that Graham was happier on his own. But I was grateful to my brother for making the effort.

I asked, half-interested, 'And mummy?'

'She's doing well.' He looked apologetic. 'The doctors say it's a wake-up call, you know, the usual thing they say. She's a terrible patient. They're telling her to change her lifestyle if she wants to live much longer.'

We exchanged dubious looks, knowing that wouldn't happen.

'You're right, she didn't like the sound of that at all,' he said.

We drove through the countryside, passing rolling hills and dry-stone walls, and rugged outcrops littered about. Grassy fields were studded with grey ewes and their white lambs, and skeletons of winsome trees were bearing fresh green shoots. Yorkshire. The land where I was born.

'How's she taking it?' I asked, even though I knew what the answer would be.

'She's giving them hell as you'd expect.'

I knew how embarrassing that would be for Dan.

Open fields gave way to suburbia and we drove past Harrogate Stray's hundred-acre park, the magnificent chestnuts like Christmas trees with their panicle displays of pink-white candles. The cherries, hundreds of them lining the footpaths across the park, had already dumped their frothy pink blossom, which now littered the ground. We turned into the hospital grounds.

'Seriously,' Dan said, 'she's been worrying about you out there on your own. She keeps repeating stories of terrorists and kidnappings. Boko Haram stealing wives and such.' He looked at me apologetic, but with a hint of enquiry of his own.

I confessed to myself I'd never thought of kidnapping, but said to reassure him, 'I'm too long in the tooth for a Boko Haram wife, and Sierra Leone's quite safe. It's nothing like Nigeria. I hope you're not worrying *yourself*?'

'No,' he said lightly. 'But it's good to have you back.'

Unconvinced I said, '*Don't* worry,' but I knew my brother's anxious nature. 'You know I don't get into situations. All the research is in Freetown. Nothing will happen to me, I promise.'

I was astonished how easily the lies slipped out, like well-oiled bearings down a greasy chute. Even my precious Danny, who knew me so well, seemed to accept them, when all the while my mind was crowded with thoughts of Arranoil; of pesticides and trafficked children.

'I *will* have to go back,' I said, 'I've barely scratched the surface in terms of data collection.'

'How's it going?' he asked.

I was desperate to tell someone, to tell *him.* Danny who'd shared my childhood, and the heartbreak and drama of dysfunctional parents. I wanted to tell him about the meetings in Kroo, and in Gorahun. The little boys at the trauma unit. I wanted to tell him about Francis. That I was considering ditching the PhD. No-one would understand better than Dan.

But instead I said, 'It's going well. I've had some great interviews, but there's so much more to do.'

WE MADE our way down the maze of corridors towards our mother's ward. Her *modus operandi* in life had always been to break the rules. To live a reckless life. A disposition not handed down to Danny or me. We were like our father in that respect. Adrenalin didn't drive us like it did our mother who smoked and drank, rode a motorbike and travelled the world for extreme adventures. That year she'd ridden a two-mile zip-wire across the Arenal Volcano Park in Costa Rica, accompanied by one of her many admirers, who'd dared not ride it himself. Thinking about it, I realised with a jolt she'd heartily approve if she knew of my affair with an African preacher.

Dan and I had been great disappointments to her; a barren daughter with a boring job and an equally boring husband, and a timid and caring gay son who managed a theatre company. No prospects of grandchildren, about which she kept reminding us.

'Karen, darling! Come here.' She held out her arms dramatically, always theatrical, always fully made-up for her audience. 'Sweetie, I've missed you *so* much,' she lied. 'Thank *God* you're back.'

She embraced me extravagantly, taking care not to smudge her lipstick, and drew me down to a high-backed chair close to the bed.

She leant out and said quietly, 'Darling, you need to get me out of here. I'm going crazy with no alcohol, no nicotine. What am I to do? Did you stop at duty-free?'

She looked hopeful, but I shook my head, 'Sorry'.

'I don't know how anyone expects to get well in this place,' she went on, irritated. 'The food's dreadful. *Margarine.* I ask you. I need to get home, darling.'

She was talking as though we'd only met the week before, rather than two years previously. That we were friends with a functional relationship, not strangers. That there had been no animosity and bloodletting all those years.

She sounded desperate, so I said as kindly as I could, 'Mummy, you have to stay until your blood pressure comes down. They can't let you go until they're happy with you.'

'My blood pressure's fine!' she shouted, reddening alarmingly. 'Dammit darling, can't you talk to them?'

'They know what they're doing, mummy. Don't be difficult.'

She calmed a little, moving seamlessly into her back-up strategy.

'It's so much better now that you're here. Tell me you're not going back to that dreadful place. I simply can't take it.' Her expression was of concern, but I'd learnt this meant nothing. She said, 'Things aren't what they used to be in the tropics you know. No real protection for ex-pats now. And I worry so. A woman like you, alone.' She gave me that look – half envy, half knowing. 'Anything could happen to you. And we don't want that, do we?'

A woman like you. She was referring to the fact that I'd inherited her looks, her height, her *presence*. She was referring to my outward appearance rather than my personal qualities. Although she'd said I made her proud, I knew I was resented.

I said, 'I'm sure you know I'm going back, mummy.' Her face set cold. 'But not before we get you home. I've come all this way. I'd like to see you settled.'

But I was thinking of Dan, not her. My mother's concerns for me in Africa were all to do with her own needs. After all, she'd travelled the globe to many tough postings with my father. She'd thrived on that particular ex-pat culture that I abhorred so much. She was jealous. And now she was in danger of becoming dependent. Of course, she wanted me home. I was of no use to her in Africa.

———

THE LAWNS at Owl Cottage were perfectly clipped, the Bramleys full of blossom. And Graham still wasn't home. I wandered around unsettled, wondering how long it would be before I could book my return flight to Freetown. The garden, a loved and familiar place, now seemed strangely disconnected from me, like something I'd once dreamt.

The sun was curling west over the bank of rhododendrons that bordered Milk Hill. Five weeks ago when I'd left for Freetown, their magenta blooms were just opening. But now their bedraggled brown heads hung weary, pools of faded blossoms littered at their feet. Looking back at the house from the terraces, I was shocked at how little the prospect of losing this idyll affected me.

Owl Cottage was much less cottage and much more manor in its size and prominence in North Keswick – a pretty village halfway between cosmopolitan Leeds and gentile Harrogate. We'd bought it, neglected and abandoned, five years ago and had restored it to its original specification. It was built of Yorkshire stone, set back from the road behind twin manicured lawns, and conical yews stood sentinel to the front door. A desirable property.

Whilst I'd been away Graham had planted the pots and

urns with geranium and lobelia. He'd repointed the stone flags in the courtyard and planted red grasses in the herbaceous borders for more structure. He'd been busy. Keeping his mind off things. In Asperger's households life is never easy, and unexpected changes posed risks to his state of mind. Even an altered lunch date resulted in panic, the deepest anxiety never far away from the calm façade that he projected to the world.

I sat on the bench looking out over the curve of Milk Hill and pulled out my phone to find my supervisor's number.

'You're back already?'

'My mother's been taken ill.'

I explained the situation, and that I was eager to get back to Freetown and continue the research as soon as I could. I wanted her help so didn't make it clear the PhD was now on hold. My professor at York University was Sierra Leonean herself and the supervision of my research was important to her, the issues close to her heart.

'What's the data looking like?' she asked.

'It's taking shape, but I'm not getting the responses I anticipated.'

'What's wrong with that? That's good research.' She was straight to the point. 'It's just as legitimate to disprove your hypothesis as to prove it. That *is* academic research.' I imagined her in the sunny office that overlooked the lake on York campus. Feet on desk, probably. Long legs clad in sharp trousers. I allowed her to continue on the theme, now a bit irrelevant for what I was actually up to.

She said, 'So people don't feel about misspent aid the way we think they should? Fine. What is it they care about? Is it education or jobs? Or even to do with the lack of graft coming *their* way? That's legitimate research, Karen. Then you juxtapose the realities with the theories and policies and build something new.'

I thought this would be a good point to cut in. 'Whilst I'm

here in the UK, I wondered if you could write a letter of introduction to the FCO with a view to getting me an interview? With a minister, I mean, that would really beef things up in terms of views from the donors' side.'

The professor, Head of African Politics, was known in government circles and regularly called upon to advise on select committees and the like. Not that her advice was ever acted upon. It was all just for show, to say they'd consulted with the experts.

She said, 'It's a possibility. But what's your line of thinking?'

'I just feel there's a gap in my interview schedule. Access to someone in UKGov would help immensely to get a broader perspective on things related to the Ebola funds.'

What I actually wanted was to get in there, to the Foreign and Commonwealth Office, and mention Arranoil. See if anyone flinched. It was just a hunch. Maybe it wasn't UKDev but someone in the Foreign Office who had sticky fingers.

'You've visited UKDev in *Salone*?' she asked.

'Yes. A bit fruitless. Thought I needed another perspective.'

There was a long pause whilst her great brain assessed my request. 'Well, I'll see what I can do but you'll probably get similar responses. Karen, is there something you're not telling me?'

'Not at all. Everything's good.'

TWENTY-SEVEN

NIA

I stood inside the Foreign and Commonwealth Office in the grandiose glass-roofed Durbar Court, its three storeys of arches and columns towering above, the stunning floor patterned with Greek, Belgian and Sicilian marble. Carved into the stone were the former names of the colonial districts in India: Goa, Rangoon, Bombay, Madras, Calcutta. This was the site of the UKGov's old India Office, from which a whole subcontinent was governed.

I'd been waiting there for some time while a PA – a young, bookish type with lank blonde hair and solid heels – went to find the man with whom I had an interview. Nigel Hurt, a minister who had once taken oral evidence from my professor at a foreign affairs select committee on the spread of Boko Haram in West Africa. He was a random minister in the FCO but known to my professor, and he'd agreed to offer me an interview on what he thought was my PhD on democracy in Africa.

Before she had gone for a second search, Nigel Hurt's PA assured me that he was aware of the appointment. The interview was in his diary and had been confirmed only the day before. The adrenalin was high. I was ready with my questions, wondering whether I would get them out before I was escorted from the building. But the minister was already forty-five minutes late and I was beginning to get that feeling you get when you know you've been stood up. Time passed. In the corner of the great court a recruitment drive was under way. A colourful stand and sails promoting the FCO's languages school and diplomatic training; student types milling around talking to the young diplomats.

The PA returned, her pale skin rosy with all the running about. She was deeply apologetic.

'I'm sorry,' she said, breathless. 'The minister has had to leave for a meeting at the Treasury. He won't be back today and sends his apologies.' Her smile was weak, unconvincing. 'We are very sorry to have kept you waiting, and for any inconvenience.'

I looked at her, unmoved, annoyed she was treating me like a fool.

'I'm sorry,' she repeated.

'Would it be possible to make another appointment? Perhaps tomorrow?' But I knew what the answer would be.

'No, I'm afraid that won't be possible.'

I watched her discomfort and waited for the excuse.

'He's leaving the country tomorrow. For Myanmar.' She shuffled her feet a bit, looking awkward.

'Right. Well, thank you for your assistance. I'll find my own way out.'

But there was to be no finding my own way out. Assertively, she escorted me back through the high-ceilinged corridors flanked with red granite columns and cold stone benches, past security and out the entrance onto King Charles Street, back into Whitehall. A City of London tourist bus was trundling past, its occupants on the open top deck plugged in and listening to audio guides.

I stood on the steps fuming.

A woman was hurrying along the pavement to where I

stood, a clutch of papers in one hand and a black messenger bag bouncing on her hip. She looked familiar; thick flaxen hair pulled back in an unruly tail. Tiny frame, Bambi-like, but strong.

'Nia?' I asked.

She was almost past me on her way into the building, but stopped on the steps and looked back.

'Yes?'

I beamed at her.

'Karen Hamm!' She rushed at me and we embraced, awkward on the steps, her sheaf of papers between us.

'My God. How've you been?' her lilting Dublin tones just as I remembered them. She was an old friend from my Masters days.

'Fine, just fine. Researching a PhD.'

'Impressed,' she said, looking me up and down as she would a puppy who'd just remembered to pee outside.

We moved down the steps, back to the pavement where an untidy group of Chinese tourists had paused, phone cameras pointing at the building.

'It's good to see you, Nia,' I said.

'And yourself.' She looked well, teal eyes magnified behind her dark framed spectacles.

'Are you working here?' I asked. New possibilities crowded my mind, though she looked too casual for the FCO, dressed in her customary uniform of black T-shirt and jeans.

'Not exactly working here,' she said.

'Not exactly?'

'Yeah, but closely connected. You know, security stuff.' She was nodding as though to halt my line of questioning.

'What…you mean…?'

'Yeah. That.'

I lowered my voice, 'You're a spook?'

'Kind of thing.'

I didn't ask if it was five or six. It wasn't the time or place to be discussing the UK's secret services.

'Never mind myself,' she said. 'What the hell are *you* doing here!'

I nodded toward the entrance to the building, 'Just been stood up for an interview.'

———

WE AGREED to meet later that day in a vegetarian curry house near Euston Station. I arrived early and waited on a heavy bench at a small table and stared at the overhead TV. The BBC World News was reporting the civil war in Yemen, young boys standing in the rubble of their city.

Nia arrived. It was years since we'd met but in minutes we'd dispensed with pleasantries, ordered a variety of dishes from the menu, and immersed ourselves in the kind of conversations we'd had in our Masters days, when we'd studied politics and security. It turned out Nia was working for MI6, the UK's foreign intelligence service, initially using her Arabic as a language specialist but now involved in things she couldn't talk about.

'Were you recruited straight from uni?' I asked, remembering that she once had plans for the FCO herself – to get in there and change the world.

'Well no, it was a complicated journey to where I am now.' She looked bored at the prospect of telling the story. She was attractive in that fragile way of the Irish, her translucent skin flecked with pretty constellations of freckles.

Nia was the brightest person I knew; an intellectual, and fearless. After her MA she'd gone back to humanitarian work, travelling to refugee camps in Jordon and Pakistan where Syrian and Afghani refugees had built tented cities to replace the shattered ones they'd left behind. In the camps she'd coordinated the disbursement of educational supplies for the hundreds of thousands of children who'd missed years of schooling. After that she'd gone to work in Ukraine with displaced families escaping from Russian-backed rebels terrorising their eastern border. There she plotted the topography of land mines that the Russians had left behind.

Nia could be trusted. I could share with her what I'd found in *Salone*.

A smörgåsbord of Kashmiri delicacies arrived: bowls of dahl and paani-poori stuffed with potatoes, tamarind and spicy sauces, cool yoghurt and vegetable paratha. We tucked in.

'Less about me, tell me about the research,' Nia said. 'Who dumped you at the FCO?'

'Nigel Hurt,' I replied. 'Just a random minister my professor knows. I wanted an interview inside the FCO, to see what the perspective was on democracy in Africa, missing aid, Ebola funds gone walkabout, that sort of thing.'

She nodded, keen for me to go on.

I explained the way the research had stalled, my unplanned meeting in Kroo and rising tensions among the former fighters I'd met there. Then the trip to Gorahun where I'd learnt about Arranoil and the treatment of the villagers. The human rights violations. It was good to talk to Nia. She was a kindred spirit I could trust. She cared about marginalised people, and listened without interruption.

'So here's the thing,' I lowered my voice across the detritus of our meal. 'Our government is the biggest bilateral donor to Sierra Leone. We're committed to sustainable development and the reduction of poverty for global peace and security. It says so in all our policy proclamations.' She looked patient, waiting for me to get to the point. 'We pride ourselves on being the good guys.'

'Everybody thinks they're the good guy,' she said, beckoning the waiter and ordering a coffee. I nodded and ordered one myself.

'After all,' I continued, 'we don't want people crossing the Sahara in their millions and getting a boat to Britain for a better life. These things are a threat to our own security.'

'We know that, tell me something new.'

'We want them to have a better life in their own country, don't we?'

'Do we?' She knew that it was a shallow policy and her reaction endorsed my own cynicism. 'The rhetoric is only rhetoric,' she said. 'It's just words. Stated aims, objectives, policy. They never have any connection to reality, what the real purpose is.' I nodded in agreement. The waiter placed the coffees in front of us. 'Is that why you hoped to interview Nigel Hurt? To get him to admit the policy is mostly bollocks?'

'No.' I moved my coffee to one side and leant in. 'Look, Nia. I think I've stumbled on something by accident. This palm oil company, Arranoil, buying up vast tracts of the Sierra Leone countryside. Everything about it stinks. They've a reputation on human rights abuses. You don't have to search far to find details about their record in other countries. Yet they're endorsed by the Sierra Leone government which at the same time is ratifying human rights legislations and writing new laws to accommodate it.'

'Just window dressing,' she said, unmoved. But I was getting excited now,.

'Ok, so I know what you're thinking – there's nothing new about backhanders for concessions in Africa.'

'Or here, for that matter. It's the way the world works,' she said.

'I know, I know. But what if it isn't the Sierra Leone government that wants bribes, or who is benefiting from the deal?'

'I'm listening,' she stirred a lump of sugar into her coffee.

'I've come across some information suggesting it's our *own people* behind Arranoil.'

She raised an eyebrow. 'Can you trust where your information's coming from?'

'I'm not sure, but this is where I hoped you'd come in.' It was out. She pulled the heavy bench in closer.

'Do you have any names?' she asked, our heads were almost touching.

'Not yet. What I need is someone on the inside to do a bit of digging.'

'Do you mean UKDev or the Foreign Office?'

'Not sure, maybe both.'

'But how's this connected to your PhD?' she asked.

'It isn't.'

'I'm liking this more and more,' she said. Then paused. 'Karen, you're not how I remember you.' I was surprised but took it as a compliment. 'There's energy in you, and urgency. You didn't have that before.'

It was good that she recognised it. That I'd outwardly changed since my return to Freetown. That Africa was making me who I needed to be: someone with purpose.

She said, 'I'll help if I can.'

'Can you do some checks around disclosure? And conflict of interests?' Nia knew everyone. Had contacts everywhere. And her job meant she could find information that I could never access myself.

'It might be possible. I do know people, but they'd be taking quite a risk. Besides, no-one with links to such a bastard company is going to be stupid enough to disclose it. But I'll do my best for you.'

I grabbed her hand, 'Thanks, Nia.'

'Be careful, Karen Hamm.' She squeezed my fingers. 'People fight for what they have with a set of rules unknown to you or me. They're in love with power and money. Nothing else matters to them. They think it sets them above us yet they lurk at the bottom of the pond, morally. The gravy train keeps rolling along and bad things do happen to people who try to de-rail it.'

—

KINGS CROSS WAS CROWDED with rush hour commuters heading north out of the city. An earlier train to Leeds had been cancelled so double the number of passengers now waited round the board, poised to rush when the platform was announced. Three texts came through from Francis wanting to know the date of my return to Freetown, asking about the health of my mother, concerned that I might not return to him. I messaged reassurance straight away. That I'd soon be back.

It had been worth coming home just for that chance meeting with Nia. I'd drawn a blank about Arranoil's directors, where they were domiciled, their backgrounds, or how they might be connected to our government. Nia might get access to something more whilst I continued digging back in *Salone*. I wanted to know about those boys, trafficked around the country, slaving away for profiteers. *Did Songola know about them?*

As I waited underneath the vast lattice steelwork of the station's atrium, daylight flooding through, the six o'clock news was being broadcast on vast overhead screens lined up beside the departure boards. The BBC was covering a ministerial meeting taking place in Downing Street; the usual shots of ministers arriving, cameras following as they walked purposefully along the street and into Number 10, nodding at banks of photographers without even breaking stride.

My attention was drawn to a woman carrying a stack of folders and following none other than my own no-show Foreign Office minister, Nigel Hurt. The woman was distinctive because of the russet-red curls that sashayed down her back when she stepped into the building. She seemed famil-iar, but I couldn't think why. The item was on a loop, so I waited for the next round to take a closer look. Then I noticed the amber pendant round her neck. Unmistakeable. This was the woman I'd seen schmoozing the Minister for Lands and Agriculture at Hill Station in Freetown. The one flirting with him, and unsettled when confronted by UKDev's Ann Wilson.

On my phone, I quickly searched for *ministerial aide to Nigel Hurt*, then selected *images*, and there she was: Bernadette MacLaughlan, special advisor (media) to The Rt Hon Nigel Hurt CBE MP.

TWENTY-EIGHT

GRAHAM

Graham sat at the kitchen table by the open windows reading the *Financial Times*, the newspaper's pink pages fluttering in a breeze that was moving down the slope of Milk Hill, across the sunlit garden into the room. He looked relaxed, reading glasses low on his nose, steaming coffee at his lips. He blew across the surface and took a sip. For all the world like nothing was wrong.

'Coffee in the pot,' he said.

'Thanks.'

Miles Davis' *Kind of Blue* was playing on the vintage turntable, the sound crackling authentically as the stylus rode the grooves. It was his comfort blanket: jazz.

Fourteen days back in Yorkshire and Graham had still not enquired as to the whereabouts of his ring, or the reason I was sleeping in the floral-papered bedroom that was usually reserved for guests. Surely he knew that whilst I'd been away something of great magnitude had occurred, but metaphorically he'd been staring me down. Now it was time to return to Freetown. To tell him I wouldn't be coming back to Owl Cottage. I had to explain about Francis, about Arranoil, and the ditched PhD.

But how to end a relationship of fourteen years and to hurt a man I cared for deeply? How to explain that my heart belonged in Africa, not with him? There were so many things to confess that he had a right to know. But I couldn't tell him about Arranoil. His state of mind wouldn't cope with that kind of stress. He may even try to stop me going back to Freetown.

I moved to the cupboard and pulled out two pottery bowls that we'd bought in Cornwall – berry-red and finely glazed – and set them to warm on the Aga. I unhooked a saucepan from the rack and placed it on the stove – added one cup of oats and two of milk. A pinch of salt.

I stood there waiting for it to simmer, stirring carefully so the milk wouldn't catch whilst Graham sat unperturbed, waiting for me to say the words. He didn't recognise emotion. He couldn't know how belittled his indifference made me feel. All those years of belittlement. Dysfunctionality that was not his fault – only a symptom of his condition – but it let him off the hook relationship wise. It allowed him free conscience whilst his victim agonised and floundered in a maelstrom of undischarged responses. That had been me, all those years.

He took a slurp of coffee, the silver spoon tinkling as the cup returned to saucer.

The phone rang but he ignored it.

Could I slip away without confessing? Leave him to work it out?

But Graham was waiting for an adult conversation – waiting for me to say it. To confess and feel the pain.

The porridge heaved and sighed as the air broke the surface and I spooned large slops into the berry-red bowls. Then a drizzle of honey, a dollop of yoghurt, a sprinkling of almonds. He sat comfortably, his square-jawed expression fathomless as always, his long fingers playing with the edges of the paper, like he was about to turn a page, but didn't.

He wasn't reading. He was waiting.

I stood over him with his breakfast, noticing his sandy curls thinning at the crown, and placed the bowl in front of him, sitting down opposite with my own.

'Thanks,' he said.

'I've a confession to make.'

He put down his newspaper and looked up, his pale blue eyes mildly interested. A trace of apprehension.

'I'm afraid the ring was stolen,' I said.

His face remained calm, unreadable.

'It was taken from my bathroom at the hotel. I'm sorry. It was my own stupid fault.'

He tasted the porridge then asked predictably, 'Have you spoken to the insurers?'

'No point. The single article limit's only one k. I'm really sorry, Gray.'

'It'll be covered under the household,' he said. 'I'll ring them.' He didn't seem overly concerned. But we both knew the ring was just a sop.

He asked, 'Was it the hotel staff?'

'That's the worst of it,' I said, grateful the real confession had been delayed. 'There was such a fuss and people lost their jobs.'

'Of course, to be expected.' His tone was the familiar know-it-all. What did *he* know? It was *me* who'd been there.

'I feel *responsible*,' I said. 'I left it in full view. Too much temptation for people who have nothing themselves.'

He blew on his porridge and asked infuriatingly, 'Are you worried about your Hippocratic Oath?' He was referring obtusely to my doctorate.

'Well *no*. I'm worried about the families whose lives I've ruined.'

'Then you *are* worried about the Hippocratic Oath,' he said. 'You can't take responsibility for the actions of others. People are quite capable of harming themselves without your help.'

I put down my spoon.

'We need to talk,' I said.

He put down his own spoon, and pushed away the bowl, saying unexpectedly, 'You've decided to leave.'

His pale blue eyes looked straight at me, no hint of hurt or surprise. Just a logical conclusion.

I stuttered, 'Gray…I,'

But he interrupted, 'You must be *happy*, Karen. We agreed. Is it what you want?'

I tried to collect my thoughts and form sentences, but the words wouldn't come. Telling the story might break the spell, and undervalue the priceless. But I owed him an explanation, so I gave him some facts he'd understand.

'I've met someone. He's what I want.'

'Right.' For a moment he wobbled. Maybe there was some regret behind the faithful eyes. Tears pricked my own. He never showed vulnerability, but I knew it was there.

'I don't want to hurt you,' I said, pathetic.

'That's not the point,' he said. His hands lay on the table, resting lightly either side of the bowl. The porridge still steaming. I studied the fair hairs on back of his hands, shining in the sunlight creeping over Milk Hill.

'Don't worry about that,' he said. 'You need to be *happy*. You *need* that. In fact, I think you *deserve* it. I know I'm not easy.'

The tears flowed freely now, and I blubbered incoherent.

'I know I've been lucky to have you all these years,' he said. 'You've been good for me.'

I wanted to hug him, tell him I was kidding, say it would be alright. I was deeply ashamed of the hurt I was causing.

'We *have* talked this through,' he reminded me. 'I know how unhappy you've been.'

I drew in a breath like it was my last gasp.

'Don't get upset.' He always said that. As though saying

the words would make it happen. 'We'll have to deal with practicalities.'

Then he started talking about selling the house.

'No!' I said. 'You *must* keep the house.' But I'd given no thought at all to practicalities.

Graham was emphatic. 'I don't want the house. It's meaningless without you in it.'

The emotion surged in my throat and I let out a violent sound, like the guttural weep of the bereaved.

He said, 'You'll need somewhere to live, unless you want to rely on this man's generosity, and I don't think you'll want that. You have no regular income until you've finished your doctorate, and I want to protect your interests, unless you fully trust him to do so himself?'

I hadn't thought it through. Graham was a kind and generous man. When I'd given up work for postgrad study, he'd supported me unquestioning. He'd encouraged me, had faith in me. Without understanding my reasons or my restlessness, he'd run with it and accepted my notions of mission in Africa. And my need for a purpose, when really he'd been mystified by such illogical propositions. He'd been the best of friends. Despite everything, he was beyond reproach. I would never have a reason to hate him.

THE FOLLOWING morning Dan drove me back to Leeds/Bradford airport. I looked out from behind red, puffy eyes at the hedgerows slipping by, dripping with the creamy blossom of Hawthorn and Elder. Cow Parsley frothed high at the roadside, its delicate flowers and fern like foliage swaying in the current of air as we passed. A magical time of year in England. It was early, and mist still lay in the hollows of the soft Wharfedale landscape. From somewhere came the plaintive and lonely warble of a curlew, persistent in its desperate cry as it circled overhead.

Dan was quiet, deep in his own thoughts. Confused, and fearful.

Turmoil had a hold on my gut. Freetown and Francis would calm me. All I needed was to re-focus on the good I'd do in Africa, not the pain I'd caused for Graham; to focus on Arranoil, and the children of *Salone*.

For the first time in my life I felt grateful to my mother. For bringing me home and forcing my hand.

TWENTY-NINE

RETURN

The return to Freetown through Lungi airport was challenging like before, but this time the estuary was calm and the water taxis were running. The small cruiser bumped its way across the open water toward its docking point near Aberdeen Bridge, passengers squashed together and rigid with fear at their proximity to the river's swell. Maybe Francis would be at Aberdeen to meet me. I needed to share with him my meeting with Nia and the prospect of getting some information on the powers behind Arranoil. The fact that Nigel Hurt's aide had been here in Freetown, probably bribing the Agriculture Minister. And my own plans to investigate child trafficking. There was much to catch up on, but he'd been out of contact for days. He would be busy with the conference for educationalists he was leading at the Mammy Yoko Hotel, a venue where many important events were hosted in Freetown. I knew his schedule was hectic and it was unlikely he'd get to Aberdeen to meet me. But still.

My neediness scared me.

Across the estuary the sound the cruiser's engine drowned out all others, assaulting the senses like the pneumatic drills on the Lungi airstrip. There was no point trying to converse with the other passengers crammed in rows under the boat's awning, their orange life jackets grubby with wear. We approached Aberdeen and I scanned the waiting vehicles for Francis' green Mazda.

The cruiser docked beside a long metal walkway that jutted out from the shore. Passengers could alight on this side of the estuary without having to be 'shouldered' across the shallows by the undignified human porterage system that operated at Lungi. I stepped onto the clanking steel and exchanged the life jacket for my rucksack with a crewman. He was wearing a vest with the logo *Albatross Crossings*. I hurried up the walkway towards the shore, passed my ticket to the collector, and searched again for signs of Francis.

He wasn't there so I took a local, yellow stripe taxi, paying extra for single occupancy, and gave the address of the Hibiscus Guest House. Traffic was light and the journey short, but I felt conspicuous in the back of the battered vehicle, and as we slowed for a rare set of lights, people swarmed the car like seagulls round a Grimsby trawler.

Everything seemed just the same at the Hibiscus as I passed through the iron gates, through the dense gardens and into the main reception. There was no-one around, so I retrieved my key from the pigeonhole behind the front desk and exited the rear doors, crossing the lawn to my lodge. I saw the maid sweeping out bungalow four. She looked up and I waved a greeting to her but she averted her gaze, continuing her sweeping. I smiled to myself – how conscientious she was. I passed the orange tree, now doubled over with the weight of its fruit.

Stepping up to the veranda I noticed a pair of man-sized flip-flops beside the wicker sofa and made a mental note to pass these to the maid who must have mixed up the rooms. Turning the key, I paused for a moment. Things didn't feel quite right. For no reason I could explain, a wave of vulnerability passed over me. When I opened the door, I could see the bungalow was now occupied by someone else. There was no sign of my belongings, my workbooks, electronics, toiletries or cosmetics. None of my clothes were in the wardrobe. They'd been replaced with jackets and shirts and two pairs of carefully pressed trousers that hung straight from clipped hangers. Men's shoes were in the rack, a stranger's wash bag by the shower.

Embarrassed and confused, I retreated quickly, disappointed that Auntie had let out my room even though I'd paid upfront for her to keep it for me. *Where were my things?* I assumed they had been moved to a different room. Maybe I'd been away too long. For sure, I hadn't expected to be gone for three weeks and would have been returned sooner had my mother cooperated with the medics and been discharged on time.

I went back to the main building to look for Auntie. It would have been nice to have received a note of some kind rather than to have found out in this way. It was only the day before that I'd emailed to let her know my time of arrival. The lodge was unnaturally quiet. I checked the kitchen where everything was spick and span, and deserted, as were the small lounge and bar areas. I replaced the key in its pigeon-hole and checked the others to see if there were any notes addressed to me. There were none. My annoyance, and another unexpected emotion – panic – started to rise. I went out front and searched the grounds. No-one. Then I went back to the porch of bungalow number four and called through the door to the maid who was cleaning the bathroom.

'Hello, can you help me?'

She came out, cloth in hand, and looked at me warily.

'Do you know where my things are? Which room have you put me in?'

The girl looked blank with no sign of understanding. She

stood anxious in her starched pinny waiting for more information. So I gesticulated toward my lodge and grabbed at my clothes and travel bag in an effort to make her understand. The girl bowed her head. My tone and expression were alarming her.

Instead I said, 'Where is Auntie? Mrs. Mansarray?'

The girl shook her head and said, 'No here, ma.'

I returned to the lodge and sat down in an upholstered chair in the bar area. Scrolling through my phone contacts I tapped Auntie's number and waited for the connection. The woman had some explaining to do, but instead my call went to message. I hung up and tapped in a text message as politely as I could.

Greetings Auntie. I've now returned to Freetown but can't find my things. Have you a different room for me?

Opening the small refrigerator by the bar, I helped myself to a chilled Coke and wandered out to the veranda to wait for her reply. The cold gassy liquid hit the back of my throat as I drank straight from the can. After fifteen minutes came Auntie's reply.

Your things are at Kangari.

I read the message several times trying to compute what other possible meaning there could be. She must have double booked the Hibiscus, but the place was deserted. No way was she fully booked. We seemed to have had an amicable relationship, I'd paid her upfront and tipped generously. I called Francis' number. He would surely know what was going on being so closely related to the woman. For a moment, the possibility of moving into his house crossed my mind, we had discussed it, and the prospect of returning to the Kangari held no appeal at all. But there was no answer from Francis' phone either, so I left a voice message. Then I tried to call Auntie again without success, so I sent a second text,

Ok. Can you tell me why? Thanks.

And a text to Francis.

My love, did you know my things have been moved back to the Kangari?

After another twenty minutes and two bottles of Star beer, I received no response from either. My feelings of unease deepened. I could hear the restless Atlantic crashing against the rocks not far away. Hitching my rucksack across both shoulders I left the Hibiscus and went out in the street to find a taxi.

THE KANGARI HOTEL was expecting my arrival. The young man in the office was in his usual place, tipped back in his chair, watching. The atmosphere was chill. I felt conspicuous in all the wrong kind of ways. The stooping porter Joseph led me to my room, now in a different block, but an exact replica of my original except for the view behind the razor wire which was now of rubbish-strewn bush.

Everything I'd left locked and secure at the Hibiscus Guest House was now in this room, laid out neatly on the bed. Whoever had affected the transfer had done a good job. But it was unsettling thinking of my personal belongings handled by strangers. Everything I'd thought I'd stashed securely had been through the hands of people unknown. I wondered about the security at the Kangari and an unease crawled over me. I was restless, wanting answers.

I DIALLED SONGOLA'S NUMBER. Whatever my new circumstances, I needed to speak to her and get on with my investigations and the possibility there could be trafficked children on the Arranoil plantation. If there were, it would be an explosive revelation especially if there was a UKGov connection to the Arranoil concession. There was no answer from Songola, just the automated voice of the local operator asking me to leave a message.

Songola…it's Karen Hamm. Please can you call me back when you get this? There's something new I want to discuss. hope to speak to you soon.

I hung my clothes in the wardrobe, found my wash bag and took a shower. Later I began organising my work. Books in an orderly pile, laptop and notebooks next to them, dictaphone, earphones, pens and diary. All there.

Next I opened my laptop, searched Google maps, and found that the Mammy Yoko Centre was only fifteen minutes' walk from the Kangari. I selected my clothes with care: long linen skirt and lilac sarong, shirt printed with tiny violas, flat sandals and a Panama hat. I swept my hair to the side and laid it over my shoulder. Grabbing a bag, I placed in it my phone, keys, and foreign currency purse, lipstick and some tissues. Then I secured the room and walked quickly down the external stairs, across the covered walkway through the dining corridor to reception, where I felt the burning gaze of hotel staff. *The English who'd brought the trouble with her die mon ring.* I felt disgraced, but walked aloof.

Joseph was at the door. 'Taxi, ma?'

'No thanks, Joseph. I'll walk today.'

The baking heat closed round me and I checked my pace, not wanting to spoil the appearance that I'd carefully engineered. The Mammy Yoko Centre was a short way down Peninsular Road, back towards Aberdeen Bridge. I'd calculated the conference would soon be ending so there'd be an opportunity to catch Francis as the delegates dispersed. His physical presence would reassure me. For sure, he'd have an explanation for my move from the Hibiscus, and all would be well. After all, his recommendation had sent me there in the first place. But intuitively I slowed my pace, hesitating. Inde-cision harrying my mind.

When I arrived at the Mammy Yoko Centre the day's events had just ended. People had congregated in small groups around the main hall, swapping business cards, making contact, chatting. I scanned the faces and there he was among them, surrounded by delegates, deep in conversation, his hands moving in the air to re-enforce his points in a way that had become familiar to me. My heart pounded at the sight of him, chest swollen with anticipation. The heat was immense, and perspiration slipped down my spine.

He was facing me but hadn't seen me, so I hovered a discreet distance away, hoping to catch his eye. I recognised a couple of the delegates in his group – the Canadians he'd met whilst I was staying at the Kangari for the first time. Then a different member of his group started talking and Francis relaxed, looking round. He saw me then, but his expression didn't change. No sign of recognition or warmth. His atten-tion immediately returned to the speaker in his group. Awkward, I made as if I was checking the noticeboard. This had been a bad idea. I'd embarrassed him. So, I took out my phone and pretended to scroll for a bit, all the while glancing across, searching his face for affirmation that never came.

After a while, I wandered outside with the dispersing delegates and soon Francis too was making his way to the exit, still in the company of the Canadians. He couldn't miss me now.

'Good afternoon, pastor,' I said brightly, wondering for the first time how he might explain me to his colleagues who were smiling warmly back.

He was deadpan, and for a moment didn't look at me. A dark, awkward silence before he said in a clipped voice, 'Miss Hamm. How are you?' Like I was a stranger.

His eyes looked past me to somewhere in the distance.

There was something else in his expression. Indifference. My gut churned. I could think of no response, not trusting myself to speak. He said some other words, but they had no meaning. He scared me. It was like I was a stranger that had just appeared at the edge of his consciousness. An irritant. The coldness of his gaze made me sick with fear and pain.

A stately woman in traditional dress walked by, and Francis fell on her with relief,

'Ah, Agnes! Miss Hamm let me introduce you to Agnes Kamara. She is working with the Ministry of Education and will be able to assist. Please excuse me.' With that he turned and ushered the Canadians in the opposite direction. I ignored Agnes Kamara, who was looking as perplexed as I, and I stood like a stone in the withering heat watching him slip away.

THAT NIGHT I didn't sleep. There was no mistaking what I'd seen in him: remoteness, hostility. Dread crept over me like a slow-moving reptile as the possibilities formed a vortex in my head.

How had he found out?

For hours I lay wrapped in a slick layer of sweat, my phone on the pillow, its blank screen tormenting me. I got up, wandered the room, took another bottle from the mini bar, flopped back on the damp sheets.

The next day came and still nothing from Francis. I stayed in my room and snapped at the maid when she tried to enter, watching her expressions of astonishment and fear. Shame covered me.

Early evening I went down to the bar to relieve the exhaustion of my loneliness. The local girls sat languid in mini-skirts and sparkly tops, their admirers hanging close. I found a high stool at the counter where I could think and brood, the noise around me comforting.

I crafted another text to Francis.

My love, I'm so sorry I embarrassed you yesterday. I shouldn't have gone to the Mammy Yoko when I knew you'd be busy. But I need to see you. Do let me know how you are when you can.

In my heart there was only fear and dread.

Ten fifteen and there was no response. I called, he didn't pick up.

The preacher knew how to torment. He must know how wretched I would feel.

Drunk, I made my way back to my room, weaving along the covered walkways, staggering up the stairs and onto my corridor where security approached with a large cleavaged girl asking if I needed 'massages'. I told them both to fuck off, entered my room, and fell on the bed in sound sleep. Later I awoke in panic, cold from the air conditioning, and remembered with shame what I'd said to the hotel staff. And how offensive was bad language in this culture. I shut off the air conditioning and fell back to sleep.

It was morning and I awoke, heart pumping, hot and thirsty, grasping for my water bottle. I'd dreamt of Francis in the arms of a prostitute at the bar. I took a draught, anguished at how the dream had made me feel. Above the bed, a chameleon clung to the wall, it's rotating eyeballs moving independently, long tail flat, its thumbs splayed out from its feet. Watching me.

Room service arrived with fruit and coffee. I tipped the boy generously, remembering my outburst, ashamed of my behaviour. I shuffled aimlessly through paperwork, pouring coffee, sipping the tepid brew, feelings of outsider-ness and loneliness growing deeper as I wondered how much of a stranger he might really be to me.

There had been no reply from Songola either.

Then he rang.

I hesitated, wondering if I could cope with what he had to say.

I answered. 'Francis.'

'Hello.'

There was a long pause when I could think of nothing to say or ask. Fear held me rigid.

Eventually I said, 'It's good to hear from you. I'm sorry. I realise I shouldn't have gone to the Mammy Yoko when you were working.'

In my heart, there was still hope.

There was silence at the other end.

'Francis, please tell me what's wrong. Why have I returned to the Kangari?'

After a short pause, he said, 'You lied to me, Karen. There's not much more to say.'

His voice was full of tension and control. The words resonated, I'd expected them, half knowing. I was mute, scared to utter a sound lest it make the agony worse.

He said, 'It seems you're engaged to be married.' An awful pause when I could deny nothing. He went on, 'With this fact in mind I can only assume I've been a pleasant addition to your so-called immersion in our culture. Useful for your research in our country.'

My throat constricted, and a wash of shame flowed over me.

'I didn't have to ring you today,' he said, 'but thinking I know or rather knew a little about your character, I felt it was in the best interests of your research for you to know I will not be in contact again. Therefore you can get on with your work. God has plans for you, but they don't include me.'

The inevitable was happening.

He went on, 'Now you need to prove you're not here living your unfulfilled dreams at the expense of others. We already have too many like that.'

The viciousness of his words stunned me.

'Francis,' I stumbled. 'Please. I never lied to you. Never.'

'As you well know there is such a thing as the lie of omission. Let's not play any more games. I've standing in this community. I put my trust in you, but I realise now it was misplaced. Please don't try to contact me again.'

The line went dead. And it felt, so did I.

THIRTY

DOROTHY

Later, I make my way home, the anger burning. I think about our pastor, and that *white*.

The hurt is like a monkey trapped inside. The monkey shakes its cage when I confess to myself, and remember that the pastor's mood has changed. Yes. It is true. He has been peaceful. Happy, like a load he has been carrying has been shared. Others have noticed this too.

Whoa…di pastor look happy today!

What has come happen?

Maybe he has new girlfriend!

This awareness cuts me deep. A violent surge of hatred comes upon me. I stop and lean against the post of someone's hut. I breathe in a way that is confusing my mind.

That *white*. She thinks she's entitled. Has she lived here! Sweated here! Laboured here like the rest of us? No. But her whiteness entitles her to what is mine?

How easy for her. Coming here from her rich and fancy country, and her rich and fancy life, and taking what does not belong.

Jealousy and hatred rise in me like a storm. Dangerous ideas fill me. Our precious pastor.

The loathing comes in a giant wave and I do not care to suppress it. No. I need to fuel it. The rage burns as I think of it. Whites coming here to save the African. No! To save themselves! Do they know how much damage they can do?

I hurry down the track into the settlement, my eyes stinging. I do not know what to do. I come to the open space where the men play soccer on the hard, rough ground. They are barefoot, shirtless, their bodies glisten with sweat. The afternoon sun is slanting low between the shacks. The men are shouting, focussed on the game. I stop, confused. My mind so busy I have forgotten to bring food from Auntie's.

I move to a vendor and buy sheesh kebab and rice, make my way through our tightly-packed residences, straddle the gutters with my quick and nimble steps. When I get to our hut my mother sits on the stoop, relaxed. She is in *Kongossa* with her neighbour; a short, thin woman of eighty years. Grey hair. Stained brown teeth. The woman smiles at me and in return I touch her arm. They observe the parcel with interest. I open it and share the food between them.

IT IS dark behind the curtain, lamp extinguished. He has gone. Anger and shame cover me. I lie on the mattress, his sweat upon me. Semen seeps from my body. His stench is poison in my nostrils. His stale breath is pungent in the air.

The sound of his zipper like a bullet through my brain.

I feel like nothing.

Then I remember. I am something.

I rise and draw the bucket. Scrub my skin with bristled cloth until it stings and shouts. Now I know that I am clean. The vile remnants of him gone. I sluice the cloth in a separate bucket reserved for his waste. I brush my teeth and swill my mouth, and spit into that bucket. The tears are flowing. Silent. Shameful.

My mother returns. I hear her slippers slap against her heels. I gulp noisily for air.

'*Wat is it, titi*?' she whispers.

But I make no reply. Lie on my clean hard mat, pull the cotton sheet across my body, wait for sleep to come, and the old horrors that sleep brings. My body stings from its violent cleansing. It reassures me.

My mind fights the battles between thoughts that come and go, disputes unresolved, plans still to bear fruit. In the confusion of my mind, something new enters. An idea about a boy at the Kangari, and a stolen ring. A diamond ring. *Her* ring.

And I realise what this could mean.

I rise quickly, dress myself, and look for the card she gave me. It is tucked in my stack of books, beneath the well-worn copy of Kant's *Perpetual Peace*. I slip it in my pocket. It is late but I know his shack is open, there will be time. My mother sits rocking, mouth agape. I exit the hut into the night without a word. And I move quickly through the dark, as slick as the dogs who know this place blindfolded, passing dim lamps and cooking fires with dying embers. The sound of the generator greats me, shaking violently outside the internet café. The shack is lit and busy with customers. When I enter, the man looks up. His face glows with surprise. Quickly he finds a place for me, special service for the one who fires his loins. The computer screen is ready. The slip of card is in my hand. I take the mouse and start my search: *Karen Hamm (Researcher), University of York, UK.*

An hour later I rise and leave. I have found what I am looking for.

THE HIGH WALL is white and freshly painted. I stand for a moment and stare. A pink hibiscus flower and the greeting: *Guest House – Welcome*, painted blue.

This is the place of Auntie Mansarray who sings in our choir, the choir at the Wellington Street Baptist Church. She is proud auntie of our dear Pastor Francis, defender of his work and reputation. She is known to me. She takes an interest in my education, impressed with the clever girl from Kroo, *bush pikin*, the one the pastor trusts to take the senior class.

I push open the iron gate and step into the shady garden, make my way along the winding path. I enter the Hibiscus Guest House with the printout in my hand.

THIRTY-ONE
THE DUTCHMAN'S LIST

The night was long at the Kangari. Unbearable. Trying to think of ways the reality wasn't so. Emotions lurching from longing to anger to despair, and wretched loneliness. His words echoing in my head – the disconnected tone that made me feel like a stranger. Like I was no-one to him.

Denial gripped me. Panic too. The brooding familiarity of insignificance dragging me down. Now I belonged nowhere. He might as well have driven a machete through my heart.

Powerlessness was unfamiliar. My heart felt sucked out. I wept with my whole body.

THROUGH THE NIGHT I packed and unpacked my things. Then packed again, frustrated with indecision, humiliation stinging like a bloom of jellyfish. His vicious words: *Prove you're not here living your unfulfilled dreams at the expense of others.* I thought of those trafficked boys and indignation rose with every ebb of despair. Four thirty in the morning, and my restless eyes kept wandering to my bags, packed and ready at the door. By six-thirty I'd unpacked, everything returned to the shelves, work paraphernalia laid neatly on the desk. What could I return to? Who was I now?

Songola had not returned my call. Had she deserted me too?

THE NEXT EVENING I went to Frank's and sat alone at a table by the water. It was a bar right on the sands at Man O' War Bay, beloved of ex-pats and somewhere I'd vowed I'd never go. But loneliness drove me there that night, away from the Kangari and its seedy bar.

Frank's Bar was open-fronted to the sea, and crowded with drinkers and diners. African grooves throbbed out across the bay and the pungent odour of charcoaled fish saturated the air. Across the water a pleasant breeze rustled palm fronds overhead. The comforting clink of bottles, the rattle of cutlery, the hum of convivial conversation.

'Every ting is good for madam?' the waiter arrived and looked concerned at the half-eaten barracuda on my plate. I assured him all was well. He nodded and leant across, emptying the last of the Chardonnay into my glass. Near to me, a cheerful group of aid workers sat chatting, cracking jokes, swapping stories, deepening friendships. Their camaraderie intensified my isolation.

I thought of Francis, and a hand inside my chest hauled something out. Offered it up. A willing heart flailing, still pumping, trembling in the careless hand that held it.

'Madam would like desert?'

I looked up, shunted from my torpor.

'Yes, no. Thank you.' I took the menu with no intention of reading it, and stared out at the brightly painted dhows drawn up along the shore, fishing nets stacked neatly against their hulls, ready for the next day's haul. Darkness was falling on the bay.

Earlier, I'd walked to Lumley Beach. All along the penin-sular road the scent of Africa had hit me. Irresistible. Dark spices, smouldering charcoal, sweet scented flowers and the earth's deep heat. And acrid smoke, sweat, and urine. Unmis-takable odours of poverty.

Africa. Still with me. Gripping like a vice on the organs of my soul.

Lumley Beach was beautiful, the sun just dipping, the shadows of the palms stretching out. The breadth of ochre sand mellowing in the sinking rays, scoured by the relentless tides that ebbed and flowed across its plane. Bright painted canoes lay upturned. I stood and watched as the fishermen hauled their catch, dragging their net and the silvery fish to shore while the women chanted, clapping rhythmically as the herring landed, jerked and slapped around, gleaming in the sunlight, waiting to die. All was peaceful, a sense of time stretching out, unhurried.

The waiter approached again, smiling and expectant.

'Just coffee please.' He retreated underwhelmed.

Songola was in my thoughts, and Gorahun. I had to salvage something from the terrible mess I'd created.

I sent another message via text:

Songola. This is Karen Hamm. Please call me when you're free. I'd like to meet up if you've time. It's important.

Frank's was buzzing now, the noise and bustle a distrac-tion. I'd drunk too much. Prostitutes sat garish on high stools at the bar, shapely legs arranged provocatively. Coquettish, knowing and practised. Feigning interest in the banter of a group of Germans drinking beer. But they weren't interested.

The Dutchman from the Kangari was still around, and in Frank's Bar that night. He was dressed in a Hawaiian shirt unbuttoned low revealing curled grey hairs as he leant across the bar. He ordered the staff to hurry up with his drink, his tanned face mean and sweaty. Everything about him shrieked subversion. The way he held his body, made his phone calls, huddled in groups. The microscopic concentration on himself and his personal dealings. Not once had he acknowledged me, although our paths had crossed many times at the hotel. Maybe he ran guns or drugs. After all West Africa was geographically key for the flow of cocaine from South America into Europe. Tonnes of the stuff passed through all the time. Kroo Bay and Crab Town had access to the sea, perfect for moving contraband in and out of the country via Lungi or sea routes.

I sat watching him, tired and inebriated, my imagination galloping along unconstrained, void of logic. I decided to take my chance.

I wandered over, glass in hand, and arranged myself on a bar stool next to him. Men were rarely indifferent to me.

'Hi,' I said.

No verbals, just a nod.

I leaned in to get his attention, smiling in a friendly way. 'I think you're staying at the Kangari too?'

He looked at me properly now. 'I am waiting for friends,' he said, in heavily accented English.

He's trying to be coy, I thought idiotically.

'It's a great bar,' I said happily. 'Good meeting place.' I took a flirtatious sip of wine. 'I'm Karen.' I offered my hand but he wouldn't take it; he just looked toward the door expectantly. It was clear he wasn't interested and, if I hadn't been drunk, I would have left it there.

'I'm here on a research project for my university,' I babbled on. 'Ages since I've been back to Freetown. Love the place. Here on business yourself?'

He looked at me, obviously irritated, and was about to say something when he spotted a man entering the bar.

'Ah, please excuse. My friend is here.'

He moved down the bar to greet a thick-set man in military fatigues, shaved head, muscled arms, pants straining round enormous buttocks. They were too far away for me to hear their conversation, and I could hardly move crablike to a closer spot, so I called the waiter, ordered a large Remy, and returned to my table.

At the Kangari my new room was right next door to the Dutchman's. I knew this because security was always there running errands for him, and through the wall I could hear his guttural tones when the local girls arrived to give him sex. One girl seemed special. During the night, I'd hear his heavily accented English, apparently on the phone.

'Where are you? I am waiting. Come now.' Cajoling and desperate sounding. There would be long pauses when I imagined him pacing the room whilst the girl made her excuses. 'I am waiting, come,' he repeated over and over. But it seemed to me the girl never came.

I sat at my table cradling my Remy watching him at the bar. A third man arrived to join the group, late and apologetic. Dressed in a black suit, he was much shorter than the others and had distinct thick black hair parted severely to one side. He was unusually handsome, perhaps Italian.

My head was heavy. I decided I must go before I did something I'd regret, and called the waiter for a taxi to the Kangari.

SULLEN STAFF MANNED RECEPTION. Their attitude to me had changed since my return.

I pointed to my key hanging on the hook, room B28, but the girl misunderstood and gave me B29. I hesitated for a moment, then thanked her and made my way across the walkways, up the steps. I looked at the Dutchman's door next to mine, then down at his key. The adrenalin rushed in. The corridor was deserted, no security, and I'd just left him with his comrades at Frank's. I slid the key into the lock.

A moment of hesitation and I was in, my heart battering in

my chest as I stood inside the room, all senses alert. It was cold, the AC pumping out on max, the curtains drawn, the bed unmade. The light in the bathroom was still on and threw a helpful glow into the room.

Quickly I searched it, wondering what I was looking for. Light weapons perhaps, or bags of white powder. But there was nothing of interest in the cupboards or the two large holdalls on the bed. I moved to the desk and turned on the flashlight of my phone to check the paperwork.

There were several folders and other documents laid out beside a row of cell phones with notes taped to them. On the notes was written a single name and number, different for each device. Local contacts, I guessed. There was also a ring-bound notebook with a list of names and local numbers, and tucked underneath was a double sheet with a table of information set out in columns. The information made no sense but it looked interesting. So I took photos, all the while feeling nauseous at the risk, trying to remind myself that, not long ago, the Dutchman had sat down to dine in Frank's. There was no way he could just walk in.

Still the adrenalin sped through my veins at the audacity of it. Here in the Dutchman's room.

Concentrating, I made sure I put everything back on the desk exactly where I'd found it, hoping I'd remembered the original layout.

Seconds later I had left the room and was on my way down to the lobby to return his key and retrieve my own. Safely back in my room I examined the photos on my phone but the columns of names – maybe local towns or villages – and corresponding numbers made no sense. I saved them to a work file in the *cloud*. The information could be important. Maybe when my head was clear it would all make sense.

THE NEXT DAY I awoke after dreaming about Francis. About the morning he'd cooked fried plantains and the way it had burnt our tongues in our rush to taste it. About the flycatchers nesting in the mango tree.

But it wasn't the dream that had woken me. It was my phone vibrating near my head. I sat up and tried to focus through the hangover. Maybe it was Songola returning my call. But instead I saw Nia's name and rose immediately from my inertia.

'Karen, it's Nia.'

'Hi!' It seemed like a lifetime since we'd sat together in London eating curry and talking espionage. I was so glad I hadn't told her about Francis. 'It's good to hear from you,' I said, almost sobbing at the sound of her voice. She was so open and wholesome. What would she think if she knew?

Straight to the point, she said, 'I think I have something. And the name that's come up is Nigel Hurt.'

She had my full attention.

'What! He's connected to Arranoil?'

'Well, not exactly. Arranoil's only a small part of a bigger holding company called Arran.Inc. And that's listed and operating out of Panama, as we know. So, alarm bells are ringing straight away. Neither company is recorded as of interest to any members. Arranoil as a company is difficult to get information on. There's little detail on its board of directors or any of its other interests.'

'Yes, I know. Is that usual?'

'It's not unusual.'

'So, what've you got?'

'I've found info on the *shareholders* in Arran.Inc., and the majority shareholder is a company called Sotone Capital Holdings, registered in the US, a private equity firm.'

'Who owns Sotone?'

'Well now, it wasn't easy establishing that. Not until I

precision searched the system and found the CEO online receiving some award for entrepreneurship in the US.'

'Who is he?'

'She's called Gabriella Cruz.'

My heart sank, but Nia went on, 'Wife of our minister, Nigel Hurt.'

'Shit!' I leapt off the bed.

'Did I do well?'

'His aide is here. I mean she's been here, cosying up to the Minister for Agriculture and Lands.'

'Really? Feck me.'

'Exactly.'

'How do you know this?' Nia asked.

'I saw her myself. Well, I didn't know it was her at the time, but later I saw her on TV when I was in London. She was heading into Downing Street with the minister himself. This isn't a coincidence.' My words tripped over themselves in my excitement to get them out.

'So he sends his aide to do the dirty work. Makes sense.'

'She's very attractive,' I said.

'No shit.'

I was standing at the window now, looking out into the bush at a large black bird flapping frantically on a branch, like me.

'It's possible that he has no idea what sort of rogue operator he's supporting via his wife,' I said.

'If he does, he'll claim ignorance anyway. But I can't imagine he could successfully claim his wife knows nothing of Arranoil's reputation.'

'Let's get this straight,' I said. 'A UK government minister is bribing a recipient government of UKAid to give contracts to a firm of which his wife is the main shareholder. The firm is well known for its human rights abuses.' I was thinking back to my conversation with David Westbrook, the UKDev contractor who'd alluded to this in a conversation at the Cape

Sierra Hotel. I wondered how the bribe was paid. Could it be aid money?

I asked her, 'Nia, what we've got here is UK government corruption, isn't it?'

I'd become aware of the sensitive nature of our conversation and instinctively lowered my voice.

'Well, not exactly,' she said. 'What we seem to have here is a corrupt UK government official. Maybe. But they say people are only as corrupt as the system will allow.'

'But it's abuse of office at the highest levels. Don't forget we're talking about human rights as well. It's not just about securing a contract that's in his wife's financial interests, it's condoning the abuse of human rights. And illegal land grabs. And everything else. What sort of system allows this?'

But the way I was joining the dots made my friend nervous.

'There's nothing new about that,' she said sensibly. 'Be careful. Of course, these people always deny it and sometimes it's just impossible to get the evidence of the actual links to the abuse. And you'll need that to make any claim or accusation against them.'

'Yes,' I replied. 'But you don't believe that really. It wouldn't stop you trying, would it?'

My mind was racing on. What did I now have to lose?

I said, 'I need to make some phone calls. I can't tell you how good it is to talk to you, Nia, and hear your voice. Thank you. Thank you.' The emotion swelled. I hoped she couldn't hear it in my voice.

'I'll keep digging,' she replied. 'You've witnessed what you think is a bribe taking place, so that's new. Take care, my friend.'

SONGOLA STILL WASN'T ANSWERING her phone but now it was essential that I talk to her. I quickly showered, dressed and made my way down for breakfast, feeling more positive now there was work to do. I would travel to Congo Cross to see Hassan. I was sure he'd be able to get a message to Songola because I needed to see her urgently.

Excited, I helped myself to slices of mango and papaya from the breakfast buffet, took some toast, and ordered scrambled eggs from the hovering waitress. A local man sat at the table next to mine mixing dried milk into his coffee. He was reading a local paper – the *Concorde Times* – and my attention was drawn to the leader on the front page. There were two photos with the article, one a head and shoulders of a young woman with her hair in cornrows, and the second of the mangled remains of a motorbike. One word in the article's title caught my eye *activist*. I chewed on my toast, but my eyes kept returning to the woman's photo and the intense interest of the man reading the article. As realisation dawned, something pulled at my gut. Of course the picture was familiar. It was a photo of Songola.

'Excuse me,' I tripped over the leg of my chair as I moved across to speak to the man and indicated the photo in the article. 'She's a friend. Can I see?' He nodded and handed me the paper. I stared with disbelief at the lovely face of Songola, killed several days before on the Kenema highway.

THIRTY-TWO

FLASHDRIVE

The worn-out yellow line taxi crawled along through Congo Cross in stifling heat. On either side, overcrowded *poda-podas* honked and belched fumes. The humidity was intense as storm clouds gathered over the Lion Mountains, a sign the rains were coming. The air pressed down like a wet blanket, grasping and stifling, sapping energy. It was hard to breathe in the vehicle and my impatience was growing as we inched along.

Amadu was now driving for CARE International, so I was travelling in a local taxi, empty when I'd hailed it, but now full of passengers. I was sitting in the back sandwiched between two market women, one with lively chicken in rickety cage, the other with a stack of fish baskets, the odour still pungent in their weave. Erect in the front sat an elderly woman with a small child, her gaze fixed on the road despite our inchmeal progress. I drummed my fingers on the canvas rucksack, conscious of the wasted time, and when the driver pulled over for another fare – a man of ample proportions carrying an electric fan – I decided it was time to get out.

From here it was only a short walk to Hassan's office and I was confident I knew the way. I stepped out into the sweltering heat, air that was thick with fumes, and paid the driver in tatty Leones. I hitched the *lappa* round my jeans, slung the rucksack across my back and headed down Main Motor Road under indigo skies. I'd rung ahead. He knew I was coming.

Without much trouble I found his neat office shack behind the empty SLAPHA building that I'd visited weeks before. Hassan, who'd welcomed me so warmly during my first days in Freetown, who'd introduced me to Sheku in the Youyi canteen, and then Songola and her work on the plantations. Serendipity had brought us together that day.

Chickens scattered as I crossed the compound and tapped on his door, pushing it open, not waiting for a reply. He was alone at his desk, looking like a man bereaved. Closing his computer, he stood to greet me and I took his hand, fighting the urge to embrace him.

'What happened to her, Hassan?'

He lowered his head and indicated for me to sit as he went to pour water.

'It seems our sister has paid the price,' he said, his body stooped in sadness.

'It wasn't an accident, was it?' My emotions were also full.

He looked at me over his spectacles, 'We have many terrible accidents on our highways, but this wasn't one of them.'

He pulled up a chair and sat opposite, legs splayed and back rigid in the manner of short men. He drew a handkerchief from his pocket, removed his glasses, and wiped the sweat from his brow and temples. I waited for more, but he was silent.

'What happened,' I asked again. 'Do you know? It's just that, well, I feel responsible in some way.'

His eyebrows lifted in surprise. I didn't really know what I meant myself. It was a struggle to find the words to explain how guilty I felt about Songola.

'I mean, I went with her on that trip to Gorahun, you

know, to see the villagers. Gather data for my PhD. I just think maybe, you know...' I trailed off when I realised I wasn't making sense and saw the astonished look on his face.

He said candidly, 'I can assure you, her dying had nothing to do with *you*. This is local politics. Our sister was an activist, and we all know the risks.'

Yes, I thought. Good people like Songola, like Sheku and Hassan, agitating for justice against all the odds.

'Don't forget,' Hassan said, 'she was also the wife of a prominent politician with controversial ambitions for our country. A *socialist*. By killing her these people have also sent a message to her husband.'

'Who are "these people"? Do you know?'

He leant back and searched across the ceiling 'Ahh...who, indeed? We have our suspicions but there will never be any proof.'

I said, 'Surely the government wouldn't...,' but he interrupted.

'No, I don't think they would. But it's true that keeping the opposition down is good for them also. And of course, there are plenty of people to do the dirty work. We'll never know for sure. There are many criminals willing to kill for cash.' I flinched, and he looked at me in a benevolent way. 'Now you are beginning to realise what life is like in our country. Sometimes is isn't very pretty.'

'What about the police?' I asked. 'Aren't they supposed to investigate accidents like this?' But I knew what the answer would be. He looked at me in the patient way I'd come to know. Many good people had shown me patience in this town.

Hassan said, 'The traffic division didn't investigate immediately. That's always a sign. Straight away they ruled her death an accident. The police even asked for "financial support" to undertake a proper investigation. And of course, the press tends to echo the government line. Journalists are fearful. They can be jailed for seditious libel if they challenge authority. It's not like in your country.' He stared at me. It seemed he was waiting for something else.

I sipped water and placed the glass on the desk, reminding myself that some things were more important than my own emotional insecurities. What I needed was to move on from my congenital and incurable defectiveness – my Western sensitivities and hubris.

The knowledge of Songola's death had galvanised me. I needed to believe that the embarrassing failures and wretched mess I'd created for myself in Freetown were just setbacks that would not define me. I thought of Songola's quiet humility, and her courage. I had already made up my mind.

'What will happen to her work?' I asked. The ceiling fan was motionless, the air thick and grasping.

Hassan shrugged. 'No doubt someone will one day try again. Sometimes we *are* successful. If we remind ourselves of that it keeps us going. You see the motorbike taxi riders…' he gestured in an easterly direction, 'they have their own influential union now. There is a big membership and they can pay lawyers to fight cases against the government.' He paused. 'Of course, it helps that most of them rent their bikes from the politicians or local chiefs. That way everyone's interests are protected.' His tone was ironic, and he eyed me carefully as my emotions rose.

I dived in, 'Hassan, I want to go back to the village and the Arranoil plantation, where Songola was working. I want to record testimonies from the people if I can. I mean, to try and save something of the work she was doing.'

Now that Songola had been killed, the stakes had risen enormously.

He looked surprised. 'Why would you do that?'

'There must have been something important she found if someone had her killed.' I was thinking about the little boys at Francis' trauma unit. 'You know, I mean, she was trying to build a union. But that's not a huge threat to government is it?' Hassan was paying close attention. I needed to get him on side.

I went on, 'Unions seem to get co-opted here, don't they? And, I think maybe there was something else she knew.' Trafficked children were in my head. I was trying to make the connections between serious international crime and Songola's work on the union. But I couldn't quite get there. 'Maybe I could dig around a bit.'

Hassan didn't seem convinced, so I tried again.

'I'm white, therefore I must have an advantage.' I figured there was zero chance the people who killed Songola would try to kill me.

He was cautious. 'Well, in some ways. Of course, you have that advantage. But why would you want to take the risk?' He sat quiet, unconvinced.

'Look,' I decided to try the truth. 'The PhD isn't going well. Since I came here, I've realised how irrelevant it is to local people.' He was nodding. The truth always makes more sense. 'I mean, I know I can't get involved in local politics.' He nodded more strenuously, 'but I think there may be something interesting to dig up on my own government. Why aren't they looking too closely at how aid money is spent? The bits that get lost and unaccounted for? Aid money belongs to *your* people. In fact,' I could trust Hassan, '...I believe there could be a connection between Arranoil and my own government.' It all came out a bit blurry, but he seemed to get the message.

He said, 'I see that you are serious. What do you hope to find?'

'I don't know exactly. But I'll need to see Sheku, to get Songola's contacts and her notebooks and any other information he has. Will he see me d'you think? I know I'm not from here, but maybe I can expose the hypocrisy around foreign investment in your country.'

'How do you think that will help?' he asked.

'You said it yourself when we first met. That I can say and do things you can't. You yourself want to know why the donors don't look closely at how the money is spent.'

He reached for his phone and said, 'Let's give Sheku a call.'

———

THE NEXT TAXI dropped me at the bottom of Hope Hill Street, and I walked the steep incline to Sheku and Songola's flat, feeling awkward and apprehensive, my sense of duty challenged by clumsy intensions of the outsider. I climbed the external steps to the flat and found the teenage boy from before sweeping fallen leaves and dust. He recognised me and nodded. There'd been no rain yet, but heavy clouds had gathered and were moving down the mountains. The wind was picking up, stirring dust from the ground, lifting leaves and foliage from the palms and fruit trees. There was water in the air. The slate cloud was low and saturated, ready to burst.

I stood outside the flat, looking at the door. They'd be mourning Songola and I'd have to move past that and cope with the emotions. Focus on the job, because that was all I could do to help them. Now Songola's death was added to the list of crimes associated with Arranoil, and I was sickened to think my own government had any knowledge of it.

Maybe UKDev had no idea the nature of deals going down right under its nose, the kind of corruption their system allowed. I'd yet to find evidence of a bribe but that didn't mean there wasn't evidence to find, and now I had the connection between Arranoil and Nigel Hurt. I just needed to understand what the connection meant. If Sheku had nothing to give me – none of Songola's notes or contacts from the village – I would go anyway. The villagers knew Songola trusted me. I had met the chief, and paid my respects and dues. Nothing would stop me going. But when I approached Sheku's flat that day, I couldn't know what it was that she had found. What had really got her killed.

The door opened and Sheku welcomed me, his usually drawn expression exaggerated by the deepest sadness in his bloodshot eyes. He beckoned me in.

'Come,' he said, and I followed him into the cosy room where the rich aroma of spices still permeated the corners of the space. Sheku indicated for me to sit on the worn sofa beside a middle-aged woman he introduced as his mother. She was holding Songola's baby and suckling him from a bottle. My heart was full. I had no words.

Sheku brought a cup of weak milky tea, pulled up a rickety stool and handed me a flash drive saying he had copied emails and documents direct from Songola's laptop. He said the smart phone she'd had with her when she died had not been found, so he couldn't pass on any of the photographs she'd taken on her last trip. It didn't matter, I was grateful for all the information he'd gathered for me. A thought crossed my mind: *what had I said in the message I'd left on Songola's phone?*

Sheku looked awkward where he sat, his angular frame folded up, his legs and arms crossed, seeming like he'd topple under the burden of all that was happening to him. Behind him, a young woman came into the kitchen and busied herself warming milk on the stove. There was something familiar about her. Then a small girl, who I remembered as Songola's daughter, followed her in and asked when mama would be home. The woman picked up the child and carried her out of the room, the warm milk in a pink plastic cup.

'What is it that you want to achieve by going back?' Sheku asked.

'I want to find solid evidence on conditions on the plantation,' I confided, 'so that I can write a report for the British
media. I want to find it for myself, first hand. People in my
country will be interested to know what's going on in the name
of international development. They'll want to know how your
people still suffer when they've already gone through so much.'

'How will that help us?' The question was reasonable and
it made me squirm with insignificance.

'I don't know,' I said honestly. 'I don't know if it will help
you. I can't promise anything will change just because the
outside world learns how corporations are violating human
rights and grabbing land that belongs to farmers and to men
promised a new start after the war.'

Sheku was waiting, his weary eyes trying to close. He'd
heard it all before.

I continued, 'All I can say is, it might mean people can no
longer pretend they don't know the cost of corruption in your
country.'

Sheku knew the full cost. He was nodding, and the argument seemed to make sense to him. Maybe it appealed to his
socialist convictions, but I decided not to tell him about
UKGov corruption, and the links to Arranoil, although I
sensed these revelations would not surprise him. It wasn't
clear exactly what had transpired between Nigel Hurt's aide
and the Agriculture Minister, but I kept thinking of the minister's words when I'd interviewed him: *It doesn't matter whether
you want a bribe or not. You get one either way.*

I stashed the flash drive safely in my rucksack and
thanked Sheku for agreeing to see me and giving me his
wife's files. It was time to go and leave the family to their
grief. Outside the window it had turned dark, the sky a
mucky shade of grey. The door to the balcony was open and
large droplets of rain began to land with a smack on the
broad leaves of the palms that shouldered the building.

Then Sheku said, 'It was the death of a child that took her back the last time.'

I stopped zipping my bag.

'The death of a child?'

'An accident on the plantation. They brought him back to the village, but no one knew who he was. My wife wanted to know more. She heard of many children who were not from the village.'

I was alive. This was it.

Remembering the conversation I'd heard in the *barrie* about children working on the plantation, I asked for confirmation.

'Was this a child helping its parents with harvesting?'

Sheku looked patient and repeated, 'This child was *not from the village.*'

'Where was he from?'

'Nobody knows,' his eyes focussed on me. 'You know there is child slavery in our country?'

'Yes, of course.' I said, knowing but not knowing. 'Is that what she'd found?'

The implications rushed my head like a storm.

Standing up he offered his hand and said, 'I wish you luck, Karen. Thank you for caring about our country.'

The meeting was over, and I stood to go, thoughts surging, my head a muddled mess. The baby had dropped off to sleep listening to his father's voice. The bud of his mouth shaped in a perfect 'O' as his grandmother wiped droplets of milk from his chin.

The younger woman had returned to the room and said to Sheku, 'She is sleeping now.'

I recognised her voice, but she had already turned away, clearing plates and putting things in cupboards, her tall, slender frame, moving gracefully.

Tentative, I said, 'Hello?'

She turned, her eyes averted, veiled and vigilant. Yes, I knew her.

'It's Moses' mother isn't it?' I said. 'I'm sorry, I don't know your name.'

She corrected me, 'Moses is my cousin.' She continued before I could speak, 'He is well, thank you.'

'That's good,' I replied. Sensing the tension, I made to go.

Then the young woman said, 'Songola was my sister. We were children together.'

Conscious that I was intruding on a home filled with grief and feeling awkward, I said, 'I'm so sorry for your loss.'

She looked at me direct.

'My name is Dorothy,' she said.

THIRTY-THREE
DOROTHY

'*Titi! Titi!*' Auntie's angry voice breaks through my thoughts.

I look up from scrubbing nasty stains from her kitchen floor.

I have been thinking of my sister who has been killed. How to avenge her. And I have wept and thrown up in the bucket.

Creeping into my head have been thoughts of that *white,* also.

How she is trying to avenge my sister herself.

It influences me.

Auntie rushes in, squeals at me, her wig askew, bosoms quivering. In one hand she holds a garment and she jabs it at me. With the other hand she is supporting her fat body on the counter. She is out of breath with the excitement of her anger.

Interested now, I look at the yellow blouse she is holding. A stain across the front, perhaps whiskey. Yes. It is so. I missed the stain when I laundered the garment.

She shouts at me, '*Yu dohn mek mistek!*'

Her face turns uglier when she's angry. There is nothing about her I can love. It is true, Auntie Turay and me, we hate each other.

Straight away I stand, put the cloth in the bucket, and say, 'Beg pardon, Auntie. I will fix it.' I take the blouse, wary of what is coming, because she is a violent woman.

She reaches for a gleaming pot, aims for the side of my head, swings it mightily in my direction. But she misses as I duck out of the way.

Auntie is confused and staggers forward, wondering where I've gone. She kicks over the bucket, and the stinking slime splashes her feet making the tiled floor slick. She goes over with a surprised expression, tipping ungainly, crashing her head against the floor. I check to see if she is dead, fear in my heart. But she is breathing. Time to clear up, for her to wake and forget what it was that happened.

This is my day with Auntie Turay.

This same morning she paraded like a queen in her new clothes. On her face a superior expression, expecting envy from a slum girl like me. She twirled her fat self around,

'*Di bodi nor bad! Di bodi fine!*' She wanted admiration, she wanted me jealous. But I did not satisfy her. My indifference angered her. I was too busy with thoughts of my sister for auntie's childish games.

It is so – I am the girl her husband takes for himself every night in Kroo. It angers her, makes her jealous. Gets the fire up in her belly.

She herself is an ugly woman. Stumpy and square. She waddles like a goose. No expensive cloth or fancy tailor will change that fact of life. Her skin is dark, and it is marked with uneven pigmentation. Under her chin lie many rolls of fat.

Today she wears a long-braided wig, lopsided as she lies immodest on the floor. She has many wigs: dreadlocks, kinky style, blonde bob, black bob, complicated braided styles – short and long. Beneath her wigs is a tortured scalp. A condition called scarring alopecia.

Auntie Turay speaks only her native *Krio*, yet her husband aspires to be a *big man*. Important. Influential. Corrupt.

Herself, she is is too lazy to learn English, when easily she could educate herself.

This is shameful to me. Already in our country there are too many ignorant, subjugated women. She chooses to be one of them. She knows he comes to my hut. It vexes her and deepens her hostility. That man has broken his wife. But he will never break me.

She stirs on the floor. I have cleaned up all around, but it is hard for her to stand. I offer my hand. She flicks it away, muttering, hauls herself to her feet by climbing up the counter, grasping at the edge with two plump hands.

'Is Auntie ok,' I ask, when really I don't care.

She screams at me to fetch some whiskey. I pour a glass but she takes the bottle, retires ungracefully to her room.

I take advantage of the fact she is drunk most of the time. It is not difficult to fool such a woman.

Like the time there was a fire in Kroo. Many homes and businesses destroyed because firefighters could not reach the fire – tiny alleys too narrow to pass. So, we fought the fire ourselves using sea water. Three hours it took to put it out. People had to sleep on the football pitch, which became a roofless home for thousands, all their possessions gone. The kids lost their school uniforms. *Awoko* reported on its front page. Auntie cannot read, but I showed her the coverage. Photos of burnt shacks, twisted metal, rubble and ash all around. The kids sitting on the football pitch. No uniforms for school. I told her the government wanted donations so the kids could go to school. She gave me twenty dollars. *Twenty dollars.*

My savings are great.

One day soon we will move to a place where I can close the door and lock him out.

IT IS time to leave for Murray Town, bring the boy home from school, then I myself can return to my hut. I move to fetch my things, take off my slippers, put on my sneakers. There is much I want to read tonight.

Auntie has slept since noon. I have heard nothing since her fall. Think maybe she died in her sleep. I spy her bag on the table. Beside it a messy pile of notes – Leones and US dollars – scattered like leaves fallen from the mango. I take a sly look. Walk round the table. She won't remember how much is there. I slide a ten dollar note, leave many more behind. I am not stupid. Slip it in my pocket, watch her bedroom door that stays closed.

I do not know that Auntie is standing on the veranda, watching through the window from outside.

———

I AM HURRYING through the alleys to our hut. Eager to get home, do my chores, sit to read before he comes. I am getting close. A neighbour catches my eye. She looks with fear. Something is wrong. I slow my pace but hasten it as well. Is my mother taken ill? I turn the corner of our street. A crowd has gathered, watching.

There is the sound of breaking things. I edge nearer. My mother stands in the dirt, our broken belongings ejected all around. There is crashing from inside the hut. The wooden rocker is thrown out in bits, my books follow it, falling at different angles, spines broken, pages torn, stained in the sludge and dirt. Clothes, pots. The mattress.

My abuser is here.

I storm inside and scream at him, 'What are you doing? Get out! Get out!'

But in his hands are my stolen savings. He gathers them, shoves the dollars and Leones in my face, shakes them at me.

'You steal from me!' he rages. 'Ha? Yes? What do you do? Make a fool of me and my wife?'

I stand mute. My future now in his ugly hands.

He takes all that he has found inside the mattress. Stuffs it in his shirt, his pockets. He looks around at our ransacked shack. Grabs me by the throat.

'Clear it up. Make tidy for tonight.'

He leaves. Strides his shiny shoes over my books, passes the gawking crowd, my mother crouched and weeping. I fall to my knees in that decimated place. Cradle my tattered books.

This is our life for now. But it does not define us.

THIRTY-FOUR
GORAHUN

The government bus pulled into the lorry park. It weaved around the flooded potholes, finding a space among the throng of coaches, juggernauts, lorries and pickups. The park was crowded with casual vendors, merchandise shacks, mechanics, and grills and braziers serving food. This was Kenema truck stop. From here I'd find a motorbike taxi to take me cross-country the rest of the way to Gorahun. The villagers were expecting me. The death of Songola had hit them hard.

The stop was a trading hub for all manner of goods coming from up-country and far beyond. I wandered through, alert to the possibility that traffickers might be in the area. Maybe Songola had the same thoughts on her last journey through this place. I searched for faces in the crowds, small boys dragged against their will by odious felons. But, of course, I saw nothing. Crimes like that were rarely visible.

There were men in long gowns and kufi caps, or shorts and T-shirts, or collars and ties; traders from all over the country selling goods and services. Scruffy boys in flip-flops hustled phone credit, gum, biscuits, cigarettes, small pouches of water, their feet muddy from the churned up ground.

Market women in variously tied and colourfully hued *lappas*, chatting behind their stalls, or strolling with head loads of fruit, vegetables, spicy snacks and drinks.

The sky was leaden with pewter cloud. More rain was to come.

A tiny woman with a shy smile stood proud behind her grill, and I bought blackened fish and cassava bread from her. It was ladled with a greasy red sauce and I ate hungrily, sitting on an upturned crate, my rucksack wedged between my knees. Inside the rucksack was a stash of phone credit, batteries and US dollars, with which I'd pay the villagers for their hospitality.

A white-haired man in fine African clothes sat nearby sucking from a water pouch. The rain began to fall in plump single drops, spreading on his robes as they landed. I watched as vendors prepared for the onslaught, constructing makeshift awnings above their goods: bread, oranges, wrist-watches, sandals, tin pyramids of tomato paste and neat mounds of groundnuts.

A shiny black cruiser entered the park, the driver weaving unhurried round the puddled potholes and rutted tracks. The vehicle looked out of place among the battered and rusted heaps, with their noisy engines, black fumes and pap-papping horns. The cruiser parked up neatly beside a row of braziers that were now sheltered under tarpaulin. But no one got out.

It felt like night, so black and heavy were the clouds.

The motorbike taxi riders sat under an enormous bread tree whose swollen ragged fruit hung low from spreading branches. The riders observed my approach, idly curious, and when I explained my destination, they looked cynical. One man waved the back of his hand toward Gorahun saying '*fah, fah*', as though it were in Egypt. Another looked warily at the sky.

One of their comrades had been killed on that bike with Songola.

One rider, a man with crooked teeth and fluorescent green tabard, negotiated me a price. He offered me a helmet, manoeuvring his bike taxi from the crowded assemblage of motors, and I climbed behind him onto the pillion. I breathed in his stale perspiration.

We exited the park under brooding skies and were soon off the highway. The dirt tracks had been softened by the rain so the driver kept to the edge of the track where the grass gave relief from the mud.

The land felt close, the passing landscape wild in a medley of green, the scent of rain and wood smoke. Thunder rumbled as we sped toward the hills of the Gola rainforest, blue in the distance. Spots of water fell heavy on my back, and in a moment it was raining pitchforks. I moved the rucksack between me and the driver, hoping my phone would stay dry.

I clung to the hand hold as the bike swerved and slid, but did not give pace. We raced through open scrub, bumping and bouncing, the driver confident and focussed, but we came to an abrupt halt when we reached a swollen river. This was a fast-running tributary of the huge Moa River, the water boiling and rushing, clay red with mud from upstream. There was a makeshift ferry – a slanting wooden barge that appeared half sunk – pulled across by a rope slung between trees on either bank. An elderly man and boy stood by, bare foot, dressed in shorts, their dark bodies gleaming with rainwater. My driver gave them some coins and the motorbike was rolled onto the raft, the boy tensioning the rope against the force of the water.

We were soon on the other bank and making good progress through thicker bush, riding under a canopy of acacia, banana, and raffia palms. I was soaked, my head sweating under the weight of the helmet; waterlogged jeans rubbing against my thighs. With one hand I held the precious rucksack, the other gripping vice like on the handhold. We sped past rows of thatched and mud-brick houses, cassava gardens, and groves of raffia palms. The journey seemed endless, but I felt no fear, only purpose.

I recognised the approach to the village, the huge moguls on the track, the haphazard arrangement of concrete bungalows on the outskirts of the settlement. The dense rainclouds were lifting, and the bike skidded to a halt. I thanked the driver and tapped his details into my phone for the return. He left immediately in a belch of fumes, fluorescent green tabard shrinking in size as he raced back along the track.

A small party was waiting to greet me, their mood solemn. They seemed wary of my return. Someone ushered me into a hut that smelt of earth and smoke where an old woman was waiting. From a gnarled wooded chest she produced dry clothes and passed them to me, indicating I should put them on, nodding encouragement. She had mismatched earrings hanging from her lobes that swayed as she bobbed her head. One gold hoop, one turquoise drop.

———

DRESSED IN *LAPPA* AND FLIP-FLOPS, I stepped outside the hut, avoiding large droplets of rain that dripped from the thatch and chicken bones that hung above the door to ward off threats from the ancestors. Waiting outside was the only English-speaker in the village, a man in a yellow T-shirt called Yusuf. The same man who'd helped me when I'd visited with Songola. He was young and thickset, with large, wide-apart eyes that made him look alarmed. He seemed uneasy, like he'd been given an unwanted job because he was too qualified for other tasks.

He asked, 'Ma, I hope the comma-day shun is ok?'

'Yes, thank you. I've everything I need.'

'Come,' he indicated for me to follow, 'chop is ready.'

I followed his broad back to a stark concrete bungalow where the headman was waiting with other villagers. Everyone fell quiet as I stepped in, and straight away I felt the tension. A meal of roasted maize, fried yam, leaf stew and rice was spread on a chequered cloth at a centre table. We ate in silence, the rain now pounding on the roof like a thousand horses' hooves, drowning any conversation we may have had. I felt awkward. An outsider. Wondering what they really thought of me. Knowing they didn't want me there. Nothing good ever came from *oporto.*

Milky palm wine was passed around – potent, heady, sickly – it tasted like fermenting vinegar, but I drank it. The rain eased off and the headman lit his pipe. Then a conversation struck up in Mende. There seemed to be differences of opinion among the group. I looked to Yusuf for translation.

His face was serious, 'They worried about security. They have bin problem.'

'Security problems? What d'you mean?'

The headman sucked on his pipe with quick short bursts, listening thoughtfully to his fellows. The plan had been that I would accompany the men's working party to the plantation, gather what evidence I could in the way of photos, statements, video clips, and audio, and then return with them to the village at the end of their day. It might take several trips to get what I needed, which was built into the plan.

But it seemed the plan had changed.

Yusuf said, 'They think is too risky. After Songola…things, they have got worse.'

'What do you mean things have got worse?' I asked, wondering if it was anything to do with the death of the boy.

'They worried about security, it is tight now,' he said. 'You have to go with me. You can not go with the men. They are checking.'

'Checking?'

The atmosphere in the room was edgy and people looked uncomfortable. Maybe I'd come this far and now wouldn't get to the plantation. Wouldn't know for sure if trafficked boys were working there. The memory of Songola kept me focussed, and I willed the group of elders to agree and let me go. The headman looked hesitant but others in the group seemed to think it worth the risk. For the first time since I'd arrived in Freetown, I felt grateful for my whiteness. It made me feel invulnerable.

I said, 'Yusuf, can you ask them about the boy? The one who died on the plantation. Is this why security has been tightened?'

Yusuf looked wary but when he spoke the mood changed. Looks were exchanged, some heads bowed, and the headman seemed resigned. They decided I could go, but I was to keep away from the work party until I was deep in the forest. Arranoil's security was now everywhere. Yusuf would be my guide.

———

YUSUF HELD the lamp that lit our way back through the village to the old woman's hut. The rain had stopped and it was slippery under foot. Woodsmoke wafted from where the fires crackled bright, and fireflies hovered in their magical dance. Throbbing pinpricks of light in a show of bioluminescence. The sky had cleared, and a blanket of stars pierced through the canopy of palms. In this remote spot, noises of the forest carried far; drums and shouting a long way off, sounds that came eerily through the trees. I asked Yusuf what they meant.

'Some body…they die,' he said.

The old woman was waiting when I entered the hut. Her face was kind, tight high cheeks the shape of apples, her body fragile and angular, grey hair cropped close. She placed the lamp beside a reed mat that was spread out on the floor, a cotton blanket neatly folded; this was to be my bed.

She indicated for me to remove the flip-flops and beckoned me sit on a stool and take water. I wondered how we were to communicate. Politely, I held up a hand and refused the drink, instead raising my skirt and making to squat. Straight away she pulled me up, put the flip-flops back on my feet, and took me outside with the lamp, leading me through blackness to a patch of grass in a small plantation of banana, not far from the huts. Raising the lamp above her head she scanned the darkness. Satisfied, she tore away a leaf from a nearby palm and handed it to me gesturing to go ahead whilst she turned her back and waited, only the unblemished darkness of the forest to protect me.

Back in the hut she let me settle. I unpacked the rucksack arranging my things carefully in the small space. There was a heavy odour of woodsmoke – its remnants stung my eyes. The old woman leant into the water pitcher, her mismatched earrings swaying, glinting in the lamplight, and scooped out a cupful. She passed it to me.

'*Tek watta.*'

'*Tenki, ma.*'

I took the cup and sipped the sweet water whilst checking my phone. There were no messages, but there was no signal in the hut. The old woman looked at the phone and said something enthusiastically in Mende. I didn't understand and wandered outside to find a signal. Eventually I gave up. There seemed to be no coverage in the village. Now I was uncontactable. Few people knew I was here. The phone's battery was full and I would use it sparingly. There was no knowing how long I would be here, or how I could re-charge the phone, which was my primary method of evidence collection.

Back in the hut my elderly host was dragging a plastic bucket across the floor. In it was a car battery. She proceeded to rig up an arrangement of clips and wires, then gestured for me to give her my phone. She looked at me with rheumy eyes, expectant. I handed it over for her to charge, chastened by her resourcefulness.

The night was long and I slept fitfully; tuned in to the sounds of screeching animals and scuttling rats, a makeshift mosquito net suspended overhead. I lay open eyed in the darkness, all the possible events of the following day running through my head like a movie.

THIRTY-FIVE

ARRANOIL

It was to be several days before the head man was happy
enough for me to leave the village and go to the plantation.
Security units had been patrolling the areas of harvesting for
days. Now they'd moved to a different part of the forest and
it was safer for me to go.

I woke at dawn to cockerels crowing, women singing and
water sloshing in buckets. The villagers routinely rose before
dawn and by the time the sun was up, the working parties
were ready to go. This time I was ready too, in jeans and black
T-shirt, my hair tucked in a baseball cap, phone and notebook
stashed in a belt around my waist.

At the edge of the village in an area cleared of bush the
workers congregated, waiting for the sound of motor engines
advancing through the trees. The company vehicles travelled
on a laterite track direct from the Arranoil estate. On the
return they took different trails delivering the workers to the
spots where they would be harvesting that day. The men
boarded into a penned trailer pulled by a tractor – similar to
the kind used by Yorkshire farmers to ferry their sheep to
market. On the side of the trailer was written *ARRANOIL*

SIERRA LEONE PALM OIL. I watched them go from the safety of the huts, and an hour later I set off with Yusuf.

It was a short journey to the point where a sign at the edge of a red dirt track announced *Arranoil Agricultural Company Ltd, Mongo-Dembila Chiefdom, Gorahun*. The road was blocked by a weighted barrier with STOP in red letters. I took photos of the sign to evidence where we were. We skirted the barrier, riding further down the track to a point where we could hide the bike in scrub on the boundary of the estate. It was as far as we could go without the noise of the engine attracting attention.

Overnight rain was evaporating from the road as the sun climbed higher in a sky of cobalt blue, all rainclouds disappeared. Now we'd be travelling on foot, a hike of seven kilometres to where the villagers were harvesting in the heart of the plantation. We hoped to reach the work site by midday.

The trek was difficult. The plantation floor was littered with discarded fronds hacked away during harvesting. We strode over them and kept a steady march through the regimented lines of stately palms.

The plantation was vast. The palm fruits ripened consecutively throughout the year, so there was never a time when there wasn't harvesting in some part of the plantation. Its immense size was overwhelming. Row upon row of identical trees as far as the eye could see, in all directions. Yusuf seemed confident of the way, and I followed his broad back keeping pace as best I could. It was eerily quiet as we trudged along. No birdsong, just the rustle of our boots as we tramped the fronds on the forest floor. The sense of isolation was heavy, and the adrenalin was pumping. All my senses were heightened, listening. Wondering what I'd do if we came across security.

It was shady among the trees but the heat was intense. Flies and mosquitoes hung in the air and settled on our clothing. Two hours in, we stopped to take water and share the flatbread baked for us in the village. Then on again, with the sure knowledge of the return trudge to come.

Then, without warning, the sounds of activity in the forest. The muted hum of conversation and the occasional slash of machete against fibrous wood. We were close. I waited while Yusuf went ahead to check the area was clear of Arranoil personnel and, minutes later, I was among them. I recognised the workers from the village, all men. The women were in a different part of the plantation working in the nurseries tending seedlings, spraying pesticides, adding liquid fertiliser to the soil. An image of the new-born child flashed in my mind.

She had died now.

The children were sitting in a group on the ground, perhaps between eight and ten years old, greedily scooping rice from a communal platter that had been brought to the site by a heavily pregnant girl. I retrieved my phone and set the camera to work, confident the old woman could keep my battery charged.

The children were anxious, but curious about my whiteness. This could be my only chance to get what I needed, and I offered them sweets. They fell upon the candy, grateful and smiling, posing shyly for photos and giggling when I showed them the results. Their feet were bare, lacerations old and new, all over their skin.

I asked Yusuf, 'Can you ask them about their villages? Their families? Do they know where they've come from?'

The boys looked blank and confused as Yusuf asked the questions. They kept looking at me, and then back to him.

Yusuf said, 'They don't know their village. They don't even know where they are now, in this forest plantation. But they know they can't go home.'

I was recording his translations on my phone.

'Can you ask them who brought them here?'

The children looked fearful when Yusuf asked the question, and went silent. They looked down at their sweets, still munching. One boy whispered under his breath, *big man.*

It seemed no one knew who the children were, or where they'd come from. The kids had been separated from their families and villages and brought to the plantation to work.

'Can you ask them if they get any payment, or who looks after them?'

The boy who'd whispered *big man* raised his head. A good looking lad with muscled arms, his skin dry and scratched, tatty blue shorts that had never been washed. In his hand he had a harvesting sickle, and he wanted to be the spokesman for the group. The others listened, anxious.

Yusuf said, 'He say they are paid no wages. They get food – rice and sauce – one time every day. They sleep together under a bungalow that belongs to the boss man.'

The boy continued talking.

Yusuf said, 'He say they are friends. They stick together because no-one knows where their family is. He say their family is poor…every boy…his family is poor.'

I asked him, 'Where d'you think they've come from? Which part of the country?'

He shrugged his heavy shoulders, his wide-apart eyes looking surprised unnecessarily.

'They are not from near this place, look,' he grabbed a boy and showed me the lacerations on his forehead, 'this is Limbo cuttin'.'

'Limbo?'

'It is far, far. In the north of the country. And this…' he grabbed another boy. 'I don't know this cuttin', maybe Guinea.'

'Guinea!' Sierra Leone's northern, French speaking neighbour. These children had been trafficked. Bought or stolen from their parents in remote locations and transported to work on far-flung plantations for no wages. An army of kids with no home, no family, no-one to look out

for them. No education or security, their only companions –
fear, and each other. This must have been what Songola had
found.

With the video running, I followed the children as they
worked. Two or three boys would together lift the harvested
fruit onto large metal wheelbarrows. The bigger boys would
lift the barrows, laden with several ripe clusters, and then
navigate the awkward paths along the plantation floor to the
collection points, some distance away, the sinews in their
young necks straining. The muscles in the boys' upper bodies
were well defined and developed, like men's, grotesque in
their undersized bodies. Some boys head-loaded the fruit to
the collection points, their young necks disappearing into
their shoulders under the colossal weight.

After an hour or so I was satisfied with all the different
evidence I'd collected, and replaced the phone and my notebook carefully in the belt at my waist. I would email all the
files to myself as soon as I could get a signal. Yusuf was waiting, ready for the return.

We set off at a brisk pace following the same track back to
where the bike was hidden. The excitement was immense. I
had what I wanted – all the evidence I needed – and in my
head I was writing the report. The testimonies, videos and
photos were damning. More than I could have hoped for.

IT SEEMED impossible to be any hotter or more
uncomfortable than on that trudge back to the bike through
unending rows of palms. There was less shade, the sun
directly above us, beating down merciless between the well-
spaced trees. My clothes stuck uncomfortably, the sweat
bright on my skin, mosquitos and flies irritating like hell. My
second water bottle was almost empty, so I took short
draughts, and several times I had to ask Yusuf to stop for a

rest. Our progress was slow, but every time we rose to resume, I checked the safety of my phone.

Eventually the grit road at the edge of the plantation came into view, our water bottles empty, we were exhausted. The relief quickened my pace when I saw the track. The motor-bike was parked close by, and soon I'd have the breeze on my face, and the comfort and refuge of the hut before dark.

Yusuf slowed his pace ahead of me. As I caught up, I saw what it was looking at and checked my own pace. On the road ahead, close to where we'd hidden the bike, an official-looking utility vehicle was parked. Cold fear paralysed me. I walked with leaden steps, my heart thumping, the blood pounding my temples. We broke cover and stepped out onto the track where two men in olive green uniforms sat in a pick-up. They got out leisurely, across their breast pockets the yellow logo of Arranoil.

'Good afternoon,' said one of them. He looked like the senior of the two, a soft fleshed, overweight man, his eyes hidden behind reflective shades. He took a drag from his cigarette.

We stood mute. No point denying where we'd been. We couldn't run. We couldn't lie. We'd be foolish to start a confrontation. Yusuf was rigid, his face a study of dread, his startled eyes staring into the bush beyond the pick-up, ready for…I didn't know what. Both men were armed with auto-matic weapons.

The first man rested toad-like against the bonnet of the vehicle. 'Miss Hamm, have you enjoyed your walk?' He smile was a sneer beneath his silver-tone glasses. He flicked his cigarette butt in the road. The second man sniggered and kept his distance, eyes roving my sweat drenched body. He was more in shape than his boss, huge biceps straining the cotton of his shirt. I felt nauseous. They knew my name. What else did they know?

When I didn't reply the first man indicated the open door of the pick-up.

He said, 'Miss Hamm, we'd like you to come with us.'

Fear gripped me. My mouth was dry as I spoke.

'Is there something wrong?' My voice sounded strange to me.

The first man tipped his head to one side in a patient manner. His lips were thick, a weak moustache clinging on, moist with sweat. 'Miss Hamm, you've breached security. Of course, you know that. You will have to come with us.'

There was no point denying I was unauthorised on the Arranoil estate. But I was sick with panic, thinking of all the precious evidence in the pouch of my belt. Yusuf stood terrified in the road. It would be futile to try and hand the phone to him; it would only implicate him more in my misdoings. I moved bullish toward the pick-up, conscious of my body drenched with sweat, trying to keep composure.

I asked, 'Where are you taking me?'

Yusuf remained where he was, silent.

The first man said, happily, 'There is no need to be alarmed, Miss Hamm, we're not kidnapping you!' He guffawed at his joke, and his sidekick joined in with lecherous snickers.

When he'd got over it, the first man said, 'You're trespassing. Our boss wants to speak with you. You're coming to the office with us.'

He was enjoying my fear and embarrassment, but I climbed into the vehicle as instructed. As we moved away, I turned to check on Yusuf, who was headed off at speed in the opposite direction.

THIRTY-SIX
NOKIA

The offices of Arranoil were in the heart of its estate. A modern two-storey building with large, heavily barred windows that overlooked the plantation. I sat anxious and alone in the stifling heat of the manager's office which had panoramic views of the palms. Regimented trees, their fronds lifting in a breeze that was steadily increasing. Oil palms. A toxic crop that ruined people's lives. I was glad I was here. There was much I had to say.

Two ineffectual fans rotated lazily overhead. Thirst was making me weak, my eyes wandering to the water cooler, my breath shallow in the suffocating air. My clothes had stuck to my skin with stale perspiration. I sat waiting for my interrogation, the phone wedged hard against my body, concealed inside the belt. The big wooden desk was empty except for an overflowing ashtray and an angled reading lamp. Maps of Sierra Leone were pinned to the wall, a couple of production charts, large metal filing cabinets and upholstered chairs. The two guards who had brought me now stood weightily outside the door, their shadowy bulk ominous through the glass. I waited as the minutes passed, my body exhausted from the trek, but my mind alert, ready for the fight.

There was a shuffle in the corridor, and the door opened to allow a short, thin man in a cool, linen shirt to enter. His features were reptilian – like *Salone's* venomous green mamba that hid in the trees, calm and agile, ready to kill you with one bite. The two guards followed him in and stood to attention either side of me. Like I was planning an escape.

'Karen Hamm,' said the boss. I felt sick at the familiarity as he arranged himself neatly on his swivel behind the desk. 'Thank you for coming to see us. I think you'll agree the official route is much more comfortable than hiking through the palms.' His tone was thick with sarcasm. He tried to smile but his heart wasn't in it, his eyes small black dots lost in deep sockets. I shuffled in my seat, aware of what I looked like, and the odour coming off me.

'How do you know my name?' I demanded.

'There are no secrets in Sierra Leone,' he said. 'Everybody knows everybody's business. It might help you to remember that.' There was no light in his eyes as he stared me down. Palm fronds rattled and slapped against the windows. The first lash of rain.

'You're aware you've been trespassing on private property,' he said. 'If you'd called ahead I would have given you a tour of operations myself, although what our business in Gorahun has to do with your research isn't clear to me.'

The guards snickered.

What did he know about my research?

Blood pumped through my throbbing temples. I hoped they couldn't see my fear.

'I notice you've children working here,' I said. 'Would you have allowed me to meet *them* during my tour of operations?'

'Miss Hamm, children work all over Africa,' he said, derisive. 'There's nothing unusual about that. Their parents are poor. An educated woman like you must know these things.'

'Of course, you're right. Children work to support their

families,' I said. 'In that case, how much are you paying them? And where are their families?'

He became a little guarded. 'Miss Hamm, you'll do well to remember you're a guest in this country. Officially, you are here to research a PhD.'

Furious, I wondered what else he knew.

'Tell me how your unofficial visit to our private plantation is relevant to the subject of your thesis.'

The flutter of anxiety crept through my stomach.

'Now,' he continued, 'if I may have your phone, our people will remove all unauthorised content collected at this site, and then escort you back to your village. In the morning you'll return to Freetown.'

I sat motionless.

He sighed. 'Miss Hamm. Your university requested permission for your visa on the grounds that you are actually *doing* academic research. You are a *guest* in this country,' he repeated. 'You'll be removed by the authorities if you are found to be doing other than your permitted research, such as pursuing an agenda liable to disturb the peace, or ignite tensions, stirring up local emotions. The government here takes a dim view on that.'

It's not me who's igniting tensions. I said nothing. But I understood his threat.

'Your phone.' He eyed me directly, and one of the guards made a move toward me. I removed it from my belt and handed it over. I didn't want his hands on me.

'Your password?' he asked.

I was silent.

'Very well.'

He nodded to his henchman who left the room with the phone. There followed several minutes charged with tension while the boss leant back in his chair and stared at his planta-tion out the window. The guard returned and handed me a zipped plastic bag containing the splintered remains of my phone. Anger and emotion rose.

If they thought this would stop me, they were wrong. I'd be back, cleverer and more prepared next time. But in my heart, the euphoria was swept away.

———

I SHOWERED in a raffia enclosure to the rear of the old woman's hut. Above my head, a plastic bag filled with water, pierced with holes and held aloft by her. The discoveries and miseries of the day I tried to wash away with the bar of soap she handed me. In the hut I dried off, stepped into clothes she'd laundered, and accepted the flatbread and sliced fruit she offered.

She eyed me curiously, no way of knowing what a disaster the day had been, but sensing something was wrong. All the evidence I needed had been right there in my hands, and now it was gone. Yusuf had not returned. He'd ridden his motorcycle straight from the plantation to Kenema where he had family with whom to lie low.

I felt vulnerable without my phone. No way of contacting my motorbike taxi for the return to Freetown. No way of contacting home, or the university if things turned really bad. I needed to get out of here, not for my own safety but for the villagers', because I didn't trust Arranoil not to punish me by proxy. The workers were now compromised and the sooner I got back to Freetown the better it would be for them.

The working group was returning to the village. I could hear the general hubbub as meals were prepared, and water splashed from bucket to bucket. Children sang a welcome song. Cooking smells filtered through the hut. A meal would be prepared for me at the headman's house, this time to debrief on the day's events. The word must have got to them that Arranoil had arrested me. An explanation would be required. People would want to know what happened and the truth would be too heart-breaking to share. What these people had risked, for nothing. But maybe I'd come back without involving them. Maybe I could still work something out.

LATER I LAY on my mat. Disappointment and anger threatened to overwhelm me. If Arranoil knew so much about me, the company must have contacts everywhere. It was better for me that I knew this.

The villagers showed no emotion at the news. They were grateful I'd returned safely. Disappointment, they were used to. Even if I'd still got my evidence, would it really make a difference to their lives? How long would it take for change to come? And whilst they were waiting, what new challenges, indignities or injustice would come to blight their lives?

The old woman moved quietly about the hut. I could see her gentle features illuminated by the lamp as I lay still and sweating.

'*Eh, ma. Tek watta.*' She leant over, offering a cup of sweet water from the earthenware pot. I sat up and took it from her.

'*Tenki, ma.*' I said, draining the cup and handing it back, the water more delicious than any I'd tasted.

She busied herself rigging up the battery again, dragging it over with the wires trailing.

I shook my head and said, '*Tenki ma*, but not tonight.' And then, '*Ah taya baad,*' trying to express how tired I felt.

She looked surprised.

'*Eh…wah?*'

From my rucksack I retrieved the zipped plastic bag that contained the broken parts of my phone and showed it to her.

'Eeeeah!' she screeched.

She looked at me with sympathy, then packing her

precious charging equipment back in the bucket, she took the lamp and stepped outside. I lay back on my mat, exhausted. I contemplated what my next strategy should be. Whether there was one. I was starting to feel the panic as hopelessness set in.

The old woman returned and placed the lamp on the floor. Sitting on the stool she looked at me intently and started to ramble in Mende, her wizened features animated, her arms and hands moving balletically to illustrate her points. I sat up, realising she was saying something important. There was no Yusuf now to translate. Sitting cross-legged on my mat, I took the old woman's hands and tried to calm her.

'*Wetin is it, ma*?' I asked gently.

She went on rambling, then she picked up the zipped bag containing my broken phone and shook it at me. I heard her say Songola's name.

'Songola? Are you talking about Songola?' I asked.

'Songola,' the old woman repeated, nodding her head, amazed at my stupidity. She kept shaking the bag with the phone.

I asked in *Krio*, '*Yu kin sho me*?'

She nodded, rose, and left the hut. She returned with the car battery and wires and tipped them onto the mat again. My fatigue now forgotten I watched her, fascinated. She linked up everything for charging as she had done the previous nights and arranged the broken pieces of my phone as though it were charging, all the while muttering to herself in Mende. Then she indicated the phone saying clearly *Songola*…Songola's phone…lifting it to her ear…and then she pointed at me saying *oporto*. Had Songola stayed at the old woman's hut on her last visit to the village? Had she tried to call me?

The old woman disappeared from the hut again and after a while returned with a young man who stood awkward at the door. He was holding a first-generation Nokia: an old camera phone. He stepped inside and powered it up with the

battery, then fiddled with it. The old woman babbled excitedly and indicated for me to look. I rose, hardly daring to
believe what might be there. A file opened on the small
screen, the young man pressed play, and I watched the movie
unfold.

AT DAWN I left the village on the back of a motorbike taxi,
waving at the small group gathered to see me off. Their
expressions were a mix of hope and resignation, seasoned
against the emptiness of promises made by Westerners. In the
midst of the group stood the old woman, her face impassive. I
longed to hold her and thank her.

The bike skidded away in the mud, and soon the small
group was indefinable in the distance behind us. We weaved
along the track, travelling through the silver gauze of rainy
season sunlight that slanted across the path. Dotted across the
landscape, luminous white smoke rising from unknown fires.
We rode under coconut palms and through tall grasses, the
vegetation dripping with water. And past acres of swamp rice
with its brilliant green tendrils, and small thatched settlements here and there. Slow-moving, graceful women stopped
to watch us pass, their slender bodies wrapped in bright
patterned wrappers and on their heads, bundles of cassava
root tied with banana leaf.

A snapshot of Africa I'd never see again.

The movies on the Nokia kept running through my mind.
They explained Songola's last trip. She'd gone there to investigate the death of a child on the plantation, and the movie on
the phone showed the body of the boy being laid out on a
cloth in the *barrie*, the villagers crowding round.

Laceration injuries to his limbs were visible, and the angle
of his neck suggested it had been broken. The child's over-
sized muscles and lacerations were identical to those of the

boys I'd met working on Arranoil's estate; but this child seemed younger, possibly only seven years old. His bruised and broken body lay lifeless on the floor, a harrowing sight. On his cheekbones distinctive long parallel scarifications, tribal identification marks similar to the ones Yusuf thought might be Guinean. And there were small puncture wounds around the child's upper body and his head, injuries possibly caused from the spikes of a falling palm fruit. These conclusions fitted with the hazardous conditions I'd seen for myself and the dangerous operations in which the children worked.

The death of that child had brought Songola back to Gorahun. What else had she found? Had she too worked out that children were being trafficked there from other regions, possibly other countries? Had she found child trafficking into slavery going on right under her government's nose? Did she guess who was involved?

I wondered who'd given the order to silence her. Arranoil? The Sierra Leone government? My own government?

There was a second movie on the Nokia. It showed Songola in conversation with villagers in the *barrie*, checking what looked like photos on someone's phone, taking copies of them. I couldn't understand the dialogue, but the seriousness of its content was unmistakable. In the second movie the old woman sat close to Songola. Now I was convinced that Songola had stayed in her hut on her last night. That she might have been trying to contact me...*oporto*. That maybe she'd tried to send me something, or alert me to something. Her files might be waiting for me in junk mail.

I had to get back to my laptop that I'd stashed in the hotel's safe.

The Nokia was now my priceless possession, tucked safely in my rucksack after an exchange of $50 with the young man who owned it. Nothing must happen to it. No-one must know about it. It was all I had left, and Arranoil was on to me. I would return to the Kangari and write up my report from the villagers' testimonials. I'd send it to Nia straight away, hoping she'd now have something concrete that linked Nigel Hurt to Arranoil. At the same time, I'd alert the British press that something big was coming. And I'd book a flight home. I had to get the Nokia safely out of the country.

THIRTY-SEVEN

KANGARI

My instincts were right. Songola's files were waiting in junk mail. And they were better than I'd hoped. She'd sent me photos of the children working on the estate. They were just like the ones I'd taken myself that had been destroyed by Arranoil. Like me, Songola had captured the boys' injuries and the awful conditions in which they worked. Child slavery on Arranoil's plantation. This must have been what old woman was trying to tell me. That Songola had got a phone connection and had emailed the photos to me, *oporto*. She'd trusted me. Maybe she'd realised how much danger she was in. That she might not make it back to Freetown.

My heart beat faster as I opened each file. Cold sweat pricked the back of my neck. It seemed she was reaching out to me. She was back from the dead and alive in my body, calling me to finish what she'd started. Tears flowed as I imagined her, lying on the same mat in the same hut, cared for by the old woman, trying to get enough signal on her phone to get the photos through to me.

Thanks to her, I now had all the evidence I needed. The Nokia, the photos, the villagers' testimonies. When the opposition parties in the UK got wind of the scandal there'd be a furore in the House of Commons, MPs would call for the resignation of Nigel Hurt. They'd demand answers from the government about the corruption of aid. Lobby groups would be energised. The British public would be outraged. Maybe something would change.

But I was still waiting for proof that Nigel Hurt had bribed the Minister for Agriculture to allow the Arranoil concession, and there was no email waiting from Nia.

Immediately I saved all Songola's files to my account in the *cloud* knowing that would be safer than keeping them on the laptop or in my regular email accounts or even on Songola's flash drive. It would be too risky to print out anything at the hotel, or in any of the city's internet cafés. Paranoia was moving in as I imagined Arranoil's tentacles everywhere, their influence at all levels, in government and in society. Spies at the hotel, in the car park, online. *How did they know so much about me?*

Fresh from the shower, I sat at the desk, the AC rattling overhead. I opened up a new document and typed *Child Slavery and International Aid*. I wrote feverishly, trying to get everything down in some order. Children as slave labour; trafficking; life-threatening working conditions; the cover up of the death of a child; aggressive threats from Arranoil; pesticides, compliance of local ministries, and possibly the corrupt use of UK aid by UK ministers. Then my thoughts were interrupted by the familiar chimes of Skype.

It was Nia.

'Karen! Thank God. Where the feck have you been?'

'Up country,' I said calmly. 'I've had no signal, then I lost my phone. It's so good to see you.' Emotions surged as I saw her pretty face and heard the Irish tones. I should send the files to Nia, an insurance policy in case I didn't make it with the Nokia out of *Salone*. It was a complicated journey back to Lungi, the airport itself was unsafe. Plenty of opportunity for Arranoil to find me, and the Nokia.

'Nia, I'm going to send you some files.' Then I imagined the line might not be safe. Maybe my room was bugged. Maybe Skype. Maybe even my email had been hacked.

'What you got?' she asked.

I was cautious, wanting to protect her as well as myself.

'Files of interest. You'll work it out.'

'Ok. You look like death.'

'Sorry. Tiring trip.'

'Right. Well, it's good to see you anyway. I was worried.' She did look worried. 'So, I bring good news. There's a link to UKDev. Seems like two hundred k changed hands on your deal. A bribe for the Arranoil concession – courtesy of your man via the CDC.' The CDC was the UK's development finance institution that doled out the aid money. She said, 'The dates all check out.'

'Jeese, Nia!'

This was it. Now I had everything.

I asked, 'How d'you know?'

'We've got access to folk's bank accounts, don't forget.'

She'd taken a huge risk for me. I was elated but had to shut her up for her own sake, and mine.

'Thanks so much for this.'

'Yeah, you definitely owe me. Hope it works out.'

'I'll be home soon,' I said. 'I'm booking a flight today. I really need to get back.'

'Things getting tricky?'

There was a timely knock on the door.

'I'll have to go, Nia. That'll be room service.' I'd ordered food. I didn't want to show up in the bar or in the restaurant.

I went to let the staff in, opening the door wide to accommodate the tray. A thick set man carrying a holdall walked straight in. Shaven head, dark glasses, sweat stained safari shirt and crumpled shorts. He slammed the door and pushed me back into the room. He smiled – bleached teeth in an unshaven face. *Arranoil henchman*. It must be.

'Who the hell are you!' I said, knowing exactly who he was and backing into the room. 'Get out!'

Fear surged my veins.

But he was busy with the door, ripping the plastic fob that covered the override locking system, double bolting the door with an expert twist of his wrist. Now there would be no access from outside. I stood paralysed, and stared in terror at the brown plastic fob, hanging there, lopsided with the violence used to loosen it. Slightly askew, limp and impotent, it hung at an angle, the metal lock rammed into place. I wondered why I'd never noticed it before. I stared at it, sticking out, useless, taunting me, and understood immediately the implications of its existence. No access from outside.

'What d'you want?' I tried to sound strong but only heard the trembling weakness of my voice. My eyes casting back to the broken fob, mesmerised by it, trying to work a way out.

He spoke in a heavily accented voice, 'This is a courtesy visit.' He leered and advanced, happy that I was terrified. It was a southern African accent, Afrikaans. *Mercenary. Arranoil heavy guy mercenary.* I felt sick. Did *he* kill Songola? Panic whipped through my heart like an icy wind. I didn't recognise the fear in my body.

'What d'you want?' I repeated, feeling vulnerable, dressed only in a towel from the shower. I reached for a *lappa* and wrapped it tight round my body.

'It's time to go home, sweet,' he said and dropped his duffle bag on the bed, unzipping it. He moved to the desk and slammed shut my laptop. My heart sank in despair. I tried to grab it.

'What are you doing!' but he pushed me away, dropping the laptop into his bag. My last lifeline.

He said with an ugly sneer, 'Just tidying up.' Then he turned to my rucksack lying on the bed, up-tipped it, collected my notebooks and diary, and stashed them with the laptop in his duffel bag. My heart hammered in my chest.

Then zipping the bag, he left it on the bed and turned his attention to me.

I shouted at him in terror, 'If you've got what you want you can get out!'

I was screaming now, knowing my voice would carry through the bathroom window onto the walkways where security patrolled on my floor. I knew they couldn't get in, but knowing they were outside might deter him. Feebly I hoped room service might still be on its way.

He grabbed me, his breath a sickening stench of stale tobacco and beer, and in one move he turned me, pulling me back against his body, my buttocks pressed hard against him. This couldn't be happening. One hand groped my breast, and the other grabbed hard between my legs, my arms locked to my sides by muscled biceps as he ground himself against me. There was no room to twist away and panic gripped me. I tried to stamp on his feet, adrenalin pumping, my heart wild at the prospect of what was to come.

He licked my ear, his breath hot, the sound sticky and sickening.

He whispered, 'My boss wants you gone, lady. But he can't see you booked on any flight.'

I struggled, trying to move my fist behind me towards his groin, realising how weak I was against the power of his massive, tattooed arms. There was no power in me. He had it all.

Then without warning, he let go.

I stood trembling, confused. He picked up the duffle bag from the bed then strode to unbolt the door, saying before he left, 'Time to fuck off home, darlin.'

I stood shaking, listening to his footsteps retreating down the steps. I hurried to bolt the door, but looked out on the walkway, wondering where the hell was security. They must have heard me shout. There was always someone close. But the walkways were deserted. The lower levels in darkness, hardly any illumination from the dim yellow lamps. Below, in the gardens, the porter Joseph stood looking up. But in a moment he was gone, backing away into the shadows out of sight.

Back in the room I stood by the bed and picked up the rucksack, upturned and emptied. I put my hand into the pocket deep inside the base. The Nokia. It was still there.

ARRANOIL NOW HAD everything it needed to confirm my threat. The report on the laptop would tell them everything. My diary would implicate others. My notes would expose my plans, and my contact list all the people I could trust.

The loneliness of fear folded round me. I went to the bathroom and threw up.

Powerlessness was new: outside forces re-directing my life. No control: someone else in the driving seat of my world. Karen Hamm, white, British, wealthy socialite, clever scholar. Now insignificant, and expendable. Unknown others had destabilised my world – my good character, kind nature – because none of that was consequential now. Good intentions held no currency. In fact, they were a threat. Full of hubris and arrogance, just like Francis had cautioned. I'd romanticised a version of a dangerous reality. I'd let go my objective brain.

I stood motionless in my room, gazing at the fob on the lock. The staff at the Kangari had been compromised. I dared not stay another night. I had to keep the Nokia safe and get myself on the next flight home. But first there was something left to do.

THIRTY-EIGHT

WELLINGTON

Still shaking, my body moving independent from my brain, I took the rucksack and a few essentials, and left the rest of my belongings and the red spinner behind, emptying the small safe of my valuables – passport, credit cards, sizeable stash of US dollars.

It was dark when I stepped outside the lobby, violent rain pelting down. I pulled my hat lower, and hitched the rucksack higher, trying to stop the water running down my back. The darkness was comforting. I moved quickly from the Kangari down the hill to the beach road and stood waiting in the deluge for a taxi to emerge unburdened with other passengers. I asked the driver to drop me downtown at Rose Bakery, an anonymous location for ex-pats, from which I planned to hasten the rest of the way to my real destination. My mind was busy with plans: none of them included the fact that I could just go home.

By the time I got downtown the rain had stopped and the streets were flooded, vehicles moving slowly, mini tsunamis washing over the broken pavements. I paid the driver and moved in the direction of Pademba Road, sloshing my way passed street vendors and hawkers.

A man shouted, 'Hey lady, I friend you?'

Another, 'Ma, come dis way.'

I moved head down like a thief, navigating the drains and fractured paving, keeping myself small, covering my face to obscure the whiteness. Traffic tooted, lurched, and splashed. The wail of *Allahu Akbar* from a mosque: its loudspeaker calling Friday prayers. Men in flowing robes moved past in one direction. Fear was my companion, bonded like a gibbon to my back.

Pademba Road was gridlocked. Thick fumes and pap-papping horns. I weaved my way through the traffic, to the monstrous concrete walls of the vast prison compound on the opposite side of the road. Beggars crowded the pavement, working the traffic. I strode through them, sweat trickling from my temples.

'Evening, ma,' said a smiling man as I moved past him, a double amputee from the war. His clothes were torn and dirty, his face friendly and warm. I stopped.

'Evening,' I said, groping in my pockets for a few tattered Leones, like a fool holding them out to him, a man with no arms, wondering if I should tuck them in his pocket, if that would be acceptable. There was a pocket in his T-shirt so I went for that.

He laughed and stepped back.

'*Tenki ma*,' he said smiling, 'please pass to di banker!'

He indicated someone on the ground. I looked down to see a man on his knees, his withered legs tucked away, a makeshift trolly underneath him, manoeuvred by his muscled arms. I mumbled something, but the second man made it easy for me, reaching up to take the notes.

He smiled showing missing teeth. 'Kine lady. Where from?'

'England,' I said, eager to get away.

They replied together, 'Ahhh, Enger-lan,' and the tears welled up. Fear, exhaustion, the turmoil within.

'No good for lady dis part of town,' warned the man who was standing. I nodded and moved on, the humidity clinging to me like a needy child, my clothes drenched, sticking to my skin. Soon I was off the main road, weaving through unlit quarters, my heart hammering. Above the city thunder rumbled in the mountains: another storm approaching.

The white walls of the church came into view, and I hurried toward them, running quietly up the steps, looking furtive left and right, stepping inside, grateful for the calm and safety of a godly place. There was no-one about, but candles burned in the side chapel. I made my way to the nave and found a dark spot to hide and dry off, trying to settle my thumping heart. In this church – Francis' church – I was safe.

The hour was late, exhaustion creeping in, but the adrenaline was still running like a current through my veins, my mind chaotic with a maelstrom of unanswered questions. The children in the plantation hadn't parachuted there by themselves: they'd been trafficked. Forced to work like men. Who knew about them? Who'd brought them there?

The storm abated quickly, and the pap-pap of horns died down, the city settling to rest. I curled up hoping sleep would come, but dread had clamped its talons round my head. Arranoil would now know what I had planned, would have read my report and have every reason to get rid of me. Just like they did Songola.

I had to move quickly before they worked out where I was, and what I was hiding.

THE NEXT MORNING, I awoke to children singing, sunlight pouring through the heavily barred stained-glass. There was a woody odour from the pews in the nave. Would Francis be working today? He was a man of principle despite what had happened, despite his disappointment in me. When he understood the circumstances, I knew he'd help. At least by coming to his church I'd saved him the embarrassment of turning up at his home.

I gathered my things and slipped out into the compound, the children playing in the early sunshine, chasing each other around puddles formed by the overnight rain. They stopped to stare before continuing their game. A girl head-loading a microwave strode by and sent a quick glance in my direction.

Inside the schoolroom, two women were preparing for the day. Francis wasn't there, but I recognised one of the women from the time I'd toured the school – neatly dressed in sky blue *lappa*, her skin light in colour, a kind of bronze. She looked up when I approached. She recognised me, but stared in confusion at my appearance, so different from before.

Cautious she said, 'Good mornin', ma.' And I wondered what she knew.

'Ma, I'm looking for Pastor Francis. I've lost my phone and need to get in touch with him. Can you help me?'

She stiffened at his name, like I'd blasphemed, and said in a measured tone, 'He not here.'

Undeterred I asked, 'Do you know when he'll be back? It's very important.'

But her expression showed she thought that unlikely.

'I don't know,' she replied.

She turned to the other woman who'd stopped stacking exercise books and was listening to our conversation. They exchanged some words in *Krio*. If he wasn't due in school, I would have to wait at his home.

The first woman said, 'He here later. Come back.'

Relieved, I thanked her. She eyed me suspiciously and watched me leave. I wandered out into the sunshine, to find a new phone and book my ticket home.

I RETURNED to the church late that afternoon. Francis wasn't there so I made my way round to the Mission School. The children had disappeared, and both women I'd seen earlier had gone. But someone was working in the library, kneeling on the floor, re-ordering the books, checking their spines, returning them neatly to their allocated slots. She turned when she heard me enter.

It was Dorothy. Aunt of the boy Moses, teacher at Francis' school, and childhood friend of Songola. She rose when she saw me, a look of concern on her face. Her lean body in jeans and white shirt, her head shaved, her skin ink black.

Her beauty smacked you in the face.

'Dorothy!' I said, smiling but feeling wrecked.

'What are you doing here? Are you okay?' She asked. Her tone was blunt and direct, and her questions spoke to the evidence that I was plainly not ok.

She stood straight-backed waiting for me to answer. She reminded me of Graham, the deadpan directness of an autistic mind, and I wondered what she knew about the pastor and me. This was the room where I'd first met him, his desk in one corner, still piled neatly with theological books and bibles. That interview seemed a long way off, like an unfulfilled promise in the annals of my imagination.

I said to Dorothy, 'I'm looking for the pastor. I hope he might help me.'

There was an indistinct reaction at the mention of his name. She stood aloof and tall, a pile of books in her hands, still waiting for me to answer her questions, her gaze fixed between my eyebrows.

'I need accommodation, just for a couple of nights.' I felt awkward saying it.

'Why have you left your hotel?' she demanded.

'I need somewhere to stay,' I replied vaguely, not knowing how much to divulge to her.

She waited a little longer, her face a composition in gravity. My appearance so altered from the previous encounters we'd had: no longer manicured, fragrant, unmistakably affluent and Western. Could she understand the difference? Could she see me now and know my vulnerability?

Eventually she said, 'The pastor is up country at a church in Makeni. The minister there has died. We are not expecting him back until the end of the week.'

Makeni was nearly two hundred kilometres from Freetown, in the northern province. Despair slithered up my spine. My heart pushed harder against my ribs. I looked blankly left and right, trying to figure what possible alternatives were left to me now.

She sensed the panic.

'What has happened?' she demanded. 'Did you go to the plantation? Why can't you stay at the hotel? Are they after you?'

She asked all the right questions. She knew about my plans because she was there at Sheku's flat when I'd discussed them, when he'd handed me Songola's flash drive, when he'd told me about the dead child.

'Yes, I went to the plantation,' I said. 'Things didn't go well.'

'They caught you on their land,' she said, like it was the most obvious thing to have happened.

'Yes.'

'They hurt you.'

'Not really.'

'Threatened you.'

'A bit.'

Her gaze was intense. She had always seemed so hostile. Distant and unforgiving. How much did she hate me now?

'I don't feel safe,' I said.

Dorothy was intelligent. She was a childhood friend of Songola. There was no other option but to trust her.

I withdrew the Nokia from the depths of the sack, held it out to her like a grenade, hands shaking, and I played to her the video.

THIRTY-NINE
KROO

'This is why my sister was killed,' Dorothy said.

Her expression was calm. The hurt all within.

There was an agonising pause before she asked, 'Who else knows about this?'

'Only the people in the village,' I said, 'but it might not be long before Arranoil find out about the Nokia, that I took it from the village. That I still have it.'

She eyed me with contempt. 'You don't understand our people. We make sacrifices to keep our business private, away from eyes and ears of big men and the corporations. We protect our comrades.'

The chastisement brought the colour to my cheeks. I felt as small and insignificant as a bug in the dirt.

'We are not helpless. We are not fools.'

She looked me up and down, taking me in now: unimpressive, work-soiled. Fearful and powerless, just like her. How could I convince her?

'I stayed in the same hut as Songola when I was at the village,' I said, 'when she was there on that last trip. She sent me some files, you know, somehow, they were waiting in my junk folder...'

She interrupted. 'What files?'

'Photos of those poor kids, working in the forest. Children that Songola believed had been trafficked to the plantation. They were malnourished and overworked, and they'd been separated from their families. Forced labour, well, slavery. The little boy who died, I believe he was one of them. I took photos myself, but they were all destroyed by the Arranoil people.'

'Destroyed?'

'They destroyed my phone.'

Dorothy was listening intently, still standing on the same spot, books in hand, her eyes now wandering around the room as she processed her thoughts.

I said, 'I need Songola's photos to write this story and send it to the media in my own country because, well, because there seems to be a link between Arranoil and the UK government. I have to write the report before I leave. Just in case…well…you know.'

Now she really was interested.

'Where are these files?' Still no eye contact. Her gaze fixed over my shoulder now.

'I'm hoping they're still safe in my *cloud* account. You know,'

'I know what a *cloud* account is.'

'Yes, but I can't be sure they haven't hacked it. They seem to know everything about me. I've got to get to it quickly so I can save them onto Songola's stick.'

'Songola's stick?'

'Flash drive. Sheku gave me her flash drive. Most of what's on it is her work for the union.'

Dorothy's mind was working through the facts. It seemed she was way ahead of me. She moved to replace the books on the bookshelves, each put carefully back in its place, and urged me to stow the Nokia safely in the rucksack.

'Come with me now,' she said. 'You will stay at my home.'

WE STEPPED into the compound to see the sky had darkened. The sun disappeared behind low clouds. The wind was picking up and rustling the leaves of the breadfruit.

We hurried through the alleys, heads down, spots of rain falling on our shoulders, the streets growing quiet in readiness. Kroo. No one would think to look for me there.

She led me to her home, a tiny tin shack at the heart of the settlement, nothing more than corrugated iron sheets atop a wooden frame; some of the walls cemented with crumbling breeze blocks. No windows, no electricity, no toilet. And a steady stream of water flowed past the door carrying flotsam and detritus.

On the doorstep sat a sleepy woman who Dorothy introduced as her mother, Grace. She couldn't have been much past middle age, but she looked eighty years old. She was sheltering from the rain under a UNICEF tarpaulin that was rigged up to form a kind of porch. She sat relaxed, smoking. But her jaw dropped when she saw me with her daughter, and she shifted her body up straight.

'Well com, ma.' Her words were slurred, but she managed a smile under droopy eyes, her fingers still wrapped around the reefer.

I squatted and took her free hand, stroking it a little, thanking her for her welcome.

Two drenched men from the Big Market arrived with a foam mattress wrapped in plastic. Dorothy had ordered it on her phone when we left the school compound. They pushed past us into the hut, manhandling it through the low front door and propping it up in the cramped space. Dorothy told them to wait as she disappeared behind a tatty blue curtain to fetch a torn and sunken mattress for them to take away. The men hustled out.

Bedraggled I sat on the step with Grace, her still holding

my hand, the rainwater pouring off the tarpaulin, splashing at our feet. After a while, Dorothy beckoned me through. Behind the curtain the new mattress was arranged on a low cot. On it was laid a cotton blanket, towel, and bar of soap. A *lappa* and blouse. All in a neat pile, ready. A wooden bookshelf was nailed to the wall, heavy with books of all kinds, some with broken spines.

This was a good place to hide.

'You will be comfortable here. There is a net.' Dorothy indicated a simple contraption holding a mosquito net that was rigged to the hut's main rafter.

She placed a red plastic bucket of water near the bed, 'For washing.'

And then put a bottle of water on the shelf, 'For drinking.'

I felt weak with gratitude for her kindness, cowed by her hospitality. I thanked her several times.

She said, 'We must go.'

Back into the rain we set out through the narrow alleys between the flimsy residences, through dilapidated shacks and muddy pathways, slippery with water moving across their surface. The Samba Drain was not yet overflowing, there was no risk the settlement would flood tonight.

Kroo was a place that overwhelmed you, saturated you with more than rain. The pleasant scent of woodsmoke, and the overpowering stench of ten thousand poor.

The rain sheeted down in one piece.

We headed to an internet café on the far side of the soccer pitch by a fast-flowing creak of the Crocodile River. The shack was recognisable by an array of satellite dishes attached to its roof and a bird's nest of tangled cables atop a leaning pole. Inside, a busy space was crammed with banks of laptops and printers, TV screens, wires criss-crossing the floor, and a Xerox copier standing stately in the middle. There was a water dispenser, empty. Ceiling fans whirring and rocking in their fixings. A twenty-first century hub at the heart of a medieval town. It was packed, every spot at the computer screens taken.

A man in a business suit, good-looking, young, was sitting at a tidy desk talking on the phone. Startled when he saw Dorothy, he hung up, standing straight away to greet her. Obviously, they were acquainted. His love shone forth, unrequited. Thoughtfully, he offered us a towel to dry off and then produced a laptop from under his desk, clearing a space for us to sit and offering us the login and password. The man was the proprietor, professional looking, friendly features. He gazed at Dorothy, his expression a composition of hope and desire. This meant we could trust him.

The man left us to work, and we waited patiently for the laptop to fire. When the screen lit up, I opened Explorer and signed into the *cloud*. Everything was there. I flicked through the files discretely showing Dorothy the photos that Songola had sent me. When I opened the images of the child, she confirmed what the puncture wounds might be: injuries from a heavy palm cluster falling from a great height. I opened Word, dragged all the photos into a document, and started to type.

A couple of hours later it was finished.

I set up a different email account and sent messages to news desks in the UK alerting them that something big was coming; an evidenced based report that implicated the UK government in the corruption of aid – and child trafficking. I figured this early warning would give them enough time to check the University of York and establish my credentials to write the piece. When Dorothy returned to the shack, I asked her to read the report and when she'd finished, she nodded at the screen.

'Is it good enough?' I asked.

'My sister would be ok with that.' The emotion caught in her voice.

I copied the report to Songola's flash drive and deleted it

from the computer. I overpaid the proprietor and we left, his gaze following Dorothy with aspirations that would never be fulfilled. She seemed indifferent to the man's yearning, but she knew it. A clever woman with a steely core, and ruthless in her relationships. I knew it was only her beloved Songola who was keeping her loyal to me. I could still feel enmity flowing from her, and I longed to understand her more.

Back in the hut, the three of us ate a simple meal before we settled for the night. Dorothy was quiet, thoughtful. I had so many questions but there was tension round her. She didn't want to talk, her face impassive, busying herself with her mat. Waiting.

FORTY
DOROTHY

I hear his footsteps on the stoop. I am ready.

He pushes aside the door and steps in, surprised to see me sitting on my mat beside my mother. No longer do I hide behind the curtain. He tries to work it out with his small brain.

My mother sits slumped and fearful, her breath quickening. She glances between him and me, back and forth.

Straight away he looks toward the curtain, now pulled brazen to one side.

The white sits pretty on the mattress, writing in the light of the lamp. African dress, it suits her – dark hair hanging round her shoulders. She looks up with interest as he enters.

He speaks to me in Temne. Anger and confusion distorts his ugly face.

'What is this…you whore!'

I am calm. The hammering of my heart he cannot see.

I say, 'She is an NGO from America.' The lie is well rehearsed in my mind. 'She has come to write for the TV, a slum diary. She will be staying in my house. I do not know how long.'

I see the rage rise in him, blood vessels pumping in his temples, protruding from skin that is slick with sweat. His odour fills the space. Fills my heart with the familiar dread.

He shouts in Temne so she cannot understand, but I feel strong.

I rise from my mat, and say to him, 'You are not welcome here. Go now.'

He looks at the white like he wants to kill her, but I know he is a coward. Instead, he rises to his full height, the top of his head resting against the roof of our small hut. He flails his arms like a child, tells me to get rid of her, then asks me how much she is paying. Inside I laugh at him.

I say, 'She pays nothing. She promises water for our street.'

He looks at me in disbelief. Nobody delivers promises. We both know that.

I look to the bed and see that the white is listening, concerned for me, not writing now. She does not know our language, but she understands well enough. This man is trouble for me.

I say to my abuser, 'She is a reporter. Do you want to find your business written in her book, on TV. All the world to know?'

He stares enraged at my strength, then at her, then at my feeble mother who reaches for the palm wine, tips the bottle, pours. The milky liquid dribbles down her chin.

The white sits quiet. She has no part in our theatre of hate. Her role is to be white. I can rely on her. In this space, the existence of one white transforms the balance of power. My abuser knows this. She knows it too. The sad and sickening reality of our world.

My plan is working. The man is a fool. Beads of sweat popping on his brow, his big hands clenched at his sides. Violence is denied him, and it chokes him not to fly his fists.

He looks at her again. She sits upright and confident looking back.

Her voice is calm as she says in English, 'Is there a problem I can help with?'

She reaches conspicuously for her phone.

He turns, his anger boiling, grabs me by the throat, spittle on his chin, murder in his eyes. He holds me there, then drops his hand and stamps his shiny shoes out of the hut, heaving the door into the drain, disappearing fast into the night.

I wait. Then go outside to find the door.

Now she is beside me. Together we heft the weighty item out the drain. The water is stinking but she does not shy or curse. We pull the door back up the stoop, step inside, wedge it back across the opening, adjust it to its usual slant. She asks no questions.

One day soon we will leave this place, and I will have the door that locks him out.

In her chair my mother sits shaking, eyes closed, one hand across her breast. I soothe her. The white brings her water, then retreats quiet to her bed. She is someone I can trust. This is how I am beginning to understand her.

WE SETTLE TO REST. Nothing is spoken. The white draws the curtain to private her space, and I hear the bleeps as she presses out a number on her phone.

She says, 'Dan, it's me. I know...I lost my phone.'

I think she is calling home. Her husband? I listen in to protect my interests.

She says, 'Yes, don't worry I'm fine. Just ringing to let you know I'll be home in a couple of days. Yes.'

There is a pause. Then she says, 'Stuff's happened... umm...everything's changed.'

I lie quiet on my mat. My mother is asleep now, mouth wide. I extinguish the lamp to listen closer.

It is a long wait before she says with voice that is low and rickety, 'It hasn't worked out. No...he...he...' She is struggling to say it, her voice is cracking. 'It's just that I can't stay here now.'

She blows her nose softly behind the curtain. I know she is talking about the pastor. My spirits rise because she knows he is lost to her now.

It was his right to know about the lies she told. About her husband – they call fiancé – an important man – the one she stands beside as he collects awards for his computing skills. For clever software he has designed for hospitals all around the world. This information is for everyone to see.

I say to you: be careful what you share upon the internet.

Now it is so – that without his new girlfriend the beloved pastor has returned to his old self. Depressed, agitated, sorrowful. Once again remote and inconsolable as when Ebola took his wife. A solitary, sullen soul. He wants no-one, and this thought makes me sad. It is not my custom to hurt those I love, because I have known so much hurt myself. The weight of guilt lies heavy on me. But I feel no shame. Never!

The white still speaks into her phone.

'I'll explain when I get back...so much has happened. I'll need to stay with you for a bit 'til I sort myself out.'

And then, 'Sunday. Yes, Gatwick. Yes. I'll get the connection north. No I don't know the timings exactly. Please don't say anything to Graham. He must hate me.'

And then, 'Thanks. How's mum. Good, good. Please don't worry about me.' But her own voice sounds worried: she is worrying enough for both of them. 'It'll be good to see you, Dan.'

She is full of an emotion that is strange to me.

Life in Freetown must be hard for her, so protected from

the everyday unease, disappointments and suffering of people like us.

But she has courage.

It influences me.

And I think this is the moment when my life begins to change.

FORTY-ONE

DUTCHMAN

The next morning I woke violently to the clangour of steel pots and sloshing of water as the settlement began a new day. A shaft of sunlight crept through the hut settling on the mattress beside my head, the storm of the night – rain pounding like automatic gunfire on the roof – had dissipated to calm. Something nagged at me. I'd dreamt a vivid dream, but it had evaporated to a vague recollection: young boys running through the forest trying to escape a Pied Piper type figure beckoning to them, luring them on. I couldn't remember the details, but it left me feeling uneasy. Like a finger tapping on my shoulder.

Children were singing down the alleys. I pulled back the curtain that separated my quarters from the rest of the space to find I was alone, the door slid open a way, the faint whiff of ganja drifting in.

There was no sign of Dorothy. She'd been quiet after the visitor who'd barged in last night, violent and threatening. She hadn't explained, and I hadn't asked. There was so much more to her to know. She was deep and troubled for sure. I'd learnt her father had died of Ebola, and that she was an Ebola survivor herself. But I felt this was the least interesting thing to know about her.

I rubbed sleep from my eyes and took a draught from the water bottle. For the first time in days, I felt safe. Hidden in the labyrinth of Kroo.

I washed as best I could, then dressed and went out to the stoop to greet Grace who was sitting in her spot, propped against the shack, legs stretched out in front. The smoke trickled from her lips. She took my hand and squeezed it.

What memories from the war kept her in this troubled state?

The night before, we had prepared for bed as modestly as the space would allow, and Grace had turned away, removed her weathered blouse, awkwardly tugging it over her head, and tipping up the three-legged stool where she was sitting. I'd moved to help her, and saw etched into the skin across her breasts the unmistakable branding of the rebels: raised scars carved into her flesh in childlike script...the letters R.U.F. Could it be that her daughter, Dorothy, had been born in the bush during the war, to rebel fighters?

We sat on the stoop holding hands, watching the water in front of the hut flow quickly past our feet: plastic bottles, paper wrappers, sticks, rotten fruit, broken flip flops, all twisting and snagging on their way down stream into the next alley. Some children came to look at me, squealed and ran away.

It was then I saw it. The shock of steel grey hair glinting against the sun, as elegant and bright as Lungi airport's architectural roof.

Just a glimpse as he moved across the space between the huts. Fifty metres away. There, and then gone.

The dream came back to me now. I'd dreamt about the Dutchman – his was the face of the Pied Piper. I leapt to my feet and into the hut to retrieve the flash drive and the sack,

Grace alarmed and confused. I squatted and held her hands before I exited.

'Don't worry Grace. I'll be back soon.'

Back up the hill through the maze of alleys, I was sure I knew the way, sweat already heavy on my brow, adrenalin pumping as I re-lived the fear of that night in his room.

I found it easily enough, just as busy as before. The proprietor remembered me and found a space for me to work, the emergency generator pounding, no electricity at this hour. Quickly I logged back into the *cloud,* hoping the photos had synced. They were there. I'd been so eager to stash Songola's files that I'd forgotten them.

The photo files I'd taken the night I'd entered the Dutchman's room.

I opened them. Printed off. Saved them to Songola's flash drive, then deleted everything from the *cloud*.

BACK AT THE hut Dorothy was pacing, anxious. She looked at me as though I were deranged.

'What are you doing,' she demanded.

Out of breath and sweating a storm, I took her hand and pulled her into the hut.

'I'd forgotten them,' I said.

'What had you forgotten?'

I sat on the bed and drew the papers from my sack, hoping she'd make sense of the coding – the numbers and letters, and other names that sounded like place names.

'Please, Dorothy. Sit with me.'

Little daylight penetrated the hut. She lit a lamp and came to sit beside me.

'Where did you get this?' she asked, and I explained about the mix up with the keys at the Kangari. How I'd decided to take a look in the Dutchman's room, to see if I could discover what it was he was doing in Sierra Leone. The memory of it tightened my gut.

Dorothy looked at me straight, her expression half shock, half admiration.

I asked her, 'Do you know what these codes might mean?'

Ignoring the question, she asked, 'Who is this man?'

I expounded on his lengthy visits to the Kangari. How I kept coming across him huddled with local men in unlikely settings – like Kroo settlement, by the Crocodile River, and by the creek in Crab Town when the government was demolishing the shanty. And then the meetings he'd had at the hotel with thugs that looked like mercenaries. And the gathering he'd had in Frank's Bar with the smart, Italian-looking man, who seemed so young and boyish. The one with a severe parting in his hair.

I said, 'I couldn't work out what he was up to in Freetown. I'd convinced myself it was nothing good – drugs, or weapons maybe.' I was speaking in hushed tones, realising the settlement itself might not be safe.

Dorothy looked at the papers. Something seemed to resonate.

'What is it?' I asked, fearing in my heart what it might be. 'Tell me what it means.'

'Here,' she said, pointing at the place names. 'These are villages up country, some of them far away on our northern border with Guinea. This village is in Kailahun, it is in the far-east on the border with Liberia.'

This was the list of names besides which were the codes.

'And here,' she said, pointing at the codes besides a village in Kailahun, 'G5, B2.'

I waited.

She looked at me, taking her time. 'Five girls, two boys,' she said.

'Five girls, two boys,' I repeated, half questioning, half knowing.

'Yes, ma. Your Dutchman is trafficking our children.'

'HE WAS HERE. I SAW HIM.'

'What do you mean you saw him?'

'This morning, today. I was sitting outside with Grace. I saw him go past the alley. Let me show you…'

'Stay here.' She'd risen from the bed and was blocking my way. 'Did he see you?'

'No, no. He didn't see me.'

'How do you know he didn't see you?'

'It was too quick. He just walked past the end of the alley. He didn't see me.'

But I didn't know for sure that this was so. I didn't know for sure that he wasn't looking straight at me before I looked up and saw him walk away.

I pleaded, 'Dorothy, I need to find out who he is. I've got to go back to the Kangari.'

I stood up and reached for my sack.

'Don't be a fool.'

'He's the missing piece. I know it.'

'You know nothing,' she said, sensibly. 'We have deduced what he is doing from limited evidence. We may be wrong.'

'But I must find out who he is.'

'And how will you do that?' She was annoyed. 'Will you idle up and ask nicely? Will you panic about and make demands? I tell you, no-one will help you there. You are the white who causes trouble.'

A slap in the face I was becoming used to.

'Sit,' she said.

Grace was now indoors looking at us with an anxious expression, steadying herself on the back of a broken chair, a hand to her throat as though gasping for air. Dorothy drew her mother onto the mattress and pulled the curtain round us.

'You cannot leave this house, only when you return to your country tomorrow. Your Dutchman might be working for Arranoil. You are here in my hut because they're looking for you.'

She was right, but I couldn't let it go.

I said, 'If he's trafficking children for Arranoil…if I don't find out who he is right now, I won't get another chance. I'll be gone tomorrow.'

Grace was looking from one to the other, her expression confused and vulnerable. She hunched up close between us.

'You will not leave this house,' said Dorothy. 'I myself will find out who he is, or what name he is using for himself.' She drew herself up to her full height, 'My cousin Charles, he works at the Kangari.'

SHE DISAPPEARED for the rest of the day whilst I stayed in the hut with Grace.

It got late, darkness falling quickly, lamps lit, braziers glowing. Earlier there'd been torrential rain and now mosquitoes whined and droned in huge clouds down the drenched alleys. Without the glare of the unforgiving sun, the excrescence of Kroo diminished – disappearing into blackness. All that was real was in the few square metres around us – in the hut and on the stoop – illuminated by a single kerosene lamp. I wondered if the violent man from the night before would return, and what I would do if he did. But he never came.

We waited.

I recalled my desire to disappear when I first arrived in Freetown. To slip like a thief into the strange and alien scene. To slink and fade, to melt into a bolder world. To live a reality so distinct from the suffocating life I had back home.

I was living that now. Songola and Dorothy had given me hope; the purpose that I'd been longing for.

Wet trainers arrived on the stoop. The clouds had burst again with a torrential outpour, and Dorothy stepped in, her skin slick with water.

'I have it,' she said.

She moved behind the curtain, stripped her wet clothing, dried, and re-emerged in a cobalt wrapper. She passed me a slip of paper with his name, passport number, and photo. I peered at it in the dim glow. Hendrikus Broekmann. Possibly a false name. But I had his photo – a good likeness. It was enough.

A lump arrived in my throat.

'Thank you. Thank you so much.' I wanted to embrace her, but I knew it was not their way.

She said nothing, looking at me as though I had the prescience of a five-year-old. She had that way. Rats scuttled across the roof, their claws scratching and slipping against the iron.

We planned my journey back to Lungi.

'I will take you to Kissy,' Dorothy said. 'We must be there before dawn.'

We would leave for the ferry terminal whilst Kroo was still in darkness. Hordes of unknowns would be jostling together in the ship's hull and the thought filled me with terror. Perhaps the same man who'd broken into my room at the Kangari, assaulted me, threatened me, stole my work. Maybe he, too, would be on the ferry. How would I know if he was standing only metres away hidden in the crowd? I swallowed hard.

'When I get to Tagrin I'll take the bus to the airport,' I said. 'Safer than a taxi.'

Dorothy nodded.

Then I'd board the morning flight to Gatwick. This was the plan, and along every part of the way opportunities for Arranoil to intercept me and find the Nokia.

THAT LAST NIGHT we ate flatbread and cassava leaf, talking well into the night, and I learnt about Dorothy's ambitions.

I asked her, 'Where do you plan to go to university?'

'Fourah Bay College. There is nothing wrong with our universities,' anticipating my reply. 'We have an excellent law college. I will receive my LLB there.'

I thought about her studying in the hut, straining in the glow of one kerosene lamp, the stinking stream outside her door determinedly rising with every breach of the thunderous clouds. She needed to get out of there.

'May I ask,' I began, 'I mean, I know it's none of my business, but is someone supporting you with your studies?' How did someone living in such impoverishment afford an education such as hers.

She hesitated. Something sticking in her throat.

'Our pastor helps me,' she said. 'I am his best student. He knows his effort will be rewarded.'

Francis. How typical of him.

I too struggled to say his name.

I asked, 'The pastor. Are you part of the Canadian programme that he's running at the Mission School?'

'Yes. That is so.'

She told me that Francis had made a promise to her father to continue to educate his clever daughter, help her realise her ambitions to work to bring justice for her community. And I saw how closely aligned were our ambitions.

Dorothy explained she was the daughter of a child soldier. That both her parents were child soldiers, news that made sense of the branding on her mother's chest, of the terror and mistrust etched permanently in Dorothy's expression. I sat in awe of her, knowing what her family had lived through, knowing the stigma that must torment them even now. How strong and resilient she must be. Twenty-five years old and born to the horrors of bush warfare, stigmatised and ostracised in school, and her mother's heart-breaking mental health and her father tortured by the war. And deep, deep poverty. By sharing this information with me Dorothy was risking judgement and revulsion. A risk that told me I was trusted.

I had to finish it.

FORTY-TWO
RETURN

The fog was heavy over the Sierra River estuary, but the ferry embarked on time, clanking and belching its way across the water.

Now, I stood upright and rigid in the chaos of Lungi's departures hall, trying to stay calm. All I had to do was get the Nokia and myself out of the country. It was hidden away at bottom of my sack, but I was conscious of it, like it was burning a hole through the canvas, only millimetres away from the hands I knew would search it. It mustn't be found before I reached London. I had to know the extent of Arranoil's power.

The queue at check-in snaked around the hall filling row after row of taped lanes that were lengthened unnecessarily by the multitude of porters with their trollies. There was the familiar strong odour of sweat and Parazone. Fear increased the perspiration flowing down my neck. I knew what airport security might do: confiscate my belongings, detain me so I missed my flight, even arrest me on some erroneous charge. It was far from over yet. How could I know who knew my business, or whose instructions these people followed, or whose pockets they were in? I tried to relax, conscious that the tension must be showing. I joined the line and waited in the stifling heat.

'Karen?'

It was a familiar voice.

'David!'

David Westbrook, a friendlier face you couldn't imagine. It was many weeks since we'd met at the Cape Sierra and discussed corruption in the UK government. I thought he'd already gone home.

'You're still here?' I asked.

'Not anymore,' he said. 'I've finished my stint. They're sending me home.'

'Oh, right.' I was thinking quickly. An idea taking hold. David Westbrook was what Francis would call an *angel from God*.

David said, 'The Ebola thing has wound down and humanitarian aspects of the programming have stopped completely.'

'Yes, of course.' I said, wondering how I could safely transfer the phone to him. How I could discretely drag it from the bottom of my bag and get it into his.

'Everything ok?' he asked. I must have looked vacant. 'How are you doing with the research. Are you done here yourself?'

I looked around, hesitating, irrationally feeling like the only person in the queue, that all eyes were on me, that anything I said or did would be heard, seen, or monitored.

I gazed over David's shoulder toward a security guard in the distance and said, 'I'm sorry they haven't been able to find something to keep you here.' Because I knew he was a competent, people-centred practitioner, and those types always seem to be sent home just as their work was bearing fruit.

'I'm sorry too,' he said, 'but I'm working on a different ticket back.'

'Hmm?' I said. 'NGO?' knowing how dreadfully that might pan out, and still thinking of a way to get the Nokia to him.

'No, I'm looking for a job in the government. Civil service hopefully. Get a real handle on things.'

I was alert now. My mind made up. 'You're kidding. Here?'

'Yes,' he smiled modestly. 'If they'll have me.' His brown hair was looking gloriously tousled and his cotton clothing spectacularly crumpled.

I scanned the crowd again, nervous. The queue had built up nicely behind us and was stationary, the check-in staff still chatting amongst themselves. It might not be so hard to get the Nokia from one bag into the other when everyone was so huddled together.

David asked, 'How did things turn out for your research?'

You were right,' I said flatly. It was David who'd planted the idea in my brain. That there was more important work to do in Sierra Leone than a PhD on the democratic process. I looked around in what I hoped was a casual way, not wanting to elaborate with so many listening ears.

He picked up on my nerves and said subtly, 'Well, that's great. Well done.'

I told him what a lot we had to catch up on once we were back in the UK. But for now, I needed his help.

———

A STOUT GUARD was standing at security in a kinky style wig. She gave my bag a rudimentary rummage, then picked it up and escorted me to an ante-room where a similarly offi-cious woman was waiting at a low table. The bag was tipped up and disembowelled of all its contents, everything opened and examined in a hopeful manner. When they couldn't find what they were looking for, the irritation showed, and they focussed their attention on me, searching my person thoroughly, exchanging lascivious glances. Discovering nothing of interest, they looked at each other perplexed.

A man of senior rank entered the room, dwarfed in size by the women. He looked at me, and then the bag, and then the women, and demanded an answer. They shrugged and stood their ground. The man took out his baton and searched the items spread out on the table as though picking through garbage on a dump. He shouted something at the women and left.

Disappointed there was nothing of consequence upon me, the women stood waiting for their bribe, staring at me keenly.

'Can I go now?' I asked.

The one in the kinky wig said, 'We are waitin'.'

'For what?' I asked.

'For our consideration.'

I stared back calmly, 'I have no money.'

They looked at each other and tittered, but before they could repeat themselves, I said, 'You've just searched all my belongings. Didn't you notice there was no money?'

'No dollar?'

'No dollar,' I replied, joyous that I had placed all my remaining dollars – all five thousand of them – in the envelope I'd passed to Dorothy when I boarded the ferry at Kissy. I figured she could find a use for them.

AFTER THE SIX HOUR FLIGHT, I stood at Gatwick immigration searching the queue for David Westbrook. He came to find me and slipped the Nokia into my hand, wished me luck, then disappeared to his place at the end of the line.

The past few days I'd spent expecting an ambush by representatives of Arranoil. Now I was in the UK, it was no different. The drama was still unfolding, because there was a final piece of the puzzle that was still to put into place.

The Nokia sat like a ticking time bomb in my pocket.

Who still knew about it?

An immigration officer signalled for me to approach the counter. He examined my passport and scanned it through the system. A young lad, blonde with ruddy complexion, he checked the computer screen, his face impassive.

'Welcome back to the UK, Miss Hamm,' he said. Smiling, he waved me through.

Straight away, a second official with a professional smile moved toward me. He took my arm gently. 'Miss Hamm, if you could please come this way. There's just an additional check. I apologise for the inconvenience.'

'What's the matter?' I asked. 'What additional check?'

'Please,' he said, 'there is no need to be concerned. It's just routine.'

He steered me by my elbow through a door marked *Security*, and passively I followed. This was what I wanted, what I had expected. A strange calm came upon me.

The security officer walked me down a series of brightly lit corridors and into a room occupied by a desk and three chairs. We waited for only a moment before another door opened and two men entered, one UK border force, the other in civvies. *Arranoil*.

This was how far the corporation's tentacles reached. All the way to the highest levels of security in my own country.

The two men had already learnt about the Nokia and the incriminating evidence it contained. They knew because I'd agreed with Dorothy that she would leak it through her contact at the internet café once I was out of the country. But what the men didn't know was that the data had already been extracted from the Nokia, and had been saved onto Songola's flash drive along with my full report to send to the press.

The man in civvies assessed me with a cold expression.

The border force official said, 'We're sorry for the inconvenience, Miss Hamm, but we understand that property has gone missing in Sierra Leone and that it may be in your possession.'

The man who had accompanied me took my rucksack and searched it unsuccessfully. I stood by, quiescent. Then I took the phone from my pocket.

'Is this what you're looking for?' I asked.

The man in civvies nodded to the official who took it from me and passed it over for him to examine. He seemed satisfied.

'Thank you for your cooperation. My colleague will escort you to immigration.'

This much I'd learnt: that a senior member of the UK government – Nigel Hurt – with influence in homeland security, had been alerted to the fact that a UK citizen – Karen Hamm – was carrying a sensitive item that might be detrimental to his career and business interests. The alert had been initiated from an internet café in a downtown slum in West Africa.

It was not a comfortable moment. Power, subterfuge, and corruption that knew no borders, and that penetrated the oldest democracies and most transparent societies in the world.

My plan would not have worked if I'd written the report in *Salone* and emailed it to the press myself. This was because I had to close the circle, capture everyone I knew could be involved. They had to believe there was still a chance to quieten me when I arrived in the UK. The corruption racket had crossed my own border, and I'd exposed my own government in the web of criminal activity around Arranoil. I felt numb. But vindicated.

THE MOMENT we entered the arrivals hall, my security companion abandoned me.

With a sense of anticipation, I wandered over to a coffee outlet where the BBC news was broadcasting on a supersized screen overhead. When I saw what was being reported, I felt a rush of gratitude for the competence and loyalty of my new friend, Dorothy.

The news loop was showing minister Nigel Hurt detained by photographers on the doorstep of his London home, and on the split screen running at the same time was some edited footage from the Nokia. The bulletin running along the bottom of the screen read:

Minister uses aid money in child slavery scandal.

Nigel Hurt looked frightened and confused, and kept repeating *no comment* as he tried to exit the scene that was about to ruin his life.

I'd needed the final search at Gatwick to prove the connection to Hurt. With me safely out of the country and in the air, Dorothy had sent the report, the photos, and the movies via an anonymous email to the press, Songola's flash drive still in her capable hands.

THERE WAS no sign of Dan who was due to meet me at Gatwick. It was unusual, as he was always on time, so I stood watching the TV screen, transfixed, emotions rising, my gut churning with excitement. All around, people stood by engrossed in the story. It was strange to know what chaos I'd created, this invisible nobody, standing among the crowd. A conduit for the courage of brave souls like Songola and Dorothy, Sheku, and even Francis.

I stood there wondering whether it had all been worth it. Worth losing Graham. My home and the old life. I'd thrown it all away like it meant nothing.

But then I noticed where the imaginary bell-jar of my former entrapment swung – way above my head, suspended perhaps forever by these ties of worth and purpose, knowing I'd achieved something truly consequential. Something for those children, working and dying on that torturous plantation, trafficked from their families, their labour and their childhoods benefitting rich and powerful Westerners. Like Nigel Hurt.

———

I WAITED, wondering what had happened to Dan, thinking I should give him a call. Then I saw a familiar figure, striding toward me, coffee in hand.

'Graham?'

He pecked me on both cheeks, then kissed me quickly on the mouth. I could taste the coffee. I wanted to throw my arms around him but instead I said, 'I was expecting Dan.'

'Yes,' he stood there in his usual awkward way, stating the obvious. 'He's not coming. It's me.'

'Is he ok?' I asked, feeling awkward under Graham's scrutiny and concerned about Dan.

'Yes, he's fine and well.' For a moment Graham looked puzzled by the question but realising I was anxious he said, 'Dan's not here. You're coming home with me.'

He reached for my bag and took it off my shoulders. The relief of the weight lifted after all those desperate days made the tears sting behind my eyes. I could let go. Exhaustion rushed across my body.

'Graham why do you want me to come home?' I asked. 'You must hate me.' Had Dan told him about Francis?

'I don't hate you,' he said, jerking the bag onto his own shoulders. 'Why should I hate you?'

His head tilted sideways, waiting for my answer,

genuinely perplexed. Logic presenting as something else in Graham's unfathomable brain.

'I've been, I've been…' the exhaustion was overwhelming, the emotions so confusing. I felt ashamed at the hurt I'd caused. But all I wanted to do was collapse into him. The sameness and solidity of Graham. His loyalty.

He said, 'You often talk irrationally. No point listening when you process things illogically.' A pause. 'You are still my best friend.'

Intolerable, inscrutable, Graham.

He could have no idea that the person behind the drama unfolding on the screen above our heads was the one standing next to him. If he knew, he'd be proud.

And now I had the name of Hendrikus Broekmann.

G5 B2.

The mission had just begun.

GLOSSARY

Ah taya baad: I am very tired
Aw di bodi: how are you?
Aw di chop: what is the food like
Barrie: a meeting place
Big man: rich, powerful, corrupt leader
Bush pikin: a child born of rape in the bush
Diamba: cannabis
Di bodi fin: I am well
INGO: International Non-Governmental Organisation
Kongossa: gossiping
Krio: The local language of the Freetown peninsula
Lappa: a colourful cloth used to wrap the body
NGO: Non-Governmental Organisation
Okada: motorbike taxi
Oporto: white person
Palaver: trouble
Pikin: children
Poda-poda: minibus
Salone: Sierra Leone (local expression)
Swit: sweet
Tek: take

Tenki: thank you
Titi: girl
Yu kin sho me: can you show me
Yu dohn mek mistek! you've made a mistake
Watta: water
Wetin: what
Wey: missing

ACKNOWLEDGEMENTS

I would like to acknowledge the following research resources: *Child Soldiers,* by Miriam Devon; *A Sunday at the Pool in Kigali,* by Gil Courtemanche; *In Sierra Leone,* by Michael Jackson; *The Bell Jar,* by Sylvia Plath; *God is No Thing,* by Rupert Shortt.

My heartfelt thanks to all my family and friends who have encouraged and supported this work. Especially my husband, David, and my grandson, Jack, for giving me the inspiration for the title of this book:

Fly Catcher.

ABOUT THE AUTHOR

P C Cubitt is the author of the novel *Fly Catcher*.

She is an Africanist scholar and during her years of research was a contributor and editor to various academic journals. Her PhD on the peacebuilding mission in Sierra Leone led to a number of journal publications, a book published by Routledge, and research commissioned by the World Bank. Subsequent work on governance in Africa took her to Liberia, Senegal, Rwanda, Tanzania and Mozambique.

During her early years, P C Cubitt travelled with her father on his various postings around the world, including to Sierra Leone, the atmospheric setting for *Fly Catcher*. These experiences, and her years of research in Africa, have inspired her writing.

She lives with her husband in Yorkshire.

Fly Catcher is her first novel.

~

If you have enjoyed reading *Fly Catcher,* please consider leaving a review or rating at your point of purchase. Thank you.

For more information and to follow her blog, visit pccubitt.com

Printed in Great Britain
by Amazon

22180958R00189